The
Spruce Gum Box

The
Spruce Gum Box

Elizabeth Egerton Wilder

Red Dobie
P R E S S

EXTON , PENNSYLVANIA

This Book is dedicated to my Dad,
Charles "Chuck" Egerton.
He kindled my respect for the 'woods'

Acknowledgments

I express sincere gratitude to my family: husband Cal and children Rob, Scott, and Cheryl, for never letting me give up my dream of writing a novel. I appreciate my husband sharing my excursions through northern Maine, driving me to museums and exhibits I had discovered on the Internet. I'm sure he was not nearly as excited as I over the trivia I gleaned.

I credit my daughter Cheryl Wilder Krass for that final little nudge. I told her I had a story swimming in my mind. I knew how it started. I knew how it ended. But I had no idea what happened in between. She told me if I wrote it, she would publish it through her company, Alexemi Publishing, and a year later I handed her my manuscript. Without her guidance through the process, I would never be writing these acknowledgements.

Many thanks to the early readers of my manuscript: Sandy Davies, Gussie Pettinati, Rob Wilder and Sabrina Wilder. Their input and encouragement gave me the confidence to continue.

Kudos to Cathy Cotter of Cotter Visual Communications for the beautiful cover and page designs. She had such patience with the back and forth.

I appreciate Bonnie Myhrum's virtual assistance as proof reader for the manuscript. My 1950's English lessons certainly needed a good review. I value her opinion as a problem solver.

Not to be forgotten, are all the nameless docents who were generous with their knowledge and didn't mind my myriad questions. Thank you.

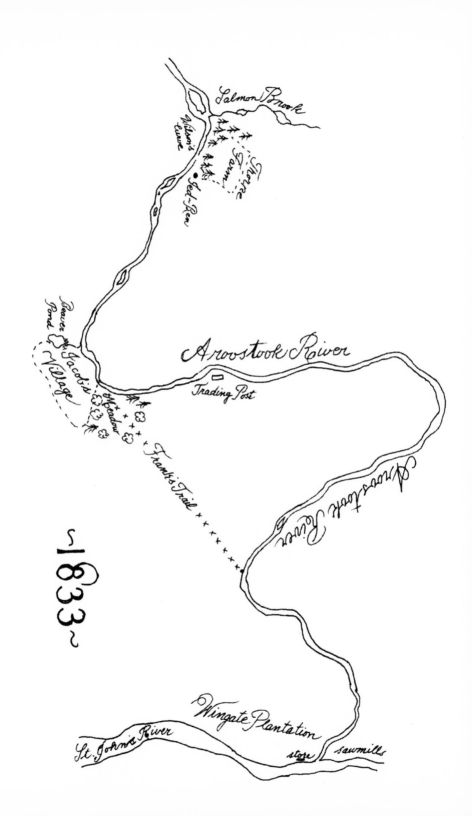

Salmon Brook

Wilson's Cove

Jed-Pen

Beaver Pond

Jacob's Village

Meadow

Aroostook River

Trading Post

Frank's Trail

Aroostook River

~1833~

Wingate Plantation

St. John's River

store   sawmills

1   The Cookee

February 1841

"Cookee, where the hell are you?" yelled Bill, who was the river landing boss of the small logging company.

"A man could starve or freeze to death waiting for you to get your skinny ass out here," growled Hiram.

The hollers of displeasure bounced from tree to tree, as sound is wont to do in the winter icy depths of an old-growth forest.

"How'd that scatterbrained ninny get to be Jake's assistant?" asked Caleb, the newest crew member.

"There's no one better at setting a bean hole than Ben. Not sure how he got the knack. It's just in delivering the goods that drives us crazy. He's probably seen some fancy bird or animal and is stalking it while our beans grow cold," growled Hiram.

Close, thought Ben, as he quietly tried to shoo his favorite turkey out of the path toward the landing workers.

"Other way, big fellow, or they'll have me putting you in the stew pot," whispered the gangling young cookee. Ben loved this particular bird. Contrary to what most believed about stupid turkeys, he had watched many grow from hatchlings and knew the complex workings of the flock. He thought this tom was the most clever of all of them, for when trouble approached he would swiftly run toward his favorite pine, spread his expansive wings and lift his heavy body into the crotch. Then he would work his way out to the limb that hung over the river. This way, neither human nor animal could get to him easily, especially when the water ran rampant in the spring.

Ben repositioned the worn hand-wrought yoke on his shoulders.
The oak was polished to a shiny patina after years of being used
to carry meals to crews that were away from the camp. Winding
his way through a patch of birch trees bent low under the weight
of winter, he could feel the warmth of the yellow–eye beans
against his right leg, balanced by the pail of hot tea on the left.

"On my way!" shouted Ben. "Don't get your woolies in a
knot." This startled a flock of chickadees, which flew across
Ben's path, causing him to stumble. He looked a bit like a drunk
trying to make his way along the slippery path without falling
down. "I should've used the push sled," he grumbled to himself.
"Especially with a new snowfall. If I drop these beans, they'll have
my hide on a drying rack."

Behind him he could hear *chick-a-dee, chick-a-dee-dee-dee,* as the
small black-capped birds sang out in order to regroup.

"Cookee!" echoed again through the trees just as Ben emerged
from the tangled brush.

"Why the hell did you come through the timber when the path
along the river is clear? You some kind of a dummy? The ice is
strong enough to hold a wimp like you if some stumps get in the
way." Disgusted, Caleb tossed his cant hook down from his place
on the top of the load on the sled, just missing Bill's foot.

"Good God, man!" yelped Bill. "Take your anger out by making
those logs mind with that weapon. The boy's here and no one
dropped from lack of food."

"Lucky for him," Caleb snorted.

Without a word, Ben carefully slid the yoke from his shoulders
and set to work opening the heavy pots, freeing the aroma of
steaming sweet, warm molasses and beans. Great chunks of salt
pork floated between the layers, completing the hearty baked
mixture. In the second pot was incredibly strong, hot black tea.
Staying warm in a tray over the tea was a batch of sourdough
biscuits.

Although his breath formed a haze in the frigid air, Ben was far
from cold. Along with his long johns, two layers of wool trousers,
two wool shirts, the exertion of carrying the yoke, the warmth
of the pots and now his growing anger at dealing with this new
crew member, even the north wind would have had a hard time
reaching his senses.

"Don't talk much do you, boy?" snorted Caleb.

Nope, thought the cookee.

"I suppose you get that from your crazy half-breed boss," continued Caleb. "I only joined up with this crew because he is the best damn cook along the Aroostook River. Now there's a man that knows how to fill a gut, but he doesn't do much more than grunt once in awhile. And you two keep a teepee. What's the matter? Think you're too good to sleep with the rest of the men?" he questioned Ben, while giving him a whack on his back.

Nope, mused Ben, *we just don't want to sleep in the cabin with your stink pole of drying wet britches and we keep our talk for something worth saying. Besides, it's a wigwam.*

Ben was grateful that the crew was small at the riverside today. He quickly filled their tins to get them off his back. It took them no time to eat and wash it all down with the tea. Ben wondered how any of them had any teeth left they liked it so strong.

Without another word, he packed up everything to wash back at the camp kitchen.

"Told you he was a dummy. Never said a word," mumbled Caleb just loud enough for Ben to hear.

"Why not give the boy a chance?" Bill said.

"Look, there he goes again. Off through the deep snow in the woods instead of the quicker way along the river. Told you he has no smarts," pointed Caleb.

"Maybe he just has some sweet thing waiting for him behind a bunch of witch's hair. Imagine what goings-on can be hidden behind a mass of intertwined branches," Hiram mused.

"Sounds like that comes from experience," laughed Bill.

"You look a bit flustered under that scrubby beard, Hiram," teased Caleb. "Have you danced a jig with a maiden under some witch's hair? Bet it was more like jigging with a hairy witch under a branch."

"Best I've heard in awhile," howled Bill, stomping in circles and pretending to play a fiddle. "Besides, the only sweet thing in the woods Ben looks for is the sap that runs in the spring."

"I don't know about that," said Caleb, finally regaining his

composure. "Haven't you seen him stare at that little lady that
rides down here with her Pa sometimes when he brings the oxen
from the farm?"

"Whoa there, crazy man," Hiram came back. "There's no way
Dan Thorpe would let his Nettie anywhere near the camp cookee.
He'd string him up in that old pine tree with the tom turkey Ben
thinks is such a big secret."

Caleb snapped back, "Are you blind, man? I didn't have to be
around long to see it. When those two stare at each other, there is
enough heat around to make the river run early."

"Would that it could," whispered Hiram.

"The thaw and drive will be here sooner than later. Now you're
full of beans, move your asses and get the last of these buggers on
the sled," prodded Bill. "Caleb, still your turn to be sky hooker.
Back on top of the pile."

The day before, Frank Ryan's choppers had used an ox to skid the
last of their newly felled trees into the clearing. The smell of fresh
balsam still permeated the air where branches had been chopped
off so the logs could be stacked.

Now Caleb labored with his hook while the other two pushed up
with their pike sticks to force the logs into place. The sled sat on
an icy strip where just a bit of persuasion from the team of beasts
in the morning would start it moving to the landing below.

The late winter sun began to slip behind the fringe of majestic
pines that had escaped the ax men. Deep blue shadows fell like
stripes on the clearing of snow and sparkled like gems when
crossing the path of ice. The only break in this feast for the eyes
was the occasional pile of unwanted boughs and stumps, which
stood like sentries.

"Hope we're going to get some help in the morning marking the
pile with the branding hammer. I wouldn't want some other crew
getting any of our harvest in their count at the sawmills," shouted
Caleb from his precarious perch.

"How about Little Bill?" asked Hiram.

"He's practicing setting the bean hole," answered Bill. "We'll get
Ben to help."

"Ben knows how to hold a hammer?" Caleb sneered. "How come

he isn't tending the beans? That's one chore where he earns his keep."

"Once the ice goes out and the river starts to flow, Little Bill is going to be cookee when Jake moves his equipment downstream to feed the drivers," explained Bill. "Ben is staying behind to work on his cabin. He is nearing sixteen years old, and Jake thinks he's is ready to fend for himself."

"You mean he is going to squat," spat Caleb. Won't last long. If the settlers don't put him out, the state of Maine will, if they get control of the Aroostook Valley."

"Bill, what do you think about Daniel Webster working on settling the border with New Brunswick?" wondered Hiram.

"It's a shame we've had so much trouble over this. So much tragedy over a problem that should have been solved years ago. If Britain hadn't claimed the same land as Maine we wouldn't have this mess."

"Do you think we'll be driving logs into New Brunswick much longer?" asked Hiram.

"Not sure. There is a settler not far up river who is thinking about building a sawmill once the border question is answered."

"Then how come Jake is going to let that Ben stay up here? What can he do if there's no logging? Also, I still don't know how come Jake made him cookee in the first place and puts up with his head-in-the-sky silliness," Caleb asked.

Hiram answered. "I heard it has something to do with Ben's father and Jake being best friends."

"What! An Englishman and an Indian?

"Could be," said Bill with a knowing smile. "Besides, what else can you do in a logging camp with someone who is terrified of the river?"

2   The Secret

Spring 1825

Ben had been born in secret, the bastard result of short but very intense liaisons between Jedediah Smythe and Adelaide Wingate over two summer harvesting breaks.

Jed was the crew manager of a British lumber firm and she the daughter of a wealthy landowner along the St. John River in New Brunswick, Canada. He was barely twenty-one; she was in her late teens. Benjamin Wingate was a domineering man; many workmen believed that the spirited Addie had pursued Jed just to get at her father, who would have preferred she stay at home practicing her needlework with her two more obedient sisters. In reality, Adelaide hated the way her father bullied her. He was not against giving her a sound slap across the face if she talked up. He tried to mold her into his idea of an obedient woman, but she had been born with a sense of independence and was totally enthralled by the sweet young Jed.

Adelaide loved to run along the river's edge so the wind could blow through her long hair, released from the strict bun her father demanded. Her hair was the color of summer straw, yet soft as down. When Jed returned from the harvest in the spring, she would fly into his arms, releasing all her pent- up passion from its winter prison.

Adelaide would pop up wherever Jed might be walking a wood lot, and it was surprising they did not ignite the forest with their antics. With joy they shared their time together, whether watching the wildlife or *being* the wildlife. Sharing their thoughts or their bodies was with rapture for them. They would lie upon the mossy slope of the riverbank and dream about exploring the world. They watched the clouds and saw imaginary creatures floating by and wondered if the creatures could see them.

Late spring was their favorite time of year. They would sit among majestic pines as the lady's slippers were starting to bloom, forcing their broad leaves and fuzzy stems through the pine needles. Each bloom grew into the form of a delicate pink slipper that appeared opalescent when pierced by shafts of sunlight falling between the trees. The two hunted for the hiding places of the wild orchids and played a game to see who could find the most. Once in awhile they found an area of white slippers; they got two points for each of those. Whoever spotted a rare yellow blossom got five points. At the end of the game the one with the most points won the prize. It made no difference who won, as the prize was always the same.

Addie would giggle and say, "Can you imagine my lazy father in his tailored breeches walking his woodlots on the plantation? And I don't think he could ever imagine the goings–on, as you do the walking for him." She would look up from her place in his arms; scan the trees and say, "Unless a little birdie tells him."

As the days of their second summer grew shorter, their visits were less frequent because Jed was beginning to map out his next excursion into the Maine territory. Addie was busy with her forced labor, helping her Mother and sister Mary with the canning of early crops. How she hated snapping green beans! On occasion she kept going by pretending she was snapping her father's neck. And she never understood why her eldest sister was allowed to spend time writing notes to her friends on fancy paper instead of helping. Mother always made excuses for Phoebe. Said she was delicate and tired easily, while Addie saw her as just a spoiled want-to-be socialite who was too lazy to do menial work, considering it beneath her.

As fall approached, she found Jed doing his security walk, making sure poachers were not taking timber that was not theirs to take.

The couple lay on a large, smooth rock, basking in the warmth of the afternoon. They looked up at the patches of brilliant blue sky where the sun shone through layers of leaves in the small grove of birches that formed a canopy over them. Most of the leaves were still green, but some had started to turn yellow. Shadows from one layer to another looked like pieces in a kaleidoscope that changed with each breeze.

Jed thought. *How perfect the day. How perfect my Addie.*

"Addie," he said. He picked up her hand, kissed the back of it and then placed a delicate cameo pin in her palm. "My Da gave this to my Mum when their love was young. I never saw her without it pinned on her dress. Its shell is pale like the color of your hair and the silhouette reminds me of you. Knowing you have it will make the darkness of winter less lonely for me as it is as precious to me as you, and my heart is bound to it," he explained.

"Jed, you know what a pompous ass my father can be. Sure, he hand-picked you on the moors to oversee his lumbering, but he demeans you all the time as being beneath the social standing of our family. Once mother wondered if you would ever fancy one of her daughters and he gave her a smack with the back of his hand, laughing at the ridiculous thought. If he saw this, there would be hell to pay and I would never want him to hurt you. The very thing that would bind us together could also tear us apart and put you in danger," answered Adelaide, putting up a hard façade.

"And you?" asked Jed.

"He would never hurt me, for if the truth were known, I believe I'm the apple of his eye.   After all, he sired only girls, but I think I'm the closest he has to a son. He likes my independent streak even though he does everything he can to smother it."

Jed laughed out loud, "There is no way you would qualify as a boy, my love. I'll take my chances with the master of all he surveys if you will take a chance on me."

Addie softened and looked at the cameo. She kissed it softly and leaned into Jed's lips and kissed him just as gently. "I shall treasure it always, Mr. Jedediah Smythe. I'll pin it inside the bodice of my dress to rest near my heart," she murmured.

Jed chuckled, "With my mind's eye I'll picture it resting on your sweet breast."

She reached out and hugged him as if to hold him there forever, then kissed him with enough passion to warm him for days. Tears clouded her eyes as she twisted free and bounded off into the brush without a backward look.

He knew his job well as a walking boss and did his best to find the finest areas to harvest. As in prior seasons, Jed worked his way a bit upriver to the mouth of the Aroostook and followed it into

Maine to work on setting camp before any crew was hired. He loved to be alone in the dense forest. The trees were so close to each other that hardly any sun made it through the branches and the peace was pierced only by the sounds of wildlife. He knew the call of every bird and could mimic most. The air was musty and the ground perpetually damp, so loggers called it the swamp.

Mr. Wingate had signed an agreement with the Commonwealth of Massachusetts, allowing him the right to take timber along a great length the Aroostook. When Maine broke from the Commonwealth in 1820 to become the twenty-third state, he assumed the agreement remained in force and continued to log the area and drive the winding waterway to Aroostook Junction for milling. Even though the border was disputed, as far as he was concerned the area belonged to the British.

It seemed that in no time it was late spring of 1825 and the remnants of the drive had been coaxed to the mills at the junction, where they were sorted by brand. Here the sawyers worked their magic on what had once been trees standing where they first took sprout along the Aroostook River. Just as the trees had screamed when breaking from their stumps, they would whine as the saw blades sliced them into planks, two-by-fours or perhaps clapboards. The bosses at the mills were true craftsmen in the way they could look at the grain of the wood and measure in their heads what would be the best use of the harvest. Before long the lumber would be shipped down river to the city of St. John and from there to Boston, London, or beyond.

Jed was weary and longed for the comfort of his cabin a bit farther down river on the Wingate plantation. It had been a tough drive and he was glad it was behind him for another year. He had lost two of his crew. One was a blackbird who had always been a whiz on the log. Spikes had never failed him and his balance was without fault. Yet he went under, jarred by a boulder hidden just under the foam of the rushing river. Something must have broken his focus, as he knew the river like the back of his hand; when the water lowered to a gentle stream in the summer that massive rock was always prominent.

The other was a young man who had come over from Prince Edward Island to learn the ways of the logger. No one knew why and figured him to be an adventurer. He was part of a trio manning a bateau. The boat was assigned to corral any wayward logs and direct them with peaveys to the right channel. This type of longboat was not something Jed was fond of and thought most of those crews were crazy to work with their cants on long poles and think they could tame maverick logs. As they went around a curve, the young man's hook caught on a heavy chain along the shore and he was yanked into the water as easily as a fisherman pulls in a trout. He fought to free himself, but became more entangled; by the time other drivers reached him, it was too late. Jed wished he had spent a bit more time learning his story, as no one knew who would be missing the boy, so they buried him there in the spring mud several feet in from river's edge. He noted it was a bit east from where the Salmon Brook met the Aroostook, so he could pay his respects at future timber harvests. Jed knew him only as Wilson, but felt no one should go to his grave without some remembrance.

The river is the master, Jed thought as he walked the path to his cabin. Even though the full force of the spring thaw was finished, the river still lapped the shore with a fury that ate away at the soil, slowly chewing away a bit each year. He had built his place on the crest of a gently sloping bluff so that if the St. John River went over its bank, his special place would be safe from the deluge. The high perch allowed him a breathtaking view of the river, and it filled his soul to watch the dawning of a new day creep over the majestic pines. Sunsets were also spectacular, as the light that fell behind him caused the water to look like ripples of rose gold. Groups of birch trees on the other shore reflected the falling sun, turning the white bark a pink-orange. This was a delight for Jed's eyes. He certainly was unusual among the lumberers who spent their off time catching up on drink and women, then odd-jobbing when the money ran out. They hardly bothered to look at a sunset and definitely never saw a sunrise.

Walking up the slope, he thought of Addie. She was the one bright spot he had allowed into his life, as she understood the long absences of his work and did not expect any more from him than what he was able to give. During the winter he had missed her popping up when she could. Memories of her high energy and beautiful eyes had warmed him on many a cold night. Knowing his cameo rested near her heart had sustained him through the loneliness that came on solitary hikes in the forest.

Soon he would walk up to the mansion to report the results of the timber harvest to Mr. Wingate. Perhaps he would catch a glimpse of Addie buzzing hither and there in the rooms. If not,

perhaps Mary would see him. She was the only other who knew
of their love, and had, on more than one occasion, managed to
save them from being caught. Addie trusted her next-older sister
with her whole heart. She sometimes felt Mary wished she were
brave enough to break away from their father's grip, but instead
she lived in a world of fantasy through them. If Mary saw him,
Addie would know he was back. If not, he would get close to
the mansion that night and imitate the song of the chickadee,
knowing she would meet him in back of the wood shed. It was
their joke that Mr. Wingate had no idea that their favorite bird did
not sing at night.

As Jed approached his cabin, he was surprised to see so many
footprints in the small amount of snow left in the shade of the fir
trees. Hardly anyone came his way, but if it were important, he
was sure the visitor would be back.

He was so proud of his front door. For over two years he had
painstakingly carved into his found treasure, a single plank milled
from one of the great white pines that the Brits would take for
the masts of their ships. It was forbidden for anyone to take
trees marked by the King's men, but in the forest many trees go
in mysterious ways. The center of the door was covered with
memories of his childhood. It showed views of the hills and dales
of Northern England with thatched-roofed houses surrounded by
a few trees and gardens. Fieldstone fences snaked through pastures
holding flocks of sheep. Jed had captured the peace of that simple
life. A border surrounded the landscape on the door. It depicted
the myriad leaves found in the forest, from those of the tallest
trees to the bushes and vines beneath them. Between each leaf
was an intricately rendered pinecone. He had carved two heavy
U-shaped handles and attached one to the door and one to the
heavy plank that formed the jam.

Before he'd left, he had threaded a heavy log chain through the
two handles and held it together with a brass lock that had once
hung on a hook at the constable's office in a small New Brunswick
town before the jailhouse burned to the ground. He had found it
in the rubble with the key still in the hole. The key had a slight
bend, but after a good cleaning it still worked. Etched on the lock
and the key was the Roman numeral III. He kept the key with him
always, attached to a watch fob that had once belonged to his
father. When he reached the door he placed the key in the lock,
wiggled it in a special way to compensate for the bend, and the

top popped up. With a twist, Jed released the chain, which slid with a racket to the stoop.

The cabin was dark and chilly. Jed managed to light the lantern with matches always at the ready on a small table by the door. How good it felt to be home. He had left the square metal wood stove ready to set, so in no time warmth began to win against the cold. He would need to pry the top off the well to draw up some water for the teakettle.

Jed tossed his pack on the hand-hewn bench by the table in the center of the room and laid his mackinaw on the cot in the corner. It was one of the warmest jackets he had ever owned. The rest of his goods and clothes would be delivered within a day or two. He was looking forward to a good night's sleep, free from the noise and stink of the camp shanty. He always slept with his crew, but hated to crawl into the bunk from the end, as they were stacked to make use of the minimal space. Many called them muzzleloaders, but he felt them to be more like coffins.

The door suddenly burst open and in stormed Benjamin Wingate himself. He was in an uproar. "Jedediah, you son of a bitch!" he yelled with the color of rage in his face. "I should have left you in the north country of Britain where I found you. I should have known your quiet ways could not be trusted! You are nothing but a damn true Smythe," he went on, "just like your father!"

"What in the world?" Jed questioned.

"I'll tell you what in the world, you bloody traitor!" Wingate roared with the look of a man about to have a heart attack. "I've been up here to your hovel three times today to tell you just what. Where the hell have you been? Your crew showed up in town last night throwing their money away like it grew on the trees they spent months bringing down."

"I stayed at the mill. Some of your logs were mixed with that Yankee owner's across the way and I wanted to make sure they were sorted and counted in your harvest," answered Jed with a questioning look.

"Would that you were so responsible all the time," retorted the irate landowner. "She never gave you up, you know. All those months she kept your secret."

"Who and what?" puzzled Jed.

"My Adelaide, that's who," answered Wingate with a tear actually rolling down his aristocratic cheek.

"I don't understand," Jed continued with a bit of trepidation. "What does this have to do with Addie?"

"She finally screamed your name in her pain. She sobbed for you in her weakness as life was nearly drained from her," spoke Wingate with hate in his eyes.

Mr. Wingate came at Jed with a bundle of some sort and it looked as if he was going to throw it. Jed began to duck, but then Wingate reached out and shoved it at him instead. "Take it," he ordered. "Take the result of your treachery!" He then shoved the package into Jed's arms.

"Good God in heaven," Jed hollered as the bundle wiggled in his arms. It looked like a quilted sack, but when he pulled back the corner, two big blue eyes with the palest of long blonde eyelashes stared up at him. "My God, it looks just like my Addie."

"You better pray that your God is looking after you. You are going to need Him because whatever you had here is gone," the landowner blustered. "And furthermore," he continued, "what you call 'it' is your son and Addie is my Adelaide, and she will never be yours."

"I had no idea. I need to see her. I need to go to the mansion," Jed stuttered in shock.

"You'll never see her again. In her spiteful manner she demanded to suckle the bastard but that came to an abrupt ending yesterday. The doctor believed she was still fragile but I thought she seemed strong enough to be moved, so I bundled her off to Boston. She'll be on the next ship scheduled for England to recuperate with my sister in London. We had to tear the little bugger from her arms. And as for the mansion, don't you dare ever set foot there again. Do you hear me?" Wingate demanded.

"But the child? What shall become of him?" flustered Jed.

"I don't give a damn what happens to either one of you. As far as I'm concerned you could do everyone a favor and toss your son and yourself over the falls above the junction. Just get off my land now," ordered Benjamin Wingate.

Jed didn't have to think twice. He knew Mr. Wingate was out of his mind with fury, so he quickly put on his coat and buttoned the baby inside, securing him to his chest by putting his leather work belt tightly around his waist. With ax and knife hanging askew, he pulled his wool cap over his ears and stuffed his mittens into his pockets. His pack on the bench had a small supply of matches, his tin cup, a couple of shirts and a few big molasses cookies called lumberjacks. His eyes flew around the room and spotted his father's wood-carving set. He grabbed it and stuffed this precious gift into the pack along with his spruce gum box from the shelf near the door. By now Mr. Wingate was spinning around the room like a man possessed by the devil. He grabbed the lantern, swung it wildly and let it fly to the cot. The straw-stuffed mattress with cotton ticking and patchwork quilt went up in flames as quickly as dry leaves in the fall.

"Jedediah! You and your bastard had better run like the wind and don't look back!" screamed Benjamin Wingate as he picked up the bench and tossed it onto the growing inferno.

The baby started to cry, adding to the turmoil of the scene. Jed stumbled a bit, but managed to swing the pack onto his back as he ran for the door. On his way past the little table he grabbed the lock and key and stuffed it in with his mittens. He hesitated for a second to trace his hand over the carved memories of his childhood; the teakettle just missed his head as it flew out the door. He ran north to the woods, doing his best not to slip on the scattered patches of snow and ice. When he reached the bend in the river, he took a breath and looked back at his cherished cabin, fully engulfed in flames, sparks reaching the top of the tallest pines. He could still hear Mr. Wingate screaming obscenities and raving, "Don't you ever come back! No owner will hire you; count on it! Don't you ever tell anybody about that bastard! Don't you ever break our secret! Don't you ever link that child to my family and me! Do you hear?"

Jed could see his beautiful birch trees glowing with a pink reflection, not from the sunset, but from his burning home. A tear started down his cheek, which also picked up the glow. He opened his jacket just a bit to look at his son's face, but still protecting him from the cold. He gently touched his cheek, and as if channeling the spite of his Addie for her father, he baptized his son with his tears, naming him Benjamin Wingate Smythe.

3 Benjie

The moon was nearly full on the unseasonably cold night. Jed wound his way into the woods, but knew he was following the edge of the river by listening to the constant flow against the thawing soil. He kept a reasonable distance so there would be no chance of sliding on the muddy ribbon and slipping into the water. Jed would never risk his precious bundle by taking chances. So when the moonlight began to fade behind a bank of clouds, he chose to stop, as it was getting hard to see protruding roots and wayward brush. He knew the safest way not to wander from an intended path was to sit against a large tree until the darkness was broken by the glimmer of dawn or moonlight.

Jed settled into the space created by two large roots at the base of a tree. Here he was protected a bit from the damp soil, but there was no protection for him from the dampness of his son. He knew the baby had not eaten since he had been pulled from Addie's breast over twenty-four hours before and knew the child needed water and nourishment. The poor little guy had given up crying out and just whimpered once in a while with a shudder.

One item he had lost in the inferno was his canteen, but it had not been filled anyway, as he hadn't had time to open the well. A tin cup was in the pack, which he gingerly slipped off his shoulder so as not to dislodge the bundle. Next to the roots of the tree he felt a patch of snow that had not lost the battle to the late spring warm-up and he scraped up some of it with his cup, melting it by holding the vessel between his hands. Next he snapped a tiny bit off one of the molasses lumberjacks and soaked it in the water until it dissolved. "Now what?" he asked the darkness, startling a passing creature that scampered quickly into the brush. "Come on Jedediah, think," he spoke to himself.

With one hand Jed explored the depths of his pack and pulled out a cotton shirt he usually wore in the warmer months. With great agility, he pulled his knife from its sheath, and with a bit of cutting and tearing finally freed a square much like the ones his mother use to patch together for a quilt. He gathered it at the center and tied it in a small, tight knot.

Jed opened his jacket a bit; even in the dimness of the light he could see little Benjamin's bright blue eyes pop open with comical surprise at the rush of cold air. "Hi there, little fellow. Let's see if you like this at all," whispered Jed. The new father dipped one of his fingers in the cool mixture, and then put it near the baby's mouth. "My Lord," yipped Jed as his son began to suck with unexpected strength. "Did you hitch onto your mother with this much gusto? Poor dear Addie."

Jed began to dip the cotton knot in the mixture and dip again when Benjamin had pulled all the goodness out. In this way he gave his son his first meal by the river. He tucked the rest of his shirt under the baby to protect himself against the ever-increasing dampness and once again buttoned his jacket securely around the baby. He laid his head back against the rough bark, hoping to catch a couple of winks of sleep and prayed the sweetness of the water would be enough to satisfy the infant until he could find Jacob.

The sliver of light that landed on his face woke him with a start. Dawn was just breaking and it took a moment for him to shake off the sleep and then he panicked. His jacket had shifted and it was tighter around his waist. He stood and opened the top button to see little Benjamin stretching as if he were reaching for the sunshine. "Good morning, little boy. I'm your Da," he whispered.

And the baby answered with a healthy stuttering cry, easily interpreted as "Hey, Da. I'm hungry."

"I'm sorry, little one. I really know nothing of human babies, just flocks of lambs that can quickly find their mum's teat without much bother," explained Jed. He took the cotton knot and rolled it in the snow and offered it to little Ben, who latched on immediately. He secured the baby again and adjusted his belt and tools. Realizing he had not eaten in a day, Jed grabbed a lumberjack from the pack before he slipped it on his back. He got his bearings and continued north along the riverbank toward the junction. By now both he and his son were wet through again, so he cautiously quickened his step.

When he started west along the bank of the Aroostook River, he could see trappers meeting traders on one of the small islands off shore. Not knowing whether they were crew from the Wingate plantation, Jed went a bit further into the woods so they would not spot him if the baby started crying again.

Jacob had always told ancient stories about his people, the Mi'kmaq, and how they would set up temporary settlements along the river. They were not an agro society, but depended on fishing, hunting and gathering to survive. However, their nomadic style of life was quickly changing because of the European traders who had come into the area. Their precious forests were being raped by lumber barons and uprooted by farmers eager to plant in the rich soil created by the swamp.

Known to most as the Micmac, some of the tribe was now scattered into more permanent settlements, while others remained nomadic, moving   according to the season. A few would find a spot suitable for fishing and beaver trapping with some fertile ground for a small garden. Many of the men took jobs on lumbering crews in the winter. Most of their income, however, came from making baskets and crafts that had been utilitarian for the ancients but now were traded or sold to merchants, to be shipped to cities abroad as curiosities and collectibles. The last Jed had known, Jacob's family was near the area where the Presque Isle Stream met the Aroostook River, so he needed to travel a few more miles through the forest. He thought that Mr. Wingate would never think of looking for Benjamin with the native people. That is, if he ever looked for them at all. Jed just wanted to do his best to keep the bully away from his namesake.

The first indication he was approaching a settlement was the sweet fragrance beginning to waft through the trees. The natives had been reducing the sap of the maple tree for centuries, first making tight containers from birch bark to catch the sweet water as it ran from the trees in the spring, then dropping hot rocks one or two at a time into the sap, to boil it down to syrup. To preserve the sweetness for winter meals, they continued to boil the syrup to the sugar stage. . When the French and then the British started trading with them, the tribe was able to buy metal vessels and tools, allowing them to prepare the sap in iron kettles hanging over a hardwood fire. Jed salivated at the memory of the morsels of sugar Jacob had shared with him in the lumber camp.

"Dear Lord, please let us find him," muttered Jed. "Let this be Jacob's clan. He may be the only salvation for Benjamin."

He heard the sound of laughter in the brush ahead, and suddenly three young boys ran out, nearly tripping over one another. All were dressed warmly in cut down hand-me-downs, yet wore remarkable beaded moccasins. They were playing an ancient game, using a ball made of tangled stems and tossing it high in the air. The objective was to catch it with pointed sticks before it hit the ground.

"Merciful heaven!" shouted Jed. "You'll be putting each other's eyes out!"

His booming voice caused the boys to stop short, leaving slide marks in the pine needles, and startled the baby, who began to wail the loudest Jed had ever heard.

"Tell me, is Jacob here?" shouted Jed. "Are you part of his family?"

The terrified youngsters turned and ran like deer toward the high pines, comically falling and leaping in turn. Jed laughed out loud as the infant wailed even louder.

"Uncle. Uncle!" Jed heard. "There is a boogey man in the clearing. He can laugh and cry at the same time. He shouts like a man but he screeches like a baby all at once. Uncle! Help us!"

"What in the world is going on out here?" a voice bellowed as the man ran from the woods. He was a well-built fellow with chiseled features and long black hair that fell over his shoulders in loose braids. He was still wearing the bright red wool shirt and dark wool pants from the drive, but the heavy leather boots had been replaced by another handsome pair of moccasins.

"Over there, Uncle. There's the crazy man," hollered all three boys, pointing in unison.

"What the hell?" Jacob questioned as he squinted in the bright noon sun. "Is that you, Jedediah? What in the world are doing away from the pasty–faced, refined aristocracy? What in the world are you doing with the savages?" he chided.

He ran toward Jed and was just about to give him a bear hug when Jed gave him a straight-arm and stopped him in his tracks.

"Thank God I found you," sighed Jed.

"Jedediah, you smell like shit," said Jacob, jumping backward and wrinkling his nose.

"Would that it were not so," replied Jed.

Just as Jacob noticed the wiggling bunch in the jacket, Benjamin let out a loud whimper, tempered just a bit by exhaustion.

"What in the world have you brought to us, Jedediah? Some kind of wild cub that needs attention? You old softy. You'll never make your keep as a hunter, now will you?" joked Jacob.

"Please, Jacob, this is serious. You were the only one I could think of. We need your help," pleaded Jed.

"We?" questioned Jacob. "What do you mean by 'we'?"

Jed opened the top of his jacket and motioned to his friend to take a look.

"Jacob, I'd like you to meet my son, Benjamin Wingate Smythe," said Jed with softness in his voice.

Jacob laughed out loud, which was at once not pleasing to the baby.

"He has not had anything more than sweet water in a day and a half. What can I do to strengthen his little body and give him a chance? It looks like you would have some idea, judging by your three nephews," observed Jed.

"So you left a little gift behind on your last drive. Would I be looking at the reflection of someone named Adelaide Wingate? You named him after the bag of wind himself?"

"He sent Addie back to England and forbade me to tell anyone of his grandson. Told me to keep the 'bastard' a secret. So what else would I name him?" Jed explained with a grin.

Jacob slapped Jed on the back—something else little Benjamin did not like. "Come, I have a good idea who could help the babe and perhaps bring you back to smelling like a human."

As they entered the settlement, Jed felt transported to a land never before seen. Although most of the clan was living in basic shanties, there was one shelter Jacob called 'wikoum' but most called a wigwam. To one side were two large kettles hanging by hand-wrought, double-end wooden hooks, one end hitched to the handle on the kettle, the other hooked over the apex of a cone-

shaped framework of sturdy saplings. Each kettle hung over a
hardwood fire tended by two women wearing blankets against
the chill. In one kettle yellow-eye beans were soaking for baking.
Soaking was something there was never time for in the lumber
camp, as they never knew when they would break for another
location.

Once again, the beautifully decorated footwear fascinated Jed.
Most of the moccasins were embellished with intricate beadwork
or porcupine quills, or a combination of both. The sound of
chatter was everywhere, but he could see no men other than
Jacob.

"Nuga, are you in there?" Jacob asked, pushing aside a heavy hide
that covered the opening of the good-sized wigwam. The rest of
the dwelling was covered with overlapping pieces of birch bark,
sturdily stitched together as in the old times, with spruce roots.

"Is that my Jacob?" a quiet voice answered. "Come in, come in."

"Nuga, I would like you to meet my scrawny British friend,"
Jacob said.

"Ah, this must be Jedediah. I thought you to be one of Jacob's
mythical characters," she exclaimed as she held out her age-worn
hand.

"May I call you Nuga?"

"You may as well, because it is easier than nou' gou' mitj, which is
'grandmother.' I reminded Jacob that nuga is Mi'kmaq for knife.
He just laughed and told me he guessed that meant I was not dull-
witted. You Europeans, the French and British in turn, have driven
our language away. Now most speak an unfortunate mess of their
tongues," Nuga said with a bit of whimsy.

"We need your wisdom, grandmother. Jedediah brings us a new
life who needs strength," Jacob said as he motioned Jed forward.

Jed opened a few more buttons on his jacket. "Nuga, this is my
son Benjamin. I have decided to call him Benjie." A stream of
sunlight beamed through the opening at the top of the wigwam,
striking the baby in the eyes and causing his pale lashes to flutter
in surprise.

"O, mon petit Benjie." Nuga gasped in surprise. "How long has it
been since he suckled?"

"Nearly 48 hours," answered Jed, "although I did manage to get a bit of sugar water in him."

"Ah, Jacob, your friend has some brains. I did not think that of a Brit," teased Nuga. "Get your sister Hanna. She is helping strip birch bark at the rapids."

"Jedediah, how old is the boy?" she asked.

"The best I can figure, about three weeks," Jed replied.

"Sweet Benjie, we will find a way," Nuga said as she stood up from her seat of cushions and blankets. She nearly tripped over several pieces of pottery, but Jed steadied her with his arm.

As Hanna and Jacob entered, Nuga barked orders as well as any leader Jed had heard.

"Hanna, take the child home to be cleaned and swaddled. There are two who are nursing right now and one about to finish. Tell them this innocent won't care who becomes his wet nurse."

Benjie was freed from the nest in his father's jacket and passed gently to his new auntie, who hurried away. "Now I understand the stench of your friend, Jacob. I figured it was the stink of the British," laughed Nuga. "This is when we need an old sweat lodge, but some warm water in your shanty will have to do."

As they turned to leave, Hanna entered, clutching something in her fist.

"We found this tied to the child's ankle with a piece of blue ribbon," she said as she handed it over.

Jed turned it over in his palm and found the delicate cameo carved on the palest of shell. He held it to his cheek and without a word put it in his pocket and walked out of the wigwam, into the light to seek his new life.

4 Beyond the Fieldstones

Jed could not believe how long he had slept. The sun was already rising above the pines when he came out of the shanty. He had heard that the Micmac were included in the northeastern tribes called the Wabanaki, which meant People of the Dawn. He could see why. The beauty of the new day, underscored by the symphony of songbirds returning to spring nesting fields, filled him with a sense he had thought lost forever —the expectation that all things were possible.

As a child he used to stretch his gangly, lean body in the field grass at his parents' farm in the north of England, dreaming of what might be, wondering if perhaps one day he would find a way to explore beyond the rows of stone fence that separated one flock of sheep from another and isolated one family from another. Jedediah Smythe was a late-in-life baby born to Agatha and Thomas Smythe. The absolute surprise of his birth smothered any chance of a deep bond between him and his parents. They abided his presence, cared for his physical needs, and in time came to appreciate him as a farm hand; he found most of his comfort in the company of the animals he tended and in his creative imagination.

Jed had been closer to his Da in the midst of the storms of winter. They would sit together under dim lanterns in the farm kitchen and practice woodcarving. His father carved native birds and small animals to sell at spring fairs, but his best work was engraving intricate scenes and designs on wood planks and small boxes. Carving was a good way of bonding for the two, as it did not involve any physical contact or much talk; teaching was mostly done by example. Each tool made a different cut and each variant of the cut was accomplished by the way the tool was

handled. Over time, Jed became quite proficient in the art. His
biggest project was making a handkerchief box with roses carved
on the lid. He had to work on it after his Mum went to bed so
she would be surprised at Christmas. Although his Da never gave
a compliment, Jed could tell his father was proud of his work by
the gentle way he ran his fingers over the finished piece. Jed was
happy that he could help provide some extra money to the lean
pickings gleaned from working the barren land.

Jed's Mum was a timid lady who took great pride in her flower
garden. He saw her smile only when surrounded by her roses,
which trailed over the rough stone siding of their small home and
climbed over the fences near the sheep pens. June was always a
glorious month, for it looked like God had reached down and
dotted the landscape with spots of brilliance that gave way to a
muted carpet of purple heather later in the season. Even though
it was hard for her to show it, Jed knew his mother cared when
she worked for hours cleaning the fruit he had gathered for his
favorite gooseberry pie and, when she was able to get currents,
she treated him to eccles cakes. Her greatest gift was her insistence
on his lessons in mathematics and reading. He never learned
the origin of her small collection of books, but they led to an
appreciation of print that would carry him away to places far
beyond his dreams.

Shortly after his sixteenth birthday, Jed heard a bit of shouting,
loud enough to carry to the upper fields. He ran downhill,
jumping the fieldstone walls as though he were part of a fox and
hounds hunt. "What is it, Da?" he shouted as he came around to
the front.

"Nothing to concern you, Jedediah. Back to the flocks," his
father answered.

"Who is this lad, Tom?" the stranger asked.

"Leave him out of this, Wingate!" shouted Thomas. "We keep
good records and none of your damn sheep are in our fields."

Jed had never heard his father raise his voice that loudly in his life.
"Da, what is going on?"

"Looks like some of my flocks have been jumping walls just to
visit yours. Perhaps for tea and crumpets," the stranger sneered.

"You've really lost your mind this time, Benjamin," Thomas
shouted. "I can't believe you have dirtied your fancy boots by

coming up where the working folks live. We keep an honest farm
and you know it."

"I don't take anything for granted, Tom. The family has purchased
land grants in New Brunswick and I'm relocating to harvest
timber for the sawmills up the St. John. The lumber trade coming
out of there is as good as a diamond mine right now. The product
is spreading worldwide and we want a piece of it."

"Figured it had something to do with money to get you out of
your fancy house in London and willing to step in shit," snarled
Tom. "What does that have to do with us? Didn't like you as the
snotty brat who thought he knew everything years ago and my
feeling hasn't changed a bit. Your family may have found a way
out, but I'm sure getting your hands dirty had nothing to do with
it."

"If I remember, Tom, these walls could tell many a story of our
families working these fields. My father just happened to be a
bigger dreamer who got us out."

"Bullshit!" shouted Tom. "He just found a way to cheat his way
out by casually sorting his sheep and counting many as his own
that never were. We knew what was going on but didn't have the
so-called bookkeepers to prove it."

"Sour grapes, Thomas," laughed Wingate. "We still own most of
these acres and my caretakers believe that someone has been re-
branding."

Jed had had enough and shouted, "No way! I have the records of
our flock and I can prove every ram, ewe and lamb."

"My goodness, Thomas, is this lad your son? Where did he get
the learning to keep records of your farm and to be so sure of him
self? I still don't see any schools up in these God-forsaken hills,"
remarked the pompous landowner.

"I'll show you!" shouted Jed. My Da is an honest man. Don't you
dare say he isn't."

"Must say he has spunk, Thomas. He must get that from his
mother; surely not from you." chided Wingate.

Just then Agatha appeared in the doorway and gave him a look
that could have cut metal.

Wingate tipped his hat, "Hello Agatha. Been a while."

She wiped her hands on her apron and spun back through the door without a word.

Over the next few days Jed found himself the center of a whirlwind. He walked the fields with his father and Mr. Wingate. They counted the flock and Jed showed the records that matched to the last hoof. He showed how he could figure the shearing and number of bales of wool they should have for market. All in all, he greatly impressed Mr. Wingate, and, if truth be known, also his father.

Soon after, Jed and his parents were having their usual quiet supper meal when there was a loud banging on the door.

"Thomas, I need to speak with you!" shouted the visitor.

"Go away, Wingate. I know who you are and we are done with you. Jed proved our stock so go back to your fancy house or ship or new country. I don't really care where, just go and leave us be."

"Thomas, I think we can do each other a favor. I want to talk to you and Agatha about Jedediah," insisted Wingate. "Don't be the same stubborn ass you have always been."

Tom shoved his chair back with such force that it fell backward and halfway across the room. Agatha jumped up and grabbed his arm and pleaded with him to hold his temper. He pushed her back and she nearly fell into Jed's lap.

"Mum, what's wrong with Da? Why does Mr. Wingate make him so angry?" wondered Jed.

"They're still holding onto childish ways. Now you finish your supper and I'll see what I can do to quiet them down." Agatha spoke softly.

Agatha yanked open the door. "Benjamin Wingate, you've been in the brandy, as usual. Still the same old bully who thought I would drop everything I love in the world and follow you. Your presence has been hanging over this house for years and it's about time I put a stop to it. Now get off our property and away from my family. The wild woods of the Maritimes are a good place for you," she said firmly with a stamp of her foot.

Jed had never seen his mother stand so firm. It pleased him greatly and answered the questions in his mind as to why things in their home had always had a cold edge.

"Really Aggie, I just want to make this up a bit and I think I've found a way to ease things for you and give Jed a chance to get off this farm and see some of the world. He's a smart boy, Agatha. You've done a wonderful job with him and his talents are wasted in the flocks," slurred Wingate.

"What's on your mind, Ben? Spit it out," Tom said as Agatha settled back into her quiet self, picked up the chair, and sat opposite Jed.

"Jed is a bright boy; with the right training he can have a good future. I need a walking boss for my lumber team. Someone who can study an area to find the best trees for a good harvest and keep track of the raw timber until it gets to the mill. I'm sure it wouldn't be a far cry from managing a flock and figuring their output. He would be paid generously and we would have London send a monthly stipend to you so you could fix up this place and hire a hand to watch the sheep. We'd see that he is settled in a boarding home and once he is on his own in the forest, I'd give him a piece of land on the river to build his own place. This is a future he would never have on the moors," Mr. Wingate explained.

Jed's eyes opened wide with anticipation as he tried to figure out what his parents were thinking. He could travel to London then the Atlantic to New Brunswick. It was hard to contain his excitement. *I can do it. I can do it*, he kept repeating in his mind.

"There's no way I would entrust him to you, Wingate. I'd sooner place him with the devil himself," scoffed Thomas.

"Give us a day to think on it, Benjamin," Agatha interrupted," when are you leaving?"

"The ship leaves in a fortnight. We'll need to be on our way to London in three days at the most," were his parting words.

"I still say he's drunk and not thinking straight," Tom scoffed.

"Thomas, leave it be," Agatha said. "We need to think on it."

The next few hours were pure agony for Jed. They sent him up to his loft and he could hear their voices rise and fall like the tide. Then silence. He could not believe it. They went to bed.

After a sleepless night because his brain would not stop spinning, Jed climbed down to the kitchen at the first peek of dawn. His Mum was already sipping tea at the table.

"I can do it Mum. I know I can. I'm a quick learner. I can help
you and Da. I can see places I've only read about. See things I've
only dreamed about. I can make you proud. Please, Mum," Jed
rattled off in quick staccato.

The die was cast. Thomas never stood a chance and knew so after
one sentence. He begrudgingly hiked over to the Wingate home
and reported the decision.

The next two days were the most hectic ever. There were clothes
to wash and mend, personal items to gather, and they needed
to find the family suitcase that had been stored in the shed for
years. Jed's emotions went up and down like the handle on the
butter churn, as he walked over his fields among the flock he had
protected for so long. He had names for many of the sheep, but
never for all. All that he knew would be left behind. But then he
thought of the adventure ahead.

The night before he was to leave, Agatha served a meal fit for a
king. She roasted a piece of beef, which was a pure luxury in this
land of lamb. With the drippings she baked a Yorkshire pudding
and potatoes were put in the bottom of the oven to bake so that
the skin was crisp, while the inside was steaming. There was lots
of thick gravy just as Jed liked it.

The morning of the parting, Wingate had the sense to stay in the
carriage while Jed said goodbye to his parents. They all knew they
most likely would never see each other again. Mum had made
some currant scones and wrapped them in a cloth napkin that
Jed stuffed into the side pocket of the suitcase. And then she did
something unexpected. She took the small cameo brooch off her
worn dress and placed it in Jed's hand. He had never seen her
without it. It had belonged to his Da's Mum and Tom had given it
to Agatha before they were married.

"I can't Mum," Jed pleaded.

She just smiled and folded it in his grip. Then she ran her hand
through his fly-away hair. They had never been able to tame the
cowlicks.

Jed almost lost his emotional control when Da handed him a
familiar flat-hinged wood box. It held some of his father's finest
wood-carving tools.

"I can't Da," Jed mumbled.

"I'm sure they will come handy on many winter nights in the forest, son. When you see your Mum's brooch and carve your own beautiful designs, you can think of us as we will be thinking of you," Thomas replied softly. He then shook Jed's hand.

In his mind's eye Jed saw his parents give him a big hug and smother him with kisses, but it was never their way.

As he turned to the carriage, he thought he saw a tear in his mother's eye. He didn't look back, as he hoped that were true. If he had turned back, he would have seen his Mum standing in the doorway cradling her handkerchief box.

Jed found nothing to like in London in the short time he was there. It was noisy and dirty and the air made him cough. It surely was not like his countryside. But when he was on the ship, the freshness of the sea invigorated him and excitement once again began flowing through his body.

The Wingate family traveled on the upper deck while Jed's bunk was in steerage, but he did see them at the rail once in a while from a distance. He enjoyed the quiet nights on deck with the moonlight bouncing off the swells, except when the Wingate's youngest was bothering him. This thirteen-year-old girl in flaxen pigtails could be quite a pest.

5   The Sagamore

Jed's reverie in the first sunrise with Jacob's clan was broken by the sound of giggles. He looked down into six of the biggest brown eyes he had ever seen. He figured his blue eyes and untamed shit-brindle hair must look pretty funny to them.

"What's your name?" Jed asked of the one he believed was the oldest. They were so close in size it was hard to tell.

"I'm Peter and I'm six. Uncle calls me Pete. He's Joseph and he's five. Uncle calls him Joe. He's Sean and he's four. Uncle calls him Trouble," Peter answered in order.

Jed chuckled out loud.

"Benjie wants you," Joe pleaded as he tugged on Jed's shirt. "He's crying; he wants his Da."

Of course he would be precocious, thought Jed. "Show me the way, boys."

"Mama has him," came from the three little voices at once as they ran in order toward their home, set back a bit from the center of the settlement.

When he entered the front door, he found the interior simple but somewhat gracious. Everything was in place, which he found incredible, given that three perpetual motion imps lived there. There were quite a few Mi'kmaq antiquities carefully displayed around the room, which served as both kitchen and living room. A double-hearth fieldstone fireplace straddled the two areas, providing heat to both sides, and there was a spit and wood oven in the kitchen side. A small bedroom was at the end of the living room. A ladder went up from the corner to a loft that seemed to run the length of the second floor. Jed cringed at the thought of the boys climbing up and down, but soon realized he was their age when he had climbed up to the loft at the farm.

"Jedediah," said Hanna as she came from the bedroom, carrying the precious bundle.

Jed was startled and turned quickly to see her with his son.

"I'm sorry Jedediah. Didn't mean to spook you. Come and see what a beautiful boy you have."

He gently took Benjie in his arms. He was swaddled in white, lightweight wool and had managed to free an arm, which he flung toward his father. The blue of his eyes was even more intense against the white wool, and his fair hair seemed to vanish.

"You'll need to take him Jedediah, I'm late to the birches. It's much easier to remove the bark in the spring while the sap is running, so we can get large pieces. The men don't make as many canoes now and only Nuga uses birch on her wigwam, but we need a large stock for the decorated boxes and porcupine art we make for trading and selling," she explained.

"Perhaps I can help you with the harvest," offered Jed.

Hanna nearly doubled over with laughter. "I can't imagine a man offering to help. The women have done the gathering for as long as anyone can remember. It is just the way."

Jed thought, *I'm sure there are many 'ways' that are going to seem strange to me.* He took Benjie in his arms and rocked him gently.

"You sure smell a lot better, little guy. How do I know when he needs to be fed and where should I take him?" he asked of Hanna.

"Birdie lives just next to the maple kettles. She has offered to be Benjie's wet nurse as Tiny Bear is just about weaned. His mother didn't produce enough for such a big baby, so Birdie helps with the feeding and Ruth helps Birdie with her other chores, especially keeping watch on the sap kettles and Birdie's three-year-old, Martha. And as for when, you'll know," she answered with a grin from ear to ear.

"Birdie? Where in the world did she get name like that? And why in the world would she want to nurse one baby after another when her child no longer needs her?" Jed asked in astonishment.

"You'll soon know when you see her, Jedediah. She's tiny and flits around like a sparrow from limb to limb, never really roosting in one place for long. Only the spirits know how such a mite can produce so much milk. She has such love for all the young ones; I think she feels it a privilege to nourish them." She continued, "You and Jacob will eat your evening meals with us, so we can discuss later where you will stay with the baby. In the meantime, he will need to be close to Birdie and she will make a hammock for him at her place."

"Let's go exploring, Benjie," Jed whispered to the now-sleeping infant, and carried him down a path that led to the edge of the river.

The sun was beating down on the two, so he found a small stand of birches that had leafed out enough to shade them, and sat on the ground beneath. There were some young girls picking sweet grass and giggling while they tried to tickle each other on the nose. A group of older girls were coming out of the woods, each with a yoke that carried two full sap buckets made of hardwood slats bound together with a metal ring. The yokes looked very much like the ones used by cookees to deliver food to the logging crew. He thought how heavy they must be, but the young ladies did not seem to mind as they meandered along the well-worn path that led to the kettles. Jacob had told him that the women once made the vessels out of birch bark laced together with spruce roots. He had thought that hard to believe. What also amazed him was that in all the activity in the settlement, he had not seen a single man—not even Jacob.

A tiny hand brushed across his chin.

"My, you already have quite a right cross, little man."

His blue eyes melted Jed's heart, as Addie's had. Suddenly Benjie's rosebud lips puckered and let loose with the wail of an infant with needs. Jed rocked him with a shush, but it did not calm little Benjie, whose face was now bright red and the wails were punctuated with gasps for air.

"Looks like this is when," Jed said out loud, starting up from the river to find Birdie. Suddenly he realized Sean had joined them and had wrapped himself around Jed's ankle. "So, now I understand the name 'Trouble'. Hang on tight and point to Birdie's house."

It was quite a sight to see—the tall Englishman dragging his leg with a passenger uphill, Sean's belly laughs synchronizing with Benjie's distressed cries. "Look at me," Sean yelled to his brothers, "Uncle Jed is giving me a ride."

Pete and Joe ran ahead and got to Birdie's door at the same time, causing a scramble as to who would open it.

"Hey!" shouted Jed, causing Benjie to howl louder. This startled Pete so that he let go of the handle and tumbled backward over the step. Joe yanked the door open and stuck out his tongue at his older sibling. Jed peeked in and spotted a tiny woman sitting on a bench chewing on porcupine quills, seemingly oblivious to the commotion. "I'm so sorry to interrupt."

Birdie took the quills from her mouth, bent them just a bit and tossed them into a bowl of what looked like tamarack bark floating in red water. "Come in Mr. Jed, come in," she beckoned. "I chew on the quills to soften them so they can be shaped to form the patterns on our boxes. Bet you thought I eat them. Sounds like Benjie is hungry and needs a dry cloth on his little bottom."

Jed flushed a bit and felt truly stupid that he had not realized the baby might be uncomfortable. He looked around the room in the tiny shanty, which seemed jammed with projects. Delicate sweet grass and ash baskets in various states of weaving were scattered on a rough-hewn table, there were several small birch-bark boxes filled with a rainbow of colored glass beads, and larger boxes with incomplete quill decorations in many hues.

The boys had made themselves at home and were chasing little Martha in circles, causing all kinds of ruckus. Birdie tucked Benjie under her arm and in a flash reached over and whacked three little backsides. Jacob's nephews yelped out the door, feigning injury.

"Don't you worry, Mr. Jed. I'll take care of Benjie and put him down in a hammock. He'll be just fine."

Jed looked around at the jumble. Martha was playing with a carved wooden doll that was dressed in an elaborately beaded dress. The doll had a tiny pine needle basket and an intricately carved cradleboard holding a tiny wooden baby. Birdie was already busy attending to Benjie's needs; Jed felt very secure about leaving him there. The sweet smell of the boiling sap added to the comfort.

When he left the house, the brilliant spring sun caused him to squint, but he could see it was Jacob crossing the yard, just by his gait.

"Jedediah, how's the new papa?" Jacob shouted. "You look more like a human being this morning and smell more like one, too."

"Sorry I slept so late. I usually win the race with the rising sun, but that little fellow wore me out. Is there any news in the wind about Benjie and me?"

"Nothing about the boy but Wingate is spreading rumors. Says you took something from him that cannot be replaced and practically threatened any landowner with dire consequences if they hire you. Believe me, there are a couple who would snatch you up in a minute as their walking boss if it weren't for that raving lunatic."

Jed smiled. "He would never acknowledge his grandson. In his mind he was nothing but a piece of garbage to be tossed. He is so full of himself and obsessed with protecting his precious family reputation that it has never entered his mind that the child is a precious part of his daughter."

Suddenly Jed was ambushed by six little hands yanking the legs of his pants, trying to get his attention. "Uncle Jed, did you know that Uncle Jacob is our sagamore?"

"Sounds like you three have been listening to Nuga's stories again," Jacob answered, appearing to be flustered. "I saw a turkey with her brood of four near the beaver dam. Why don't you head into the bushes and try to find some of the little ones to chase? Bother them and not Jedediah. Who knows, you might find a feather off some tom."

Jed laughed and watched the brothers fall over each other as they disappeared behind a broad oak. "Just what is a sagamore, Jacob? Your nephews seemed quite proud of this tidbit of news."

"It is someone that I'm not. In another time, the sagamore was the leader of his tribe. The Micmac split into family units and he was one of the stronger older men who took charge. He made decisions for their needs."

"Sounds like that fits you perfectly," noted Jed.

"I like to think we all work together. We've managed to settle our group in this one spot for three years, while other families

still jump around, moving from place to place. They pack up the
canoes and head out to build new shelters near good hunting
or fishing or gathering grounds. I've been trying to establish a
more permanent village, but foresee an uncertain future for us.
People are buying up the land along the river; once a landowner
seals a claim, our people become squatters. I moved us farther
in from the junction, but this territory is still being claimed by
both Britain and America. No matter if this land becomes part of
Maine or part of New Brunswick; it will be lost to the Micmacs.
I have heard that some tribal families are already being relocated
to small reservations in New Brunswick. That would never do for
my people. We are all working hard and saving every coin in the
hope that we can claim and buy this piece of land from whatever
government takes over. Then we can form a township. You can
almost see where large towns will develop along the Aroostook.
I hope we are far enough removed to not be gobbled up by the
money people. "

"Sounds like the thinking of a sagamore to me," chided Jed

To which Jacob whacked him a good one on the arm and set off
on another of his seemingly endless chores.

The two men had become quite close over the past two lumbering
seasons. It was not easy to find a kindred soul in the rough-and-
tumble of a lumber camp, but during any off time they would
walk the woods or sit by the frozen river with hardly a word
spoken. They communicated through their wonderment of the
world around them. Most would find winter in the northern
forest harsh, but they shared an ever-curious appreciation of the
environment and the creatures that lived within. Those creatures
may have found it amazing that two humans could be so close yet
still be alone, sharing solitude.

One of the wiser moves by old Wingate was to hire Jacob as a
cook. Wingate had heard of Jacob's potential from other owners
and because he had money, he was able to lure Jacob to his crew.
Those close to him knew him by his given name, but all others
called him Jake.

Fiddleheads

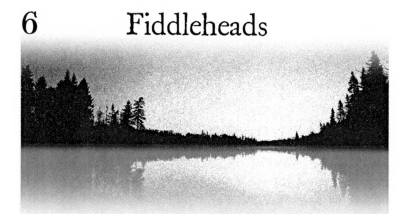

From the minute he walked into Hanna's kitchen, he knew a treat was ahead. The aroma of bread in the fireplace oven brought him swiftly back to his Mum's kitchen. He had worked the churn with zest at the thought of the butter on warm crusty nubs. He could see that Hanna had set out a bowl of honey to spread on the bread for the meal. The young men must have had great success at the beaver pond this morning, as their share of the catch was more than ample. Several fillets were sizzling in a large, flat, three-legged pan that stood over the coals in the fireplace. Another small kettle held dried apples from the fall crop. They were soaking in warm water and beginning to plump up. In a kettle suspended by its bail over the coals were greens that Jed didn't recognize, but he thought it rude to question. They were simmering with a small piece of salt pork.

The day had gone swiftly, between his frequent visits to cuddle Benjie and his effort to explore the area. Obviously the baby was adapting well, as his color was pink and Jed could swear his face was rounder.

He had watched Tiny Bear's mother work the reducing maple sap until she could tell it was ready to sugar. With swift dexterity she ladled the thickening syrup into squares carved out of small planks of cedar. When the syrup had cooled she turned the wood over and popped the chunks of maple sugar onto a large pottery plate. From there she packed the sugar into square birch-bark boxes and put on a tight cover. The maple sugar would be either stored or sold to traders. Any scrapings of sugar left in the kettle were put in small pots and sent off to the kitchens in the village. He made a mental note of an idea of carving fancier shapes for the molding.

Jed had found the beaver dam on the brook and marveled at the
engineering that went into the design. When the beavers slapped
their tails hard against the water to warn of his approach, the
residents of the branch-and-mud house quickly disappeared under
water until they felt he was of no danger.

At a narrow sluice to the side of the dam, a conical weir of
twigs had been built to trap any fish that might be swimming
downstream. He had noticed several fish drying on a rack in the
sun. Those were to be stored for a leaner time.

He had watched the boys digging ashes and stones out of their
bean hole not too far from the boiling kettles. He was fascinated
at how they started by arranging kindling with stones and placed
hardwood on end around the sides. *So this is where Jacob learned
his knack at baking beans*, thought Jed. Not many of the cooks
along the river served them, but he predicted before long all the
crews would want this baked meal, as it sure stuck to the ribs.
He made plans in his head to come back when they started the
baking. It shouldn't take long, as the beans were already being
soaked.

About mid-afternoon the three boys had skipped by, pretending to
be galloping on horseback. As they galloped by, without missing
a beat, Pete handed Jed a piece of molasses gingerbread in a small
ash basket. When Jed yelled out a 'thank you,' all he heard was
three neighs as Pete, Joe, and 'Trouble' disappeared down the path
to the meadow. Jed hadn't felt hungry, because Jacob had left him
two large biscuits, a bowl of cider applesauce and a kettle of tea
on the small metal stove. Although it had turned cold, Jed had
enjoyed every morsel and sip. The molasses gingerbread reminded
him that it was time to eat.

Jed sat on a stump at the edge of the woods to eat his lunch. He'd
stayed clear of the river's edge after seeing some canoes go by; he
wanted no chance that he would be spotted.

In the late afternoon he went to see Benjie, who had just nursed
and was still awake. Jed cradled him gently and spoke softly to
him. "I'm your Da, remember me? I'll always hold you close.
You'll not wonder for a second if you're loved. I may not be that
good at words, but you'll know by my actions."

Jacob gave Jed a nudge when he came through Hanna's door.
"Have you had a good day of exploring?"

"I feel like I have found a new world."

"Hey Hanna, we have a great explorer out here who has discovered an appetite." Then Jacob observed, "I'd say from the quiet in the house she is out rounding up her own little tribe."

Suddenly the peace was broken by the yelps of what looked like three drowned rats. Hanna had stopped by the rain bucket and given them a good splash. She grabbed a piece of cotton fabric from the counter and after some scrubbing, found three little faces under all the dust and muck.

After putting the food on the table, Hanna sat between Peter and Joseph on one bench while 'Trouble' plunked down between Jed and Jacob.

"Hanna, has it been settled where Benjamin will stay? With his father or Birdie?" asked Jacob.

"I nearly forgot. Birdie thinks the baby should stay with her, as it is so much easier for her to have him near. Besides, I think she would have a hard time letting him go right now and she knows you will be there whenever you can," Hanna said, looking at Jed.

"Whew, what a relief," sighed Jacob. "I thought he might bunk with us and what in the world could I do to help? I certainly don't have the right equipment," he chuckled. "I'm going to have enough to do just keeping his father busy."

Jed dug eagerly into the fish Hanna had prepared for dinner and poured honey on a thick slab of sourdough bread. He eyed the greens with curiosity and then tentatively ate one of the coiled pieces.

"What you think?" asked Jacob.

Jed felt every eye in the room on him. "Really not bad. Tastes a bit like the asparagus that I picked on the farm in the spring." Jed tasted another. "What in the world is it?"

Three little voices answered in unison, "Fiddleheads."

Jacob came out with a belly laugh. "Just enjoy, Jedediah. I'll take the mystery out of them for you after we finish."

And what a nice finish. Hanna served the warm apples swimming in fresh maple syrup.

Jed surprised all when he helped side the table to the work area near the dry sink and fetched a bucket of water from the well.

"Watch it, Jedediah. Take a walk with me before the rumor gets around that men help in the kitchen," said Jacob.

Always helped my Mum, thought Jed.

The sun hung low in the sky as the two men walked the path to the river. The water was calm but rings were visible where a fish had jumped for the bugs that plagued man and beast this time of year. Jacob took a long breath. "Isn't this beautiful, Jedediah? I chose this location at the bend where the water flows on three sides. Certain times a year, we see both sunrise and sunset. I must make it work so that my family can stay here."

"What about the reservation?"

"I've great respect for my heritage, Jedediah, but take a close look at us. I just don't feel we belong; not one of us is full-blood Micmac, including Nuga. From what she says, her grandparents were respected among the tribe. One of her treasures is the tall, pointed ceremonial hat her grandmother wore. The quill art is exquisite."

"I saw that in Nuga's wigwam but had no idea it was so old," marveled Jed.

"Nuga's mother Sarah was an only child. She was married quite young in a Catholic service to a French missionary in the area of Acadia that is now New Brunswick. The French had been quite successful in converting the Micmac and Nuga's parents felt it was very special that she married a man so devoted to the Christian God. Too bad that it turned out he didn't act like a man of God."

"Did he mistreat her?" wondered Jed.

"Physically and mentally. Things started well. Then his selfish side surfaced and he became very demanding and abusive. She never complained, as Micmac men looked after their mates and she was ashamed that her parents might find out. She felt it was her fault and that perhaps she was not as worthy as a white woman. After all, he had chosen her and she adored him. When Nuga was born, he was full of himself and took the baby everywhere, showing off his beautiful baby. He named her Cateline, from the French word for purity, and had her baptized in the church with no family present."

Jed chuckled, "As if he had given her life on his own."

"What Sarah did not or perhaps not want to see was that he never showed the baby to any French businessman or landowner who came to the chapel. None of them knew he had taken a native woman for his wife. It became clear to many that he had married this beautiful young woman for his own pleasure, expecting her to tend to his every need."

"How long did that last?"

"Just until the coward left in the middle of the night to flee to France so he would not be caught up in the great deportation of the Acadians by the British. He was not about to bring any savages back to his homeland, so he abandoned Sarah and Cateline."

"And Sarah?"

"She carried her shame back to her parents and the story goes that she pined her life away. Nuga was left in the care of the Micmacs, where the sweet Cateline was raised in the way of the tribe."

Pointing to the muddy edge of the river, Jacob said, "over here Jedediah, before we lose all the sun. Take a look."

Jed bent close. "All I see are some ferns coming up. What am I missing?"

"Nothing at all. Look at the tops."

"They haven't opened yet."

"Look closer. Humor me," said Jacob.

"Some leaves have started to unfurl; others are still tightly closed."

Jacob pressed on. "The ones not open. What do they look like?"

"At the top of the stem, they are coiled. If I use my imagination, they almost look like the end of a fiddle."

Jacob chuckled, "Sort of like a fiddlehead?"

"Good God, I've been eating weeds!" yelled Jed.

Jacob let out a belly laugh, which was echoed by giggles in the bushes behind them. "Scat!" he shouted, causing a squealing cloud of dust to run up the path. "Let's get a good night's sleep. We'll set off at sunrise in the canoe. I'll tell you more about my family away from three sets of ears attached to chattering mouths."

Jed yawned. *Guess there will be no bean hole tonight.*

7 Trouble on the River

Jed woke to the aroma of frying bacon, something he didn't have often in the lumber camp. *My,* he thought, *the home of a great camp cook was a smart choice for my sanctuary.* It didn't take Jed long to get up, ready, and out to the table.

"Thought that would get you out of bed," laughed Jacob.

On the platter with the bacon were large flapjacks. "Never could figure how you make these so light. Some I've had could be tossed as weapons."

"A person needs some secrets. That makes me a bit more valuable to a boss who wants to keep his crew happy."

"I'd better slow down or I'll sink your boat," said Jed.

"Would take a lot more than your appetite to down a good old birch-bark canoe." Jacob added, "I know you're eager to check on your boy. I'll meet you at the landing."

There was just enough early dawn light to allow Jed find his way past Hanna's place to the other side of the settlement where Birdie lived. He felt surrounded by deep peace, broken only by the wake-up calls of spring songbirds happy to be back at their summer home.

The door of the small cabin was slightly ajar, most likely to let in some of the wonderful early fresh air. Quietly, Jed peeked inside. A dim glow from a lantern on the table was the only light. The tiny lady was sitting cross-legged against the wall on a thick pile of blankets. Cradled in her arms, Benjie was nursing with great gusto. Jed felt the warmth of embarrassment creeping up his cheeks.

Birdie looked at Jed with a great smile.

He formed a silent "thank you," which made her smile grow even larger.

As he left for the river path, Jed saw that the sap kettles were empty and the bean hole was covered. *Looks like I'll miss the digging up, too. Next time.*

The sunrise was doing its magic on the river, turning the water into shimmering gold. Jacob handed a paddle to Jed and nodded for him to get in the front of the canoe. It was about 17 feet long and beautifully crafted from what appeared to be a single piece of birch–bark, rather than overlapping pieces sewn together with spruce roots and sealed with spruce gum.

"Where in the world did you find a piece of bark this large?" wondered Jed.

"That's one secret I'll keep. The tree has to be over ten feet in diameter and able to produce a single sheet twenty feet long. Once we find an old stand of those wonders, no one tells where they are."

"No seats?" queried Jed.

"Nope, just bend those long legs. We'll be paddling the way I was taught, kneeling down. The newer canoes have seats, but to me they get in the way, especially when I have a lot of goods to carry. I have a pole so I can stand to push the canoe through the shallows."

The river was fairly quiet and the two friends slipped across the surface as if they were gliding on ice. A couple of girls were snapping off fiddleheads where the water lapped the shore and putting them in a basket woven of thin strips of ash.

"Hey look, Jedediah, they're pulling up some more weeds for your next meal," Jacob teased. "They'll soon unfurl into fern fronds and our spring treat will be over for another year, just as the sap has started to stop flowing in the maples and birches. That's why so many are out of the settlement—they need to harvest as much as they can while it's available."

"Are we heading somewhere special?"

"Bear sent a message down that he got two deer with his flintlock rifle. They are about two miles in and I need to pick up the fresh meat and the hides for tanning. Not a scrap will be wasted. In the good old days, the hunters would leave the game where they killed it and the women would go back to dress it," chuckled Jacob.

Jed shifted his weight, setting the canoe rocking. "Sorry, I'm not used to kneeling in one place for so long."

"Not a religious one, huh?"

"I find nature's world a spiritual experience," explained Jed.

"The Micmac are very spiritual; that is probably why they were easily converted to the Christian God. Some of it is based on superstition, but much came down from the ancients as a deep belief in goodness and respect. They believed that if they took the life of an animal for sustenance, they had to thank its spirit and waste none of the sacrificed animal. A use was found for every bit, from the meat to the bones to the brain to the antlers and hoofs. They did not want to make the animal's spirit angry, for they feared it would turn on them. Nuga tells stories of hunters who would first take the animal's eyes so it could not see who killed it."

"Think I'd rather hear more about your family. By any chance has Bear anything to do with Little Bear?"

"My, aren't you a smarty. My cousin Bear is his father."

"Let me guess, he's a big fellow," Jed chimed in, waving his paddle through a swarm of black flies.

"Guess I better get back to the family tree. We left off with Cateline, who is now the grandmother or grandmother-in-law or 'Nuga' of most of this crew and she knows each and every soul. She is much better than I at keeping track of them," said Jacob, deftly doing his job of steering the canoe past a log half in the river and half out.

"I hope that's one of Wingate's. Wish I had shorted his count myself."

"Cateline did not learn much from her mother's tragedy. She fell head over heels for a French fur trader who regularly came to the Micmacs to pick up pelts and leave glass beads, cotton material, metal tools, kettles, and so on. A few French were still around, even though the British had taken over governing, and he was no threat, as he did not try to settle the rich land and timber plots the Brits coveted. He also found prime furs for the beaver top hats favored by the gentlemen in England. So at the tender age of 17, Nuga married the much older Pierre Croteau."

"So that fine, elderly Micmac lady living in the wigwam is named Cateline Croteau," Jed noted, shaking his head in disbelief.

"She didn't leave the tribe; he lived with her when he came by on his trading travels. They had four children—my uncle Henri, my mother Angelique, and twin boys who died shortly after birth. So Nuga's children had more French blood running through their veins than Micmac. They spoke French and a smattering of their native language, which was much more difficult to learn. The European missionaries pretty much forced the language out of the children; they were not allowed to speak Micmac in school or church."

"I can see now why she tries to teach the children Micmac words and history, great sagamore."

At that, Jacob lifted his paddle and swooped water all over Jed with great glee. Jed turned to complain just as they went under a low-hanging limb that whacked him on the back of his head.

"That will teach you, you skinny Brit. After all, this is the land of the savages, and the spirits of the trees are in my command."

"I surrender, Chief. Get back to your story."

"I'll try to put it together quickly—Bear and his older boys should be around the next bend."

Jed got back into the rhythm of the stroke.

"My uncle Henri did quite well. He was a trader like his father, but built a permanent cabin near the river where he bartered with the Brits, French and Micmac. He was more or less a go–between. Each group could come to him and find what they wanted. Some supplies he would buy outright and turn a profit. Over the years, he slowly added rooms for a trading post, which is still here, just about a mile from us, where the river turns north   It is in a perfect spot for all concerned—hunters, fishermen, farmers, lumbermen and the Micmac. No one knows if the settlers will be allowed to stake a legal claim once the border is settled. I know he has been saving in the hope of buying that piece of land.

He married Amy Wilson, the daughter of one of the British merchants, much to the chagrin of her father; he didn't want her to settle for a mixed breed. I don't think the Micmac heritage bothered him as much as the French. Henri and Amy were the parents of Jacques, known to most as Bear. You'll soon see why. Jacques was such a large boy that some say Aunt Amy did not have much baby-making material left when she gave birth to her tiny daughter, Beatrice. You know her as Birdie. A few years later they had another son, Philippe who still lives with them and helps run the store."

"You didn't tell me Birdie is your cousin."

"Well, most of the clan is just that—one big family. Bear's wife is Ruth. She is mostly Micmac with a smattering of French. They have two boys and a girl in their teen years. Then along came Tiny Bear, who is nearly two. Ruth has some of her siblings here with their families, so Bear has in-laws near. Everyone pitches in. The younger boys try to slack off, but as I remember, most do at that age."

"Now it's coming together," exclaimed Jed. "The woman helping Birdie is her sister-in-law Ruth. What about little Martha?"

"That's a bit sadder. Birdie married a fine young man from one of the other Wabanaki tribes, the Passamaquoddy. She went over to the coast to live with his family in the Perry area. They are fishermen. While she was carrying Martha, her husband drowned in a tragic accident. She came back to be with Nuga for the birth and stayed. Aunt Amy wanted her to live at the trading post, but she wanted to be with us. We built her cabin and she more than earns her way with all the beading she does and the baskets she makes for trade."

"Hey there," came a booming voice from on top of the knoll.

"My word," exclaimed Jed. "That has to be Bear."

One of the biggest men Jed had ever seen tromped down the embankment and grabbed the front of the canoe before it bumped onto some rocks. He tethered it to a sapling.

"Bear, like you to meet my friend Jedediah" said Jacob, handing him a basket of jerky and molasses cakes from Ruth.

"So you're the skinny-assed Brit I've heard about," exclaimed Bear with a whack on Jed's shoulder that nearly toppled him into the river. "Yep, you're right—never seen such hair."

Jed could feel the flush filling his face.

"So what do you have for us?" asked Jacob as he started climbing the slope.

"Good-sized doe and a wonderful buck. His rack will bring a lot in trading. Some snooty English gentleman will pay a goodly sum to have a trophy that was brought down by some savage. Got each with one shot to the head so there will be no holes in the hides," bragged Bear.

"You're so full of yourself," scolded Jacob. "You're just too cheap to waste any shot."

"I've put some of the meat in the basswood hunting bag to share with the folks. Better cover the bottom of the canoe with pine boughs to protect from the mess. We'll toss the hides over and you should have plenty of room for long legs there."

"What will they do with the rest?" Jed questioned as they pushed off.

"In a minute. Bear's trying to get our attention."

"By the way," Bear shouted. "There was a canoe from the Wingate Plantation up here earlier. You know which crew. They're out looking for your buddy and I don't want to know why."

Thanks came in unison.

"Keep a keen eye out," warned Bear.

"What should we watch for?" asked Jacob.

"One wears a raccoon hat with a tail and the canoe has a red star on each side of the bow."

"I know the two brutes," spat Jed. "They could be back to the junction by now."

"I'll stick as close to the shore as possible so we won't be so easy to see."

"Good idea," said Jed, shifting his position to get more comfortable. "Now finish up about the rest of the deer."

"They will carefully remove the slab muscle across the back. That makes the best sinew for sewing. The next best is found in the lower leg. Much of the meat will be dried for the winter. There is no waste—every part has some use. I'm sure the brain is in the bag we have, as that is used for tanning its hide. The women will do that."

"Goodness. Let's talk about something else. We've talked about Henri. What about your mother and father?"

"My mama married Joseph Buck, a full-blood Micmac she had known for years; they went to school together at the convent. I understand they were inseparable from the day they met. She was his world. When she turned eighteen he asked her to marry him in the ancient way. She sat in Nuga's and Grand Papa Pierre's wigwam. According to custom, my father came in the front and tossed a stick in her lap. If she threw it back it, she refused him. If she kept it, she accepted. They say she kissed it and held it to her breast. An ancient couple would then go off alone to the forest, returning as husband and wife when they had killed a deer and gathered food for the wedding feast but Nuga would have none of that and they were married by the priest."

"So" injected Jed, "I finally know your full name: Mr. Jacob Buck, or shall I say Chief Jacob Buck." Jed ducked in case more water came his way.

With a bit of nostalgia, Jacob continued. "My father was so proud when I was born. Nuga says that as soon as I was able to toddle, he had me in the woods teaching me the ways of the animals. One day we found a perfect turkey feather and Mama made a soft hide headband with an ornate porcupine quill design and I wore the feather in the band. When I was nearly six, they told me I was going to have a brother or sister. Part of me was happy, while another did not want to share my parents and grandparents with anyone. Mama let me lay my head on her belly so I could feel the baby move and I began to love it before the birth."

"And that was Hanna?"

"Yes. When the baby started coming my father sat vigil by the wigwam and Grand Papa took me for a long walk along the river. He loved it so and would tell me stories from when he was a child in France and lived next to a river much like it. When we were coming back I could hear the screams of my mother and tried to run to her but Grand Papa held me back. He picked me up in his strong arms and I can still feel the way his heart beat against me."

"It's true that the memory of a certain touch stays with you," said Jed, remembering his mother's hand running through his hair as he was leaving England.

"Suddenly the screaming stopped. The silence was deafening.

Then I heard Nuga let loose an ungodly wail and I knew in my young soul that my mother was gone. "

Jed seemed in deep thought about what he was learning. Suddenly he pointed to the one white elongated cloud floating in the clear spring sky. "That looks just like a fish. It even has an eye."

"That's my British dreamer. I was wondering where your imagination was hiding," Jacob laughed in appreciation of the change of mood.

"Damn," Jed yelped.

"What's the matter? Did your fish-cloud turn into a monster of some kind?"

Jacob followed where Jed was pointing downriver. The red star on the bow of a canoe was appearing around a bend.

"Quick, lie flat in the boughs under the supports and don't move a muscle," ordered Jacob. As fast as lightening, he laid the extra paddle along the side, pulled some of the boughs over Jed, tossed the bundle of meat on top of that and then covered everything with the hides.

By now the Wingate crew was close enough for Jacob to see the raccoon tail flying in the wind.

"Ho, half-breed," came a shout from one of the men, who was waving a paddle at him. "Have you seen that British boss you hang out with at the camp?"

"Haven't seen him since before the drive started. I moved my equipment a few miles toward the mill while the ice could still hold me. That way I'd have vittles ready for the drivers. We usually don't meet up again until early winter. Didn't he make it back to the St. John?

"He sure did and somehow made old man Wingate so angry he tossed him off the plantation and torched his cabin."

"What in the world did he do?" Jacob shouted back.

"Wingate said it was none of our business but he sure wants to know if he perished in the woods or if he's hiding somewhere. There's a big bounty for anyone who finds him, dead or alive, and can guarantee he won't come back."

"I'll keep an eye out. Could use the money myself."

"What you got there, Jake?" one asked.

"Bear got a couple of deer and I'm bringing some meat and the hides back to the settlement," Jacob answered as the two paddled closer.

Under the pile Jed was trying his best not to gag as blood dripped around and on him. It was getting hard for him to breathe—the hides were much heavier than he had imagined.

"Look like fine hides. Want to sell them?"

"Sorry. The women are waiting to use these for moccasins and pouches. If I don't bring them back in one piece, they'll have *my* hide instead."

"They sure are fussy," laughed one of the men. "How come you're hugging the shore? I wouldn't want to go that close. Too many rocks."

"Bear said he thought he saw a moose in this area. I was just checking it out for him. Their hide makes thicker leather that protects the foot better."

As they started to turn, one yelled back at Jacob, "If you hear of the Brit, let us know and we'll cut you in on the bounty. Never did like him—a strange one.

Jacob leaned down and pulled some of the pile aside so Jed could get some fresh air. "Stay put for now. I'm going to paddle to the mouth of the brook, then you can slip over the side and work your way up to the beaver dam. Take a good wash in the pond and I'll bring you some dry clothes."

"Do you know how cold that water is?"

"Would you rather stay smelling like a slaughter house? Not quite as bad as baby shit, but not far behind. The dogs would be knocking you down."

It seemed like an eternity before Jacob came trudging through the woods to find Jed, curled up and shivering. "Why Jedediah, you look like you were in a birling contest and the spinning log tossed you for a mile."

"Ha-ha."

They got back to Hanna's place just in time for the evening meal. The boys nearly fell off the benches laughing when Jed walked

in wearing an old pair of Jacob's pants that were too short. The
leather had been softened with wear and age and the fringe up
both sides of the legs was getting tattered. Above the pants he
wore a red wool lumbering shirt that also had seen better days.
On his feet were handsome moccasins.

Hanna knew better not to ask.

The beans had been baked to perfection in the hole. Not as
much salt pork was used, so they were not at all greasy the way
the hungry axmen liked them. They had a more delicate flavor
because they were sweetened with maple syrup instead of dark
molasses. Hanna had cooked another mess of fiddleheads and
made molasses bread.

When the good-sized fried venison steak was plopped on his plate,
Jed's stomach turned upside-down. *This is going to be hard to
swallow*, he thought.

8   Brothers

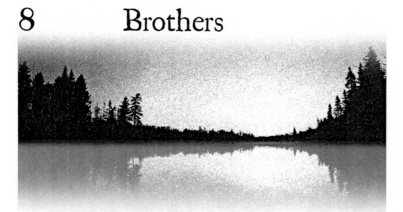

Jacob met Jed just outside Birdie's shanty after his evening visit with his Benjie. "How's he doing?"

"He's doing just fine, but Birdie nearly split in two with laughter when she saw my new style," grunted Jed.

Jacob tossed Jed's wool hat at him. "Put it on."

"Good grief, why? My brain will boil. It's warm tonight."

"Better your brain boil than have it smashed to bits by one of Wingate's thugs. We have to do something to hide that very—shall we say—*unusual* hair of yours. It could be spotted from the river even if your skinny, tall body didn't give you away."

"I'm leaving, Jacob. I didn't mean to put your family in danger," Jed said suddenly.

Jacob gave him a quick whack to the head.

"What was that for?"

"Just seeing if I could knock some sense into that dense British brain. Let's take advantage of the full moon and walk over by the brook."

The two friends settled on a large log near where the water flowed over a ridge of rocks smoothed by years of current. The rhythm was somewhat soothing and the moonlight on the bubbling surface was hypnotic.

Finally Jacob asked, "Just how would you care for your child? You're going to take him away from the breast of a woman who loves him? Birdie is so attached, it would break her heart."

"Guess I hadn't thought that through. I just don't want anything to happen to your family."

"Benjie will stay in his cradle board when he's carried around the yard, so he'll look no different from any other infant in the village. As for you, we need to knock the proper English look out of you and create an everyday man of the woods —mix you up as Micmac with a dab of French, a dash of English, a dollop of Irish."

"Irish! Where did that come from?" exclaimed Jed. "I'd just as soon not be stuck with some of that."

"From what I've heard tell, the feeling goes both ways."

"Just where does the Irish come in?" Jed wondered.

"Well, when Hanna helped our Uncle Henri at his trading post, a lot of men took interest in her, but she would have none of it; her heart yearned for a full-blood Micmac like our father. But fate stepped in when she tripped off the porch one day and toppled straight into the arms of a strapping young Irishman who had worked the lumber season as an axman and took a turn at trapping in the summer. He was bringing in some pelts."

"And I suppose that is where Sean got that reddish glow in his hair," teased Jed.

"And I suppose you would be right," Jacob snapped back with a big grin. "His name is Francis Sean Ryan. That's what Hanna calls him when she is fed up with his foolishness but everyone else calls him Frank."

"Good Lord," exclaimed Jed. "How in the world did he get into this neck of the woods?"

"His parents came to New Scotland, which was once a section of Acadia before the French were expelled. Now, most call it Nova Scotia, but Nuga was always unhappy when the king of England wanted them to use the Latin, so to us it is still New Scotland."

"She sure is strong-minded for a little lady."

Jacob continued, "The Ryans were potato farmers, particularly the Blue Nose variety. Sean wanted adventure more than farming, so he came our way. When he found Hanna he never once thought of going back. He charmed her with his fine Irish blarney and his fiddle. My, how he can make that instrument sing!"

"When will I meet him?" wondered Jed.

"He's down in the city of St. John picking up some fresh seed. When we found this piece of land, he set some potatoes and discovered the Aroostook Valley was a perfect place for growing. He works on clearing a larger field every time he is home. One of his friends has cleared a fairly large plot further inland. I don't think you have met Dan Thorpe. Many use his hay and grain for the hovels and sometimes I get him to part with a few potatoes as a treat for the woodsmen. He got a grant for the timber rights from his farm to the river. Not sure this will hold once the boundary problem is settled, but he's sure farsighted. We're trying to be the same."

"So that's why everyone is working so many odd jobs; you want to make this a permanent village."

"That's the dream."

"May I ask what happened to your father?"

"My mother's death put him over the edge. He cradled her body for hours, never once looking at Hanna. When he came out of the wigwam I ran to him, but he stopped me cold with his eyes. He gave my hair a tousle and walked into the forest. All he took was his flintlock and pouch."

Again, Jed could not help but think about parting with his Mum and how she had run her hand through his hair.

Wistfully Jacob continued, "My father never came back. Not even for the funeral. I sat by the river for days, then weeks, hoping to see him walk out of the woods. So many times I imagined running into his arms. We heard that he took up drink, which can be deadly for an Indian, especially a full blood. He occasionally did some cooking for a random logging crew, probably to get his hands on the alcohol in the lemon extract. Then he faded out of sight. Nuga and Grand Papa Pierre took us in and we were raised by the tribe."

Jed laid his arm around his friend's shoulder and they sat quietly for a while, watching the brook trout jump at the swarms of mosquitoes over the water. When one particularly large fish jumped, the spell was broken.

"Look at that," Jacob murmured, "I'll have to tell Bear's boys to drop a line there."

"How many family members do you have here?" asked Jed.

"This time of year about 43, but it grows to nearer 50 when the odd jobbers come home. We want you to make it 52. How about it?"

"Will I have to cut my palm to become your blood brother?"

"You've been reading too many Indian stories in the chapbooks," laughed Jacob. "How about a handshake?"

9 Fiddling Frank

Summer 1825

A plan was developed. Jed would stay away from the river, at least until the initial search by bounty hunters had subsided. Benjie would keep to the same schedule he had now. When Birdie was needed for the planting, Benjie would be carried in the cradleboard to Nuga, who really could not wait to get her hands on him. When he started to outgrow the infant board, she would weave a small rush hammock for him, which could be string between the trees while she was telling the older children about their heritage and teaching them moccasin-making, beading, or quill decorating. None ever questioned why Jed and the child came to them. They just knew that they loved Benjie very much and they liked the way Jedediah was such a good friend to Jacob.

Jed was to help around the settlement in any way he was needed. Jacob demanded he not do dishes and housework; that would make things difficult for the other men. He did this very ceremoniously with tongue in cheek—sort of. He was not to carry the cradleboard, as this would very much be out of character and would be noticed by anyone passing on the river. He would keep his hair cut short so the tangle of cowlicks would not be as obvious, and he would dress in the mishmash style of the men. Most wore trousers and shirts of the type used by the woodsman. Ruth gave him one of Bear's old fringed shirts, which flapped in the wind because it was so big for Jed. Until one of the women had a chance to take it in, he strapped his work belt with knife around the waist. Hanna fixed him up with a pair of Frank's trousers that were plenty long enough, just a bit big. Jed's leather belt took care of that. He would have to become accustomed to the moccasins Jacob let him wear; the soles were soft and protected his foot, but he could still feel small rocks and sticks under his feet.

Standing outside Jacob's shanty, Jed watched a wisp of a cloud floating by, tinged on the edge by the early dawn light. His thoughts turned to his parents and their troubles the year after he left for New Brunswick. *What do you think, Mum? Would you ever believe I would be living with a tribe? We used to read about the savages in the woods of northern New England. It's not true, Mum. I think the Brits just wanted the Micmacs to look evil because they supported the French in their wars with the English. The Micmacs are kind and generous. Do you know you have a grandson? I wish you had not succumbed to the influenza. It must have been lonely for you after Da had his heart attack. If you should bump into him in heaven, please tell him I said 'thank you' for all he taught me. I think he would be proud of my carving. Also, please tell him that I know it will be hard, but I will be the best Da I can be for Benjie. Let him know that in my heart, his name is Thomas.*

Jed's silent prayer was suddenly ended by the gibberish of three small voices talking at the same time.

"Uncle Jed, you are needed to help clean out the bean hole and set the wood and stones for later."

Now it begins.

"Race you to the hole, boys." He gave them a good head start. "Look out, I'm catching up."

As usual, the trio were running over each other, falling down and scrambling up again.

Hope they don't run that way if a bear is chasing them. Jed laughed out loud, causing them to turn around and fall again.

On his way past Birdie's home, Jed tiptoed in to see his son. He could tell he was well-fed and comfortable from the way he was sleeping in his little hammock. His cheeks were rosy, which pleased Jed no end. His long pale lashes fluttered just a bit, perhaps from dreaming things that only babies know of.

"Da's here, little boy," Jed whispered, so he wouldn't disturb little Martha asleep on a pile of blankets in the corner. "Sure wish I could take you in my arms for a walk near the river. It would be so pretty right now under the new light of day. Your Uncle Jacob says there is a mother duck with six hatchlings paddling their little hearts out to keep in a straight line behind her. Perhaps they could teach Pete, Joe, and Sean a few things."

At this, Birdie let out a giggle from where she was working by the light of the morning warming fire. She was beading a wallet of dark blue wool from a scrap left from several yards she got in trade at the post. The two inward folded flaps had been decorated with a combination of quills and white seed beads. The curve on the edges of the folds distinguished the pattern as Micmac. She was doing the edges with narrow white ribbon and more white beads. It was lovely and would certainly bring a good trade. It is the type of small item the Europeans liked to take home as a gift.

As Jed passed her, he laid his hand on her shoulder as a gesture of thanks. He could not help but wonder how such a frail shoulder could carry such burdens. She surely was Benjie's angel.

As he passed the hanging kettle he saw that beans were already soaking. One of Bear's and Ruth's boys and a cousin were waiting for him by the bean hole. They had a roughly smithed metal spade that was used to remove the debris from the last baking. Jed soon learned that lifting the ash from the hole was not that simple, because as he scooped it up, much would fall back or get carried back by the morning breeze. After a few demonstrations by the boys on how to hold the ash close to the side as he scooped, he managed to finish that part of the task. Next he began to lift the stones from the bottom of the pit; surprised by the weight, let out a few grunts. At this, the boys giggled and stomped their feet.

Never knew Micmacs giggled so much. "Now what?" questioned Jed, who looked like a poor chimney sweep in middle London. Patiently the boys showed him the placement of the tinder at the bottom of the hole and hardwood standing on end along the sides. Then they piled the rocks back on the bottom and set the wood afire. Once the hardwood burned down, the stones would be hot enough to place the bean kettle in the hole.

In the meantime, he was to help the boys tie a deerskin to an A-frame constructed of saplings. The hide had been meticulously cleaned by some of the women, who had carefully removed any meat remaining under the skin and scraped away the hair on the other side. Holes for tying had been made around the edges. Now the hide was soaking so it could be stretched onto the frame.

"Come on Mr. Jed. Grab a hold—it won't bite. Lift the hide so we can start stretching it to the frame and tying it off."

Jed tugged on the deerskin and found it was slick and much heavier than he had imagined. It was difficult to keep it in place as the boys laced it to the frame with sinew.

"Come on Mr. Jed, hold it steady. We have to get it drying before Jacob comes to check on us."

So that's what he does all day. Walks around and checks. Sounds like the job I use to have in the woods. At least I had hard leather soles on my boots, thought Jed with a chuckle.

Just as they finished tightly stretching the hide, two young girls walked by with their yokes and pails filled with water from the village well. As they passed, they giggled in unison.

Jed didn't know if they were giggling because of the boys or because he was covered with water that was turning the soot from the pit into rivulets of sludge running from his head to his toes. *There has to be an easier way. I've never seen any other mud men running around. This will surely make the dynamic trio run from their Uncle Jed in terror.*

"Just when I thought I'd seen it all," hollered Jacob from the thicket. "I told you to disguise yourself, but I think becoming a mud monster is going a bit far."

"Keep on walking or I'll show you how much of a monster I can be," shouted the disgruntled Jed.

Jacob retorted, "I suggest you take a quick dunk behind the beaver dam before the boys show you how to set the bean kettle."

Good grief—not the pond again.

Jed splashed his face and hair with the cold water to remove the mud. There was no way he was going to strip and take a dunk so soon after the canoe incident. As he walked back to the kettles he noticed the day was warming nicely as the midday sun neared its peak. For this he was most thankful.

At Birdie's place he found the door open and the house empty. He spotted her sorting quills and beads in the bright sunlight. In the shade nearby, Benjie was strapped comfortably in a cradleboard leaning against a tree. He had managed to free his right arm and it appeared that he was waving at his Da.

Ruth was stirring a kettle of parboiled beans. When she saw Jed and the boys coming, she grabbed a large cover of woven reeds and began to drain the water from the kettle into a smaller pot. Jed was amazed at her dexterity in manipulating the big pot, which was still on the hanger. Next she scored the rind of several pieces of salt pork and dropped them in the beans along with a good portion of molasses and a heaping spoon of ground mustard seed.

"Why not maple syrup like the other day?" asked Jed.

"We have finished with the sugaring for another season and the prepared syrup and sugar have been stored for leaner times. Some of the blocks of sugar have been sent to the trading post. This is one of our best products of the spring."

"Not fiddleheads?" joked Jed.

"Those are for our own pleasure. You know, the weeds we savages eat," giggled Ruth.

There goes the giggle again.

She took a long paddle and gently stirred the beans, then took a deep scoop that had been carved from a branch and returned enough of the drained water to just cover the beans. Next the boys placed a flat metal cover on the kettle. The cover had been forged with the edges bent down so dirt could not fall into the beans but the bail could still be pulled up for carrying.

"Clever," said Jed. "You have a blacksmith here?"

"Not yet," replied Ruth. "We hope to someday. Right now there is a traveling smith that stops at the trading post. He figured out the cover for us."

"How were the beans baked before that?"

"Nuga taught us the way of the tribe. Until we began trading with the Europeans for kettles, pottery jars were put in with the stones with the necks just above the ground. Nuga said her people used maple syrup and bear fat with the dried beans. I'm much happier that we can use salt pork."

"I must say, bear fat would not take my fancy," grumbled Jed. "So this is how Jacob came to bake the beans for my crew."

"You wait. All the lumber bosses will want them soon," said Ruth. "Dried beans are much easier to transport and they keep a man's gut full for much longer than pickled beef, boiled cod and biscuits."

The boys came to the pot with a sturdy long metal rod.

"They ready, Mama?"

"Yes, show Mr. Jedediah what to do next before the stones cool."

Ruth's boy slipped the rod under the bail. "Pull it through Mr. Jed, so we can carry it to the hole."

Jed definitely had a height advantage, so both boys took the other end to keep the kettle from sliding. Jed thought it was like lifting a stubborn ram from a path.

"Use your legs," he could hear his Da say.

They carefully placed the kettle in the hole and covered it with dirt, leaving the bail sticking out of the ground. The trapped heat from the rocks would do their magic over the next few hours.

Birdie brought Jed and the boys a basket of big chucks of sourdough bread and a jar of molasses for dipping. Ruth came out with mugs of hot strong tea.

"Thank you," said Jed. "You must have read my mind."

"We are good at that," the women laughed.

Just as Jed lifted the mug to his lips, the high-pitched shrieks of three banshees came up behind him and before he had a chance to move, they bumped into him, causing his mug to shoot straight up with tea flying in every direction.

"What the—," Jed cried out as the jumble of energy headed for the path to the meadow.

"Papa—Papa—Papa," were the cries heard around the settlement. In their path a large turkey took flight in fright.

Jed had never seen such a sight. The bird ran faster that Jed thought possible before lifting itself to the tallest pine in the area.

Nuga was laughing from the opening of her wigwam, not at the boys but at Jed, who had a layer of tea over the mud on his borrowed shirt.

"What was that about?" shouted Jed.

"Listen closely," Nuga shouted back.

He thought it was his imagination, but he could swear he heard the sound of a fiddle faintly bouncing off the trees. Several others were gathering in the clearing by the kettles, some clapping their hands in rhythm.

Jed ran over and stood with Nuga, while Birdie went to retrieve Benjie's cradleboard from its perch against the tree.

As the music became clearer, he turned to Nuga, "How in the world did all of you hear that so far away? Do Micmacs have superior hearing?" he asked in a half-joking way.

"It comes from generations of practice staying out of the way of the likes of you," she answered, also half joking.

Just then Jacob stealthily crept up behind Jed and nearly scared him to death, clapping his hands behind Jed's head.

"I suppose being that sneaky also comes from generations of practice in prowling around the Europeans," exclaimed Jed.

"Actually, stalking game was more important to our survival than hiding from the white man. We could usually sense you clods miles away. And by the way," Jacob continued, "you've added another layer of stains to your shirt. Trying a new tea bath?"

Just then a burly young man came out of the woods with a greatly loaded mule following, apparently of its own volition. Jed thought the man to be handsome, but it was hard to tell under the bushy red beard. When the three scamps reached him with cheers of "Papa," he didn't miss a beat on his fiddle. In an instant, Pete was marching in the lead, Joe had taken the reins of the mule and Sean had attached himself firmly to the lower leg of his father, who kept fiddling like Jed had never heard before.

Suddenly a squeal of delight came from the background and the group parted to let Hanna through to meet her husband. As she ran toward the path, Pete grabbed his Dad's fiddle, Joe hung on tight to the mule and Sean tumbled ass-over-teakettle off his father's foot. As though she were flying, Hanna landed in Frank's arms, her legs wrapped around his waist.

Jed could tell from Nuga's face that she was thinking this would never have happened in the good old days.

"Oh boy," Jacob mumbled.

"What's the matter?" muttered Jed.

"Just take a look at them. He isn't even up the path yet and she is probably already pregnant."

Jed piped in, "And he isn't even fiddling."

To which Nuga rolled her eyes and went over to Birdie's to hold Benjie.

"Jacob, my brother!" Frank shouted as he lifted him in a bear hug. "I think I managed to use our investment well. Over and above the seed potatoes, I got a great deal on beans and if the soil is as good as I think, we will be able to raise our own crop. This will save us cash in the long run over the winter. If it works well, we can grow enough in the future to trade.

"Nice thinking. Now will you stop with the hugging—save that for my sister."

"And who is this string bean—someone you dragged home from the drive?"

"This is my good friend Jedediah Smythe."

Frank blanched at the name and grabbed Jacob by the collar. "What the hell have you done? Don't you know this man has a bounty on him? How dare you bring him here? My family is here. If Wingate finds he is with us, we could lose everything we have worked for. Good God, Jacob!"

Just as the Irish temper was hitting the boiling point and Jacob began to clinch his fist, Nuga stepped between the men. Her little body barely came up to their chests, but the power in her eyes stopped the crisis before it went any farther. She opened the flap to her home and with a nod of her head, the three men walked in without a word. They looked a bit like Frank's trio after being caught scrapping.

The red of Frank's face began to subside as Nuga told him about what had happened to Jed. How Benjamin Wingate had practically thrown the baby into Jed's arms. How he torched Jed's home and chased him and the baby into the forest. How Wingate had sent Adelaide off to England after taking her baby away.

Nuga continued to tell Frank that hardly anyone in the family knew the circumstances of Jed's arrival or that there was a bounty on him. Only someone traveling to the St. John River would have heard that and even then, wouldn't know about the baby.

The flap parted. Birdie walked in with little Benjie and placed him in his father's arms.

"What am I to do, Frank?" asked Jed. If I take the child into the forest, he won't survive. If you wish, I'll let you turn me into Wingate's crew so your family can get a share of the bounty. But please, let my boy stay." Jed continued, "I have some money saved that would keep him for quite awhile."

Jacob cut in, "You know they won't take you back alive. From what I hear, Wingate wants total revenge. That means your permanent disappearance. No one will ever know why, but they won't care as long as they get their blood money."

"I'll do anything as long as my son is safe. If anyone asks me about him, I'll say that my son perished to the harshness of the forest. Then they can do as they want with me."

Frank took Benjie from his Da and looked into his wide blue eyes as the baby wrapped his hand around his finger. "No, no—that will never do."

"I think we can make it work, at least until things calm down," said Hanna who had been sitting quietly at Frank's side.

"How many know the whole story?" asked Frank.

As the group looked around at each other, Birdie spoke up. "Only those here. Bear told Jacob he didn't want to know the story and Ruth has never asked."

"Then that is the way it has to stay. Henri and Philippe must not hear of this as there are too many outsiders at the trading post and it would be too hard for them to not let it slip. I know Amy would help if need be."

"So be it," Nuga finally chimed in.

"I can really use the help clearing more land to plant. Yes, this could work," mused Frank as both Jacob and Jed showed great relief on their faces. "Tell me, what have you named this fine boy?"

A few giggles filled the space as Jed cleared his throat. "Benjamin Wingate Smythe."

Frank let out with a loud guffaw, which set Benjie wailing. Birdie quickly picked him up to comfort him.

As the tension continued to melt away, the flap opened and Pete and Joe breathlessly tried to speak at the same time, and of course they made no sense.

"Peter, tell us what is wrong," said Nuga.

"Sean was down by the river talking to the man with the funny raccoon cap while another gruff man sat in their canoe."

Frank jumped up, "Where are they now?"

"Sean is bringing the man up the path to see Uncle Jacob."

"Trouble is his name," whispered Jacob.

Hanna shushed everyone, especially the boys.

As Frank exited the wigwam, he was greeted with, "Hey Frank. Didn't expect to see you here. Back a bit early, aren't you?"

"Wrapped things up in St John quicker than expected."

"This little redhead happen to be yours?"

"Sure is."

"I was just paddling by and gave a shout to see if there was anyone new in your camp and that was just what he said—'sure is.'"

Frank bent down, swooped Sean onto his shoulders, gave him a spin and asked, "Just who might that be?"

"Silly Papa. Benjie of course."

"Of course. I was away when Benjie came."

Just then Birdie came out of the wigwam carrying Benjie, who was wrapped in a brightly colored blanket that covered his fair hair. It was quite evident he was feeding at her breast. She sat on a log bench and continued nursing.

The uninvited and unwelcome guest appeared flustered; Birdie just nodded with a big smile. He backed away and stumbled a bit down the path. "To hell with it," he yelled. "I've wasted too much time chasing this bounty. That weird Brit is most certainly rotting some place in the forest. That's just what I am going to tell the old man. He better pay something for all the trapping time I've missed. That's it. I'm done." His rants continued to the canoe and slowly faded away as he and his friend paddled their way toward the St. John.

"Where's Ruth?" Frank yelled.

She and Martha came from the kettles.

"You must have some beans ready. Call the boys to dig them—I'm starved."

As the sun began to set and the fires were lit, the big table near the kettles was laden with breads, molasses cakes, honey, and stewed apples. Everyone carried out something to add to the feast. Jed finished his job at the bean hole by digging away the top layer of dirt and grabbing one end of the pole to help pull the kettle out. When the top was off, the aroma of sweet baked yellow-eye beans filled the clearing.

Dusk settled in, the turkeys settled high in the pines, the tree frogs began to croak, and the creatures of the night scurried away from dancing feet. Jed picked up Birdie and spun her in circles with joy. Well into the darkness, the lilt of Frank's fiddle echoed up the valley.

10 The Porcupine People

The next several weeks flew by. Jed said hello to muscles he'd never known he had. Sowing seed was one thing, but making farmland of forest was quite another. He was quite a hand at planning the downing of a tree, but was used to leaving stumps and piles of brush. This certainly wouldn't do when preparing land for planting. He could see why it took so long each season to extend the gardens and he was glad his efforts led to a fairly large extension to the potato area and allowed room for a good number of rows of yellow-eye beans. While Jed and Frank toiled over the preparation of the new soil, the women planted the usual crops of squash and corn.

Once in awhile Jed helped stretch more hides, but he was thankful he did not have to do any of the tanning. He was walking by the women one morning, peeked in a warm pot, and saw the brain of the deer soaking. This turned his stomach more than the bloody trip on the river. He still was not used to seeing them wetting the hides with the solution from the brain. Each time the hide dried, they wet it again until the hide became supple. He never asked, but often wondered how the Indians knew the brain had enough of the oils needed to turn the hide into the soft waterproof material used for so much of their clothing, moccasins and accessories. Hanna once told him that each animal has a brain with just enough oil to tan its own hide. The last step after tanning was to hang the hides in a smoke house to do the final setting. Again, he wondered how they learned to do that.

Jed remembered helping his Mum with the weeds in her little kitchen garden. He was content to let the women of the settlement do the weeding when the seedlings began to push their way through the soil, while he chopped firewood from the trees felled to clear the land.

"We need the blanket," came the cries. "Where's the blanket?"

"What the—," uttered a startled Jed.

The three boys came running across the field, deftly hopping from row to row, never harming a single newly sprouted corn plant. "We need the blanket!"

Jed noticed that the women did not seem a bit concerned.

"Auntie Ruth!" they shouted as they bounced over the last few rows. "Auntie Ruth, do you have it?"

Ruth brought her finger to her lips. "Nuga has it. Both Benjie and Martha are asleep and she will be none too pleased if you wake them."

Simultaneously, the trio started running on their tiptoes toward the wigwam. This brought more of those endearing giggles from Ruth and the other women in her family.

Jed stood in wonderment when someone suddenly tapped him on the shoulder. He jumped and spun around to come nose to nose with Jacob.

"What the hell are you? Some kind of Indian spirit that can materialize and disappear at will? You made the hair on my chin stand up straight!"

Jacob laughed. "I noticed you are adding another piece to your woodsman disguise, and that with the help of my breakfast and Hanna's cooking, you are losing that clean-cut skinny look. It amazes me how you Europeans can grow such beards. With my Indian blood, it would take months, if ever."

"You keep sneaking up on me like that and it will soon turn gray and nobody will recognize me. What in the world is going on?"

"Give the ax a rest and let's see just how good you are at stealth in your own m'kusins."

Jed was beginning to get used to the moccasins and it was the first time he had realized they had been made just for him. Just then he caught sight of Pete, Joe and Sean out of the corner of his eye. They were slowly making their way into the woods with a large wool blanket that once had probably been white, but was dingy with a few holes throughout.

With a wag of his finger and a whisper of let's go, Jacob began to follow the boys.

Jed thought for sure his spirit friend had learned to walk an inch off the ground, for as hard as he tried, he still snapped a dry twig here and there.

Jacob raised his hand and pointed through a break in the new foliage on the oak in front of them.

The boys were standing in a semi-circle around a porcupine that was not pleased at the intrusion and was puffed, ready to let go of some quills if they got any nearer.

Jed thought of the story of two-year-old Sean who had tried to pick up a baby skunk to bring home for a pet. The creature's mother had not been pleased. The swimming pond had gotten a lot of use for a while. Jed imagined Sean coming home this time with needles in his nose.

Pete and Joe took opposite sides of the blanket and pulled it taut. Sean held onto the back edge.

The porcupine was stamping its feet and clicking its teeth in displeasure.

As the animal started to turn his back in defense, Pete nodded his head and his brothers followed in rhythm. Suddenly the boys tossed the blanket over the hapless animal and pinned him under.

"Hang on tight," yelled Jacob.

The porcupine started grunting louder and louder.

Jed laughed as he thought how much it sounded like his old pig on the farm when he teased him in play.

"Now!" Pete ordered. The boys released the blanket so the forward edge was loose and the porcupine began to struggle to escape. "Pull back!" he yelled, and the three of them held back as hard as they could. As the animal pulled away from under the blanket in a speedy escape, the boys went flying backward on their behinds.

"That's my nephews," said Jacob as he ran up to lift them off the ground. "Good job."

Jed stood with his mouth open, as if trying to understand what had just happened.

"Show Uncle Jed what you did."

The boys held up the blanket; the underside was covered with porcupine quills.

"Well, I'll be," exclaimed Jed.

"Off with you to Aunt Bea. She will be happy."

Captain Peter, as Jed was beginning to call him, carefully folded the blanket and led the pack back toward Birdie's.

"I thought the porcupine shot the quills at you," quizzed Jed as he and Jacob followed the boys.

"Nope, they run backward into the intruder, flapping their tail. The fishhook-type ends of the quills attached themselves to the skin and expand, making them hard to remove and quite painful."

"Sounds a bit like the voice of experience".

"Believe it or not, I was once young and in charge of the blanket. When a porcupine shows itself during the day you need to act quickly. They usually roam at night."

"Auntie Bea," the trio sang out.

When Birdie saw the blanket she was more animated than Jed had ever seen her. She carefully laid the treasure on the work table by the kettles and gave each boy a big hug. Then she went into her shanty to get each of them a good-size piece of maple sugar candy.

"That will keep you busy for a while, Birdie," said Jacob, patting her on her little back. "Could be more than a thousand."

"Isn't that just a bit exaggerated?" scoffed Jed.

"Not according to Nuga. She tells me there are many thousands and they grow back."

"I take it as gospel if Nuga tells it. Bet that particular porcupine will run like the wind whenever he sees that gang."

"Jacob!" came the angry cry from the edge of the river. "Jacob, that son-of-a-bitch did it again. Where are you?"

"Sounds like Frank is having one of his fits. You stay back here and I'll go down by the canoes and find out what has him in a stew."

Jed watched through the brush as the two men met halfway up

the hill from the water. Frank's hands were waving like the tail on a deer running off in fright. Jacob was obviously trying to calm him down and then trying to get his point across, using his finger in punctuation on Frank's chest. Then he pointed up to where Jed was hiding.

Damn, I hate this. I want to be able to walk where I please, especially near the river.

Frank threw his hands up in disgust and headed for his place. His three sons skipped along behind him, just to make sure they didn't miss out on anything.

"I think it is about time we got you into this conversation, Jed," exclaimed Jacob when he reached him. "Meet with us in Nuga's place late tonight after we get the rest of the place settled. We had some plans in the works with the help of Dan Thorpe, but my dear cousin Philippe has smashed some of our hopes. We'll explain it all tonight. Frank is ready to strangle him, so we need to try to keep his head cool. In the meantime, visit your son. Looks like Birdie is inside nursing him."

Jed tapped on the door jam.

"Come in Mr. Jed, I just finished wrapping little Benjie.

"Thanks, Birdie. I'd like to spend some time with him."

Birdie laid Benjie in his father's arms. "He'd like some time with you, rather than being bound in the cradle board. Just remember that Jacob does not want you to walk outside with him."

Jed could see that Birdie was eager to get back to the blanket. Releasing the quills from the wool fibers was tedious work. She needed to back the fishhook end out carefully in order to not damage the shaft, and then soak the quills in warm water to clean them.

"Hi there, little boy. I wish I could be walking along the river's edge with you. There are so many fun things to watch. We'll just have to walk from wall to wall in here and pretend."

Jed got such joy looking into little Ben's eyes. He could see Addie looking at him.

"I worry about your Mum, little boy. She should be the one holding you now. I hope I'll be able to let her know that you are safe and loved."

Jed laid his son on the pile of soft blankets in the corner of the room where the sun made its way through a small window. He sat down beside him.

"Look. You can see the bright blue sky peeking through some of the leaves and there is a mother bird carrying something to the nest she has hidden in the branches. Someday we will go looking for those little fuzzy babies. Just wait, Benjie—we have so many wonders to see."

Jed reached into his shirt pocket and pulled out a small box he had carved like a spruce gum box, but he had placed small pebbles inside rather than gum. The box, which resembled a book, was carved from a solid piece of wood that was hollowed out and had a thin piece of wood on a track to open and close the top. On the outside of the box, Jed had carved BEN on one side and an intricate chickadee on the other. He held it in the light and gave it a shake. The rattling of the pebbles quickly caught Benjie's attention and his bright blue eyes followed it from side to side.

"Won't be long, little man, and you will be able to hold and shake this all by yourself. I have something else I'm carving that I think you will like, too."

"What a lucky Little Benjie," Birdie exclaimed as she entered carrying a tray of drying quills, all sorted by size. "What a pretty rattle box. Your father has unknown talents."

"A gift from my Da." He carried the tired little boy to his place in the hammock and then stopped to look at the quills. "I had no idea there were so many lengths," Jed marveled.

"Many are longer or shorter, but these are perfect for weaving on my next birch box. The tiny ones are out in the dye pot with red I have made from boiling hemlock. I'll use those to finish this pair of moccasins." She showed Jed a piece of soft deer hide that was already cut into the pattern that would be folded and sewn into the footwear. She had started a geometric design with many colored beads and tiny quills that would end up on the top of the foot of the moccasin.

"Perhaps I can use some of your dyes for some figures I'm carving for Benjie?"

"Anytime, Mr. Jed. Anytime."

Just then Jacob popped his head into the doorway. "Bear has all the boys on a turkey hunt now that the new broods have hatched. Will you give me a hand with the bean kettle?" he asked of Jed.

"Bit early, isn't it?"

"Sky is getting dark. Think there could be heavy rain. We need to pull the beans so everyone has a chance to get them home before the storm."

"Think they're ready?"

"Folks can give them some more time in a pot at home if need be."

Jed knew the routine and he and Jacob dug up the pot without a word. They had just put the rod under the bail and begun to pull the kettle out when they heard the first clap of thunder.

Jacob stood in front of Birdie's place and let out a piercing whistle; Jed had never heard one so loud. Suddenly the three brothers came running out of the woods and stood looking up at their uncle.

"Tell Aunt Ruth and her family that the bean kettle is out and to send someone with a pot before the rain comes. Then you get your Mama's pot and bring it here. Then get Nuga's. Better make it fast."

"What about that whistle," asked Jed putting his hands over his ears. "I didn't know anyone could pucker enough to do one so loud."

"That's our emergency whistle. No one uses it unless they are practicing or there is a real problem. Peter is getting pretty good at it."

"Of course, he is the captain."

"He must have delegated, as here comes Joe with Hanna's pot and Trouble with Nuga's. The rest should be soon behind, so let's get this lid off."

Jed loved the aroma that escaped from opening the kettle. Birdie ran out with the stick and gave the beans a quick stir, then ladled them into Hanna's fairly large kettle and filled the small container for Nuga and the boys were off again.

Just as Peter came running back with Ruth and two of her nephews, a streak of lightening flashed from one side of the river to the other. The clap of thunder caused little Martha to run out and grab her mother around the waist. Fearing the kettle would burn her; Jed swooped her up in his arms and carried her back into the cabin. He cuddled her as he checked on Benjie, who was sleeping soundly.

"Good boy," he whispered. "I used to try to sleep my way through these storms myself."

The next lightening strike was so close that the sound of the thunder seemed to fill the clearing. One of the large pine trees behind the bean hole had been split in half. It was smoking, but there was no further fire. At that, the scene around the bean pot became frantic. The last of the beans were scooped into waiting pots and carried as fast as possible to each home.

Birdie came in with her share of the beans. She took Martha, who nearly jumped from Jed into her arms. Jed looked out and saw Jacob struggling to pull some of the fresh pine boughs from the downed tree over the bean hole. He gave Benjie a quick, light kiss on the cheek and ran out to help, as he knew who was going to have to clean it out if rain filled the pit and turned it into muddy ash.

"Spread as many of the full branches that you can," Jacob yelled.

Soon there was a fairly large green brush pile over the bean hole. Just an occasional wisp of smoke made its way through.

"I think that will help some, as long as we don't get an unusually heavy downpour," Jed said, just as the heavens opened with that downpour.

The two men ran as quickly as possible toward Hanna's home and nearly straight into Frank, who was coming from the opposite direction. Lightening in the sky lit the way, as the afternoon had become as dark as midnight.

"I pulled the canoes half way up the hill," shouted Frank. "If this keeps up, the river will run rapid and we may lose the new landing. Don't want to lose any of the boats."

Another tree behind Nuga's took a hit and came down with a crash like thunder itself. It barely missed the wigwam.

"We should go get her," exclaimed Jed.

Frank answered, "She's been through more of these than all the rest of us put together. She knows what to do and the base of her place stands on a knoll that is well-protected from the water."

Jed was amazed that he had never noticed that mound before.

The three men reached the door at the same time. Hanna had made it home from the gardens before it started to rain and the three boys were huddled in their loft. They all started laughing when what looked like three drowned rats fought their way in.

Dinner was simple. The beans had a bit of bite, but were as delicious as always. Hanna sliced some salt pork and fried it crisp, made some sourdough biscuits with honey for dipping and topped it off with big molasses cookies. Their discussion over tea was of their worry for the newly planted beans with the sudden heavy rain, whether the landing would hold, and if another well should be dug, since the population of the clan was increasing. Seems that Tiny Bear was not going to be Ruth's last child.

Once the clamor of the meal was done and the boys had settled in the loft, Hanna settled herself in the rocker next to the fireplace, where she still had enough light to work on some mending. It was still raining quite hard when Jacob motioned for the other two men to set out to Nuga's.

"Will she still expect us in this storm?" Jed asked.

"I'm sure she is quite eager to get this meeting going," answered Jacob.

"For all the good it will do, with her grandson Philippe being such a bastard," growled Frank.

Hanna just shook her head.

Jed thought, *this must be important, for us to go to the wigwam on a night not fit for beasts.*

11 The Wangan

Here we go again.

Jed was not at all happy about running back out in the deluge. His clothes had just dried from the first dousing. Of course the water- and mud-filled holes didn't help any, as he tripped in one and landed face-first, sliding several feet on his chest.

This better be something important and worth all this aggravation.

As they entered the cozy wigwam, Nuga looked up and smiled. "Jedediah, you certainly are hard on clothes. Was your mother always busy with her mending basket?"

"Come to think of it Nuga, she spent many nights putting together what I had torn apart."

She motioned for the three men to sit as in counsel around the small fire in the middle of the floor. It was in a pit surrounded by stones edged with some sand.

Nuga's wigwam was domed and Jed was impressed by the clever construction that allowed smoke to leave through the top while not allowing rain in. He had only seen drawings of the cone- shaped shelters. The floor was covered with soft pine boughs, which Nuga had covered with blankets.

Jacob broke Jed's reverie with, "Are you with us, Jedediah, or are you deep in sweet thoughts?"

"Sorry." The rain seemed to pick up, if that were possible. "It's raining cats and dogs," Jed exclaimed.

Nuga looked at him quizzically. "Tell me Jedediah, just how can that be?"

A bright smile filled his face. "My Mum told me that when most of the cottages in England had thatched roofs, they were usually warm from the fires within. On cooler nights, cats and dogs would climb up and settle on the roofs to stay warm. If it started to rain hard, the thatch would get slippery and the animals would slide off. Thus, it rained cats and dogs."

Nuga laughed and slapped her hands together. "I like your mere."

"I know she would have loved to meet you."

"Let's get down to business," Frank snarled.

Nuga looked at him with a scowl. "Then you let him know our plans."

"I'd say they were more like the plans we *had*. Let Jacob tell the tale."

Nuga nodded at her sagamore.

"I wanted things in place before I mentioned it, Jedediah. I am not going back to the Wingate crew. I sent word to him with the men that floated his wangan and horses back to the plantation."

"Wow. I bet the tyrant didn't like that at all."

"From what I understand, he called me things I would not want my grandmother to hear. He threw a vase across the room and let the world know to never trust a savage."

Jed shook his head. "Looks like the esteemed Mr. Wingate has taken to throwing fits."

"He pulled out all the stops to make sure no other owners hired me as their cook. Another of his power plays."

Jed interjected, "Jacob, your plans for this settlement depend on the wages you bring during the forest harvesting. How can you make that up?"

"That jackass was not in our way. We had worked out plans to do an independent drive to a smaller mill and allow for a bigger share of the money."

"Now you have my curiosity piqued."

"We have been talking about Frank's friend, Dan Thorpe. He has put a lot of thinking into the future of the land grants he received from the Bay State Colony. When Maine broke away from Massachusetts in 1820 to become a state, he was worried he might lose his claim to the land he was clearing, but a few months ago he got a deed from a Maine Land Agent for the 50 acres of land he had worked for his farm. He also recorded a claim for a good-size tract of woodlands along the Aroostook River that he could purchase from the state in the future. The only concern is the fight that is brewing over the actual border between New Brunswick and Maine. If Britain is found in control, what will happen to him then? Will he lose his claim? Right now the only access to his land is by water. If settlers start moving inland, how will he protect his farm? In the meantime, he is saving as much money as possible to secure the land before any newcomers try to claim it. He doesn't want a large company to harvest the timber; he's seen the destruction left behind. He needs the extra money the logging would bring in, but doesn't have the time or experience to work it himself. If we can work out the details, he will let us manage the timber claim for either a share of the profit or a stumpage fee per tree."

"How large a crew?"

Frank piped in, "I was planning on heading up the axmen and picking them up as needed. With Jacob as cook, there should be no problem finding odd-jobbers. So the crew would vary."

Jacob added, "Bill Mayfield was ready to jump in as crew boss for the landing, but now his missus is pregnant and due in the middle of winter. She was his sweetheart in England and left her family to move here to be married. He doesn't want to leave her alone and so will try his hand at trapping for this season."

"Would his wife stay with us for the winter?" asked Nuga. I'm sure Hanna or Ruth would find a space for her and she will have plenty of help when the baby comes."

Jacob smiled, "No way. She's already afraid there might be a savage behind every tree. Imagine her staying with a whole family of them."

"I've survived," Frank butted in. "By the way, is making babies contagious? Dan Thorpe's wife is due this winter also."

"Careful," Jacob came back. "We don't want you and Hanna to catch the bug."

Nuga just grimaced.

Frank quickly changed the subject. "We have a plan for the Bill situation. The overwhelming problem now is Philippe. Uncle Henri's favorite son has shot down all our big ideas. Sorry, Nuga. But your grandson is a miserable skinflint."

"What in the world does the trading post have to do with a lumber harvest?" Jed asked.

Nuga pointed at Jacob, "You'd better explain. If Frank tries, the heat of his temper will drive us out of here."

"First let me check to make sure we are all alone. It sounds like the heaviest rain has stopped," remarked Jacob as he opened the heavy flap to look around.

"Leave it open a bit," said Nuga. "I have a feeling we may need a bit of fresh air before we figure this out one way or another."

Jacob began to explain. "We would have to rely on our own supplies. Wingate has the biggest wangan and there is no way he will let any of our crew buy goods there. Also, he'll do his best to stop any of the others from opening their company stores to us. Our men will need replacement tools, clothes and boots and such."

"Can you imagine pipes with no tobacco? No spikes for the boots of the drivers? Damn Philippe."

Nuga gave Frank a 'keep your mouth shut' look.

Jacob continued, "I've always wanted my own wangan, but it takes a great deal of money to put together even the minimum supplies. We thought that among all of us, we have enough to start a crew and made a mistake in assuming that Uncle Henri would order us enough wholesale goods through the trading post to stock a wangan. We offered a percentage of the profit as well as regular payments on the original order with interest. We didn't mention starting a lumber crew and camp."

"Come on, we did more than assume," interrupted Frank. "We presented a written plan that was reasonable, with the wangan profits being shared. Henri and Amy were quite excited for Jacob. Then that son-of–a-bitch social wannabe squashed it."

"Frank, watch your mouth. He's family." Nuga was more than aggravated.

"I'm more part of this family than he will ever be. I haven't got a smidgeon of Micmac in my veins but I have 100% in my heart."

In an attempt to quiet things a bit, Jed asked, "Jacob, what would it take to get a start on your supplies?"

"A miracle," exclaimed Frank.

"Pretty much true," Jacob replied. "To get down to it, here is what we planned based on $1,200. Over the past few years Frank and I have managed to put together $300.00 each by working as much odd-jobbing as possible outside of lumbering. That is why he has been in St. John working on the docks as soon as the drive was over. I've been building a couple of canoes each summer and cooking at any place that will have me. I'm surprised that Birdie is not blind from all the beading and fine work she does. Ruth has been making baskets from the materials collected by her girls. Everyone has been trying to do something extra over and above what his or her family needs. Nuga keeps the young ones busy. In all they have raised another $200. That gives us a kitty of $800."

As if Jed did not know, Nuga chimed in, "Pretty much a fortune for savages." She winked at him in jest.

"Yes, but not enough for this dream," Jacob continued. "We figure we need $400.00 to payroll six to eight men for the season. This should cover it as many will spend at the wangan and that will be subtracted from the final payout."

"Sounds reasonable."

"Frank and I will not take a pay, but will work for our share of the profit. That will help stretch things."

"What would be other expenses?" Jed asked.

Frank answered. "Most of the needs of the families are met by selling and bartering at the trading post, but we think it important to leave $100.00 here for emergency supplies. Bear and his boys will stay here and do the winter hunting and watch over the security of the settlement."

"What about the other $300.00?"

"Have you forgotten how much a working crew eats?" Jacob continued, "I usually prepare four meals a day and will need about $10.00 a month per man, since Dan is going to supply potatoes and yellow-eye beans from his garden. He is also going to help with expenses by letting us use his oxen for the winter and will also provide their grain and hay."

"How many nights have you lain awake as your brains worked all this out?"

"Too many," came three answers at once.

"I see a couple of missing pieces from this puzzle. Could those be the holes in the plan Frank is stewing about?"

Jacob turned to Nuga and his brother-in-law. "See, I told you he has a quick mind."

Jed looked at Nuga with a smile, "I suppose you expected less from the Brit in me."

"Jedediah, you have made me rethink my surprise. But I'm not saying this applies to all of you."

"And just what holes do you see?" wondered Frank.

"First thing that jumps out is Bill."

"We were hoping that you would fill the hole of landing boss. Also, Jacob tells me that you are quick with figures so could help with the books."

Jacob continued for the family. "Working as an independent should keep you out of the way of familiar lumberers. We would need to change your name. Jedediah is not that common. Most men who worked closely with you before will be staying with Wingate. You would share my wigwam so you could keep out of the camp house. Nuga and Birdie will happily continue to tend to your son over the winter. You'll not need to worry about his safety."

Jed began to put together most of it. "Somehow I don't want to ask about the Philippe problem. Should I duck, Frank?"

"You know, Jacob, I'm beginning to like this Brit. At least about as much as an Irishman can."

This brought a broad smile from Nuga that went from ear to ear across her face, which was chiseled by the wisdom of years.

"Okay," said Jed. Let's hear about the fly in the ointment that's keeping you from getting the supplies you need for the wangan."

Jacob began. "Nuga met with Uncle Henri and Aunt Amy and told them about the plans we were putting together to start my own wangan. She explained the profits would help keep our family independent and in turn make this land a small village to be recognized someday by Maine or New Brunswick. She had a list of what would be needed to make a good start to cover the needs of the lumber crews—not only ours, but those traveling through. Not all small operations have a company store and not many large operations allow outsiders to buy at theirs. Their investment would be the other $400.00 for wholesale goods that we can price for a profit.

"If they are able to take the cost, sounds like a good plan."

"That's the problem. Henri and Amy felt it quite doable and a good investment. When Philippe caught wind of it, he blew his stack. I've never seen such disrespect for his parents."

"Wish I'd been there," growled Frank. "If I had been there, I would have helped him blow his stack, that selfish piece of—" Frank caught himself when he saw the look in Nuga's eyes.

"It's your uncle's trading post. Why does Philippe have such a say over the affairs?" wondered Jed.

Jacob explained. "Unknown to us, a few months back Philippe convinced his father that the day-to-day running of the post was becoming too much work for him."

Frank interrupted, "Philippe has no idea what work is until he comes out and clears fields for crops. That lazy son-of-a-gun wouldn't know which end of an ax to hold."

"Let me finish," Jacob came back. "Philippe convinced my uncle how much easier his life would be out from under the stress. Henri signed the management over to him lock, stock and barrel. Of course Henri stipulated that in due time, Bear and Birdie would be compensated."

"They can kiss that inheritance goodbye," sneered Frank.

"Please, Frank," spoke Nuga just above a whisper. "I must admit that I did not think my son so old that he was addled. Amy is very upset. Philippe says that the trading post simply can't afford to risk so much money, especially for a fairy-tale idea."

Frank added. "The only fairy-tale idea is that he thinks his wealth will buy him into the favor of the timber barons, or at least into the favor of their daughters. This is the one big reason he should never find out about Jedediah. Just think how his standing would rise if he turned him in to Wingate. The land baron might even overlook the bit of Micmac running in Philippe's veins and offer one his daughters.

Run Mary, run, thought Jed.

"The only offer he considered," added Jacob, "was to deal with the agent in St. John and get us a discount because it would go through the trading post. For what we were looking for, he would want around $650. Of course that would mean we would have to jack the prices up for the crews that buy supplies, which is something I would never do."

"For God's sake, is he crazy?" yelled Frank. "If we didn't have the $400 to buy wholesale, how the hell would we get that much money? If we had that cash in hand, I know the agents on the docks and could get the supplies myself without going through that jackass."

Jacob tried to calm him. "Hey, the entire family doesn't need to hear about this."

The wigwam went quiet as if each of them suddenly went into his own cave of deep thought.

Suddenly Jed stood up and walked out.

Startled, Nuga looked bewildered about where he had gone.

Frank shrugged. "He's probably just gone to find a tree."

"He'll be back," said Jacob as they all sank back into thought.

The gentle rain had picked up again when Jed came back into the wigwam, making sure to close the opening behind him. He was carrying his pack. They were all intrigued as he started to fish around inside with his hand.

"Aha," he said, as he pulled out a good-sized spruce gum box. It was a larger wooden book, hollowed like Benjie's rattlebox with the same type of sliding closure on the top.

The amazing intricate carvings on all sides immediately fascinated Nuga.

"Did you make this, Jedediah? May I see it?"

Jed smiled and passed the box to Nuga.

"Beau. Tres beau," she whispered in awe.

"Thank you. Many of the lumber crew work on boxes like this to fill with spruce gum to take home to their sweetheart at the end of the drive. I made this one for Benjie's Mum. It has many of the things she loved carved on it. I knew she did not have a liking for spruce gum, but thought she could keep special trinkets in it."

"Why do you have it?"

"Addie cried when she saw it. We talked about each of the memories carved on it and then she handed it back to me and said that if her father ever saw it, he would know there was something going on."

"Figured that old buzzard had something to do with it," Frank commented.

"She was right, you know. I was caught up in the moment and joy of making it. I wasn't thinking."

"Such a shame," said Nuga as she passed it back to him.

"As I was carrying it over here, I had a conversation in my heart with Addie. I needed to know if what I was thinking was right. Suddenly, peace came over me and I knew she had answered."

Jed slid open the top and pulled out some folded letters from his Mum. Then he pulled out a small, light wool bag by the tie that gathered the top closed. He opened the bag and with a slight sigh poured a collection of coins into his palm, mostly silver, but a few were gold. He picked the three biggest and put the rest away. Handing the coins to Jacob, he asked, "Will these cover your start-up inventory? There are two gold sovereigns and one half–sovereign, which at last check were worth in the area of $400 in total. Since they are British, I know they will be welcome in St. John."

"My good Lord, Jedediah. Where in the world," gasped Jacob.

Frank picked up the coins from Jacob's hand and was struck dumb. He had not a thing to say.

He passed them to Nuga, who clutched them to her breast and whispered, "Jedediah, we couldn't take these."

"When my Mum died, Benjamin Wingate bought my family's farm, which included a good amount of acreage, the house and a large flock. He always wanted to add to his working estate. When he gave me the note I had it turned immediately into coin, as even then I didn't trust him. I only think it fitting that he should be responsible for funding the wangan that someday will outsell his."

Everyone clapped and laughed. Jacob nodded to Nuga and she placed the treasure in her pouch.

"The coins come with some strings," chuckled Jed, as he looked the men in the eyes.

"Anything," came the response in duplicate.

"First, I need some clothes. Some that fit and don't smell."

"Absolument!" exclaimed Nuga.

"And one of those leather hats with the floppy brim that some of the woodsmen wear."

"Got it," answered Frank.

"I want to be a partner in both funding and labor, so will work for no pay. That will save \$40-\$60 this year that you were going to pay Bill. I will work hard to ensure my Benjie will have his needs met for many years."

"More than fair."

"I want this written down, including Dan Thorpe's offer to work his timber. Right now Thorpe has a binding grant to that land."

"Got it."

 I want the agreement signed by all involved and left in a safe place in case someone suddenly sees the potential of the wangan and tries to get one on that land.

"Like cousin Philippe," grunted Frank.

"Looks like we finally have a business head in the group," Nuga interjected. "That Wingate person must have taught you something even if it was what not to do."

"She's a wise one," said Jacob with a tender smile for his grandmother.

"That brings me to the most important request. I want you to get me as close to the Wingate plantation as possible and help me contact Addie's sister Mary. I need to find out how Addie is doing and to get a message to her that her son and I survived.'

"That could be riskier than harvesting the wilderness, but I understand the need and somehow we will make it happen," Jacob agreed with a nod from Frank.

"It must remain quiet, with as few people as possible knowing of the arrangement, especially the funding."

"Who would ever believe a partnership between an Irishman and a Brit that also includes a savage? I think we're very safe," laughed Frank.

"What? No sharing blood?" exclaimed Jacob as the three stood and shook hands.

In the background sat a sweet lady weeping with joy.

12   Partners

After a night of tossing and turning, Jed awoke to find Jacob
sitting in the kitchen sipping a cup of freshly brewed tea.
Apparently he had had a sleepless night also.

"Shouldn't you be on your way to wherever it is that you go early
in the morning?" Jed mumbled as he helped himself to the pot on
the little wood stove.

"I don't seem to be able to concentrate on anything but last night.
For years I've tried to find a way for this opportunity and now my
head is spinning as to where to start."

"Do you have any writing materials?"

Jacob opened a small dome cover trunk and found a few sheets of
paper and a snub pencil used for marking logs.

"We really need to do this in ink."

"Didn't think of that. I'll have to run over to Hanna's. She usually
has some ink and pens for Nuga to use to help the children
practice their letters. I'll see if Frank can join us. There is some
leftover corn bread on the table and molasses in the jar. Really
didn't feel much like cooking this morning."

"No problem," said Jed. "I don't feel much like eating."

Jed stood in the doorway of the shanty and listened to the birds
sing their wake-up songs. The air was clear and cool as the sun
just started to peek through the tall pines. Two white-tailed
rabbits scooted by, stopping once in awhile to nibble through a
fresh blade of tall grass.

"You'd better hop on by fellows, before Jacob spots you and
pictures you in a stew.

His voice sent the startled creatures off toward the river.

Soon Frank and Jacob came meandering toward him. All three men looked like they had been awake for days.

Frank was carrying his own mug of tea and grunted a greeting to Jed. "You look like you've been on a bender in Bangor."

"I'd say you must have been with me."

"Hanna thought so too. She knows something is in the works. I never made it to bed."

Jacob let out with a laugh. "No wonder she thinks something big is happening. There is no way you would miss a night wrapped around my sister."

Jed did his best to hold back a blush. He actually wasn't thinking about Frank and Hanna, but his mind flashed back to many a tangle between Addie and himself.

Jed closed the door as Jacob lit the oil lamp and placed it in the middle of the table. He and Jed sat on the bench and Frank pulled up a barrel.

"As soon as we get this out of the way, we can start the real work of pulling the rest together. Jed, you take care of the writing."

Jed felt as though he were back at his Mum's kitchen table; he sat up straight just like she had always said and dipped the pen point in the ink.

"Before we start, Frank and I think you should get the largest percentage since you put in a hundred dollars more than we did."

Jed already had prepared an answer for that proposition if it appeared. "I want that extra hundred to go into the amount the family saved so that each share is equal at three hundred. They have earned more than I can ever give for their kindness, protection and the care of Benjie. In that way, the financing for your plans to establish a village can grow faster."

Dumbfounded, the brothers-in-law agreed.

The breakdown for the disbursement of the profit was planned at 10% each for Jacob, Jed, Frank, and the settlement. Dan Thorpe would receive 20% for the use of his forest land, plus supplies as needed. The remaining 40% would be turned back into the company for growth, including future payroll and increasing the stock of the wangan.

Jacob was to go to Thorpe's farm as soon as possible and tell him they had the funding and about the partnership. Jacob did not feel there would be a problem getting him to sign off, as Dan was trying to get as much money in as possible without having to work another job. His potatoes and beans, as well as grain and hay for the work animals, were beginning to be in demand from more than one lumber camp. Once it was sure Dan was on board, Frank would travel to the docks at St. John and secure the order for the supplies.

Frank asked if Hanna could be brought in on the plans, as it would be hard not to speak to her about it.

"It would make sense because Nuga is going to need someone to talk with, since she won't be able to confide in Amy," said Jacob.

"Never thought of that angle," thought Frank out loud.

"From what I hear, your cousin Philippe sure would be curious to know how you got around him. Eventually he is going to question the funding when he realizes the wangan is going forward as gossip comes up from St. John about your purchases," added Jed.

"Right now the only gossip he's interested in is about the social circles on the St. John River, and that curiosity is about the young ladies. With his mother's pure English and father's French blood, he feels his Micmac heritage is pretty well hidden, especially with his green eyes and light brown hair. It will be awhile before he realizes there may be a problem with his first love—making money," spat Frank as he grabbed the pen and wrote his sprawling Francis Sean Ryan.

"I only hope I am in our growing village when it hits him that we have somehow worked around him. I will wager part of my share that it will be the one thing that brings him up into the midst of his family," said Jacob, adding his signature of Jacob E. Buck.

"Just what does 'E' stand for?" questioned Jed.

"Nothing you need to know of."

Standing behind Jacob, Frank mouthed 'Ezekiel' to Jed.

With great flourish, Jed dipped the pen in the ink, and using his middle name and the more popular spelling of his last name, he wrote J. Thomas Smith.

"Was wondering how you were going to get around that. Very creative," exclaimed Frank.

"Thanks—it's also legal. He turned to Jacob, "By the way Zeke, just call me Tom."

"I'll fix you for that, Frank. As for you—you know I can be fast with a paddle."

"Only the beasts of the forest will ever hear it from me," Jed pledged.

"Well that takes care of three. We need two more. First Dan and then I want Nuga to sign as the representative of the family," said Jacob as he carefully rolled the document and wrapped it in a small piece of deerskin.

He took his quiver off its peg on the wall. The tube had been formed from a sheet of birch bark and laced with spruce roots. The bottom had a solid plug of wood. The top had been dipped into the red dye pot to make a border that had a single row of blue glass beads along the bottom edge. Then a lining was added of more bark. He pulled out six arrows, placed the document inside and then replaced three of the arrows and hung the quiver back on the wall by its soft leather carrying strap.

Frank just shook his head. "All this legal business stuff when a good handshake would have done it for me."

"It seems like we got a firm handshake from Uncle Henri."

Frank answered with a grunt.

"Now, before all the family wonders what kind of mischief we are into, we need to survey the damage from the storm. We would have heard by now if any of the shanties needed major repair. I'll check out the canoes and the landing. Frank, I'm sure Hanna is already at the gardens. See if she needs any extra help if there is reseeding to do. You'll know best how the potatoes are faring."

"And me?" questioned Jed.

"First, go check on Birdie, Martha, and your son. Then walk the woods behind Nuga's and the kettles. We know at least two trees came down. Round up the trio and have them collect pieces that are the right size for firewood before we take the ax to the rest. For some reason, they don't seem to mind taking orders from their Uncle Jedediah."

This pleased Jed. "Before I leave, what about the money? Where is it kept and who doles it out?

"Nuga holds all the money and portions it out when it is needed. I'd like her to continue, as she seems to have a perfect safe hideout, as I have not figured it out. I think she has told Hanna which will be perfect. She is another quiet strong woman who will do anything for her family, especially for her nou' gou' mitj."

13   The Quiver

The dawn sky had started to turn pink when Jed stretched at the open door, drinking in the fresh morning air while munching on sourdough bread and molasses. He figured Jacob had left in the moonlight on his rounds of the settlement.

He had slept very soundly, most likely due to the sleepless night before and the work of the day cleaning up the downed timber from the storm, which had given him aches in muscles he never knew existed. Hanna had served a wonderful meal of venison stew followed by maple-drenched stewed apples over dumplings. He had had to force his eyelids to stay open while cuddling Benjie and just made it to his bed before dropping off into a dreamless stupor. Jed barely remembered seeing Jacob when he passed through the shanty on his way to bed; his head had been down on the table, papers with notes and figures scattered around him. This morning all was in order. Perhaps it was a dream.

Starting the walk over to Birdie's, Jed saw Jacob coming up the path through the woods from the meadow and gave him a wave.

It was early, but Ruth and Birdie were already sorting beans on the worktable. Deftly they sorted through and picked out even the tiniest pebbles that sometimes were mixed in with the beans at harvest. Just as quickly, they tossed the beans into the kettle where they would soak for a few hours.   Cheerfully watching the scene was Benjie, snuggled in his cradleboard and making sounds in his own language.

"He won't fit in here much longer," said Jed while he knelt down to grab Benjie's hand. "From the strength of his grip, he'll be freeing himself from the bonds."

"He is a tall one, too. Tiny Bear didn't last long on a board. When he was born some felt he should be the one carrying it," laughed Ruth as she began to pour water over the beans.

"Don't push, you two. He's still just a babe. They grow too fast as it is," remarked Birdie with a wistful glance at little Martha, who had just come out hugging her own little doll.

"I want to go—please! Please!" came shouts in unison from the threesome.

"Now what in the world," said Birdie tossing her arms in the air in exasperation. "I swear those three should be used to send messages up and down the river. You can hear them everywhere."

"We're supposed to go after the turkeys, not the grown-ups," hollered Sean.

Jed could see now that Jacob was on his way out of his shanty with his bow and the quiver holding three arrows over his shoulder.

"I'm going out in the canoe, boys, not in the woods."

"We want to come too," the trio shouted out.

"Not this time. I need to go up the river and make sure things are clear after the storm. We don't need to find wayward logs in our way, especially at night. There may even be some trees down blocking safe passage."

"You never take your bow and arrows unless we are going for turkeys," observed the captain with a stamp of his foot.

Jed was surprised by the action, as it was usually Sean doing the demanding. Peter usually did the thinking and leading, while quiet Joe went merrily along with the group.

"You said this year I would get myself a turkey for sure. I've been practicing and practicing and can hit the target, at least most of the time."

"Yah, we wouldn't take up much room in the canoe," pouted Sean. "I won't even rock it this time."

Joe spoke up, "Uncle Jacob. You never go hunting turkey in the canoe."

"Look boys, I need to go inland and check out the terrain. You know that before long, we'll have to plan on the timber harvest and the drive. We need the summer to clear out any obstacles in the water. I just thought if I should happen to come across any turkeys on my way, we sure are ready for some nice fresh meat. Don't you think?"

"You promised!" came the cries.

With this, Jacob raised his index finger and the boys stopped mid-complaint and dragged their feet back toward their place, sulking all the way.

"Wow, that's a powerful finger. You'll have to teach me that one," winked Jed as Jacob approached.

Jacob shouted to the boys, "When I get a chance, we'll take Jedediah out to look for some turkeys. We'll see just how well he can do with a bow."

At that the dragging feet turned into skips.

"You want me to spend an afternoon in the forest with those three carrying bows and arrows? I thought we were friends."

"Speaking of which, Frank and I are working out a plan to get you close to Wingate's place. We both still think you are crazy to try, but we gave our word."

"It's very important to me."

"I'm on my way up to Dan Thorpe's and if all goes well, I'll be back before sunset with another peg in place. Get your list ready for what personal supplies you need. Frank is spending the day figuring what supplies he thinks his axmen will need and I'm going to think out my food supplies as I paddle. We all need to meet tonight to write an overall inventory for the wangan—from socks to pipe tobacco—trying not to miss anything in between. I know we'll make mistakes, but after working with the supplies of other crews, I think I have a good handle on that."

"Are we moving too fast?"

Jacob answered with a shake of his head, "We have no choice. Working with Henri would have given us lines to supplies without trying to negotiate with the wholesalers. Frank has a lot of work to do at the port."

With that, Jacob started down the hill to the spot where they had left the canoes, well above the water line. He picked up his by the supports, slipped it into the river with no apparent effort, hopped in, and without looking back, started paddling.

Jed watched his friend glide over the river making hardly a ripple. He saw the arrows move up and down in rhythm and thought about how the next chapter of his life was sharing the quiver.

14   The Plan

After another fairly sleepless night, neither man was very talkative.
Jacob did take a break from his usual early morning excursion
and cooked a great breakfast of sourdough pancakes and fried
up some salt pork. Jed thought maybe this was to help regenerate
some energy in both of them.

Jacob had returned much sooner than expected the previous day.
He had one arrow left in his quiver and two turkeys in his hunting
bag. He put the boys to work cleaning the innards and plucking
the feathers. It was not a job they liked, but they were told if they
were going to be hunting the birds, they had to know how to dress
them.

Jacob had found Jed piling hardwood for the bean hole. It seemed
that Dan was so enthusiastic about the prospect of having his
wood lot harvested by a crew that knew what they were doing,
he signed with hardly a question. He wondered about this Tom
Smith, but accepted the fact that Jacob had known him for quite
some time and that he was a full paying partner. He could also see
that he had a good business head.

Once the area settled down, they met again at Nuga's wigwam.
It was hoped Hanna could be there too, but finding someone
interested in staying with the boys even when they were asleep,
was not to be. Making the shopping list was tedious and depended
on how well Frank could deal when it came to supplying the
wangan. Jed's needs for clothes and supplies was pretty succinct,
right down to the woolen long johns. He had hired one of Ruth's
sisters to make him a tunic with fringed sleeves out of tanned deer
hide, He longed for something that fit his long lanky frame. Birdie
wanted to do some sewing for Benjie, so Jed gave her money for

cloth with some extra for Martha. Jacob had a plan for his food order. Things would be brought to the settlement for storage a bit at a time over the summer months, and then he and Jed would take it up river to Dan's acreage, making several canoe trips. They didn't want to be seen hauling large loads, in order keep the arrangement as quiet as possible for as long as possible.

They showed Nuga the final paperwork and she added her own Cateline Dondo in the careful script drilled into her by the nuns. They rolled the document back in the deerskin and left it with her to put in her safe place, wherever that was. She would give Frank one of the gold coins to start negotiations when he was ready to travel.

This morning the three men were meeting in the gardens to discuss schedules and a plan to get Jed to the Wingate Plantation.

All this was spinning around in Jed's mind when the hot, strong tea finally started working and his stomach was well full of breakfast.

Jed started over to Birdie's and bade good morning to the hopping pair scurrying toward the sweet grass. "Looks like your luck is still holding," said he.

Birdie had some carefully cut rectangles of birch bark laid on the outside worktable. She was using an awl shaped from bone to punch holes along the edges and sides of the bark. These rectangles would be the bases for intricate patterns of porcupine quills stitched with sinew through the holes, up through the hollow centers of the quills and down again through the next hole. The quills had been dyed many shades and were sorted by color and length. Some had been cut into tiny pieces the size of beads. Once the pieces were decorated they would be joined with stripped spruce roots, using the holes along the edges. The finished boxes would be magnificent and would bring good value at the trading.

"Okay to use the dye pots?" Jed asked Birdie.

"Help yourself. There is no blue. I won't be able to fill that until the blueberries ripen in a couple of months."

Jed reached into his pockets and pulled out some carved wood animal figures that had a piece of sinew threaded through a center hole. He dipped the porcupine into the brown dye created by boiling cedar, then tied it on a nearby twig to dry. He did the same with a duck dipped in yellow from cherry wood, a rabbit dipped in ochre from boiling earth from the gardens and a bird in the red from bloodroot.

"They are wonderful, Jedediah!" Birdie exclaimed.

"I may be away for a few days and want to finish these for Benjie before I leave. I'll do that later this afternoon."

He peeked in at the two sleeping children and made his way up the garden path. The brothers-in-law were standing in the middle of a row between sprouting potato plants. The earth looked a bit soggy, but with some sunshine it would dry up enough to save the crop. Jacob was wagging his index finger and Frank was doing his shrug with an occasional toss of hands in the air.

"Looks like a typical early morning," Jed shouted.

The men waved to have him join them in the very obvious meeting place that at the same time was the most private, for anyone coming would be easily seen.

Frank started. "I still think this a ridiculous chance to take, but it's your skin. We must leave later today with enough sun left to get us to the spot on the river where I board Zeke and pick up my canoe for the journey to St. John."

Jed looked quizzically between the two. "Why the name Zeke?"

Frank let out a belly laugh. "What else would you call a hard-working mule with a bull-headed stubborn streak?"

Up came Jacob's finger. Then he had to let out a grin of his own.

"I thought we had several days to work out a plan. Why are we rushing now?"

Jacob answered, "I wanted to work out a couple of ideas with Frank before I said anything."

"So that was the arm and finger-waving discussion I witnessed when I came out of the woods."

"Hey, as I said, it's your neck. But I'm not sure it is worth the risk," grunted Frank.

"Tell me. What if it were Hanna who did not know if you were alive or dead?"

Up went the arms in surrender.

Jacob interrupted. "Dan Thorpe told me that he is going to the general store in the village on the edge of the Wingate place in the next day or two. His wife wants a certain trim for the baby clothes she's sewing and it's something the trading post doesn't carry."

"Philippe doesn't think it necessary to carry any 'fancy stuff' for the people he serves up here. Actually he's just too cheap to add that kind of stock and the silly ass has worked right into our hands," Frank blurted with great satisfaction.

Jacob continued, "Dan knows the Wingate sisters and sees them whenever he goes that way. They seem to have a routine of picking up a few supplies mid-morning every day. They are always with their mother. Miss Mary never misses. He thinks it is because it gets her out of the mansion and away from the old man, even if only for a bit. Miss Adelaide also never missed, but he hadn't seen her in a while; he was told that she went off to London to spend some time with her aunt."

"Sent away against her will is more like it," Jed spurted in anger as he clenched his fists and his face turned red.

"I asked him if he thought he could get a message to Mary without causing any questions. He doubted he could ever pass a note, but since he always greets them, might be able to whisper a very short message."

To this Jed let out a great gasp of emotion.

"It may not work, but it is the best I could come up with. I could see that Dan wondered if he should ask why, but knew from my silence not to pursue it further. We made some plans to meet and just shook hands."

"Won't this add another to our circle of secrets? Will it jeopardize Benjie's safety?"

Frank answered, "If all works well, he will never meet you until we set up camp this fall, so there should be no connection between you and this request. We will pass information back and forth through Jacob. Dan knows that a strange Irishman will raise eyebrows if he talks to the ladies and there is no way in hell a savage will get anywhere near them. Once I drop you on the shore near where I leave Zeke, I'll take the canoe down the St. John River right away to start negotiations for supplies."

Jacob broke in. "You and I will make the final plans. I'm going to take my canoe over and will meet you and get whatever the message needs to be so I can take it back to Dan before he goes into the store."

Jed understood why Frank took Zeke overland and then picked up a canoe. The Aroostook River took a path due north not far from Jacob's settlement, then bent east and then south again. When he looked at a rough map, he could not help but smile at how the course reminded him of one of his mother's fancy hair combs. A trip to the same spot by water would take a lot longer than the hike across.

He asked Jacob, "Will I be walking back? It would be just like the trip I made with Benjie when we ran from Wingate."

"Just for a bit. When we finish, you will walk back just west of the junction and I'll pick you up at sunset and take you the rest of the way back here by canoe."

Frank continued, "Ruth is going to bring you some clothes. She'll be at Birdie's as usual when they start the beans. She said there is something extra for you and seemed quite pleased about it. Hanna is working on some provisions. When I leave, the boys like to walk with me for a bit, but I always turn them back before they leave the meadow so they won't stray too far away. So, you can meet me beyond the meadow. Try not to let the little devils see you leave or you'll have so many questions to answer, we'll never get away from here."

All this information from Frank left Jed's head spinning. "Where should I start?"

Jacob answered, "With your pack. Wear your forest boots, but take your moccasins. Spend some time with Benjie as usual. Finish your pack once you get your shirt from Ruth. Watch for Nuga. She is going to keep the children busy with stories and treats down by the river so you can sneak off. You'll need to be past the meadow before Frank leaves. That always causes a commotion, so you will know when he is coming."

"Whew. And you claim not to be a sagamore."

"Papa! Papa! Nuga's going to tell us some stories of Glooscap later ," chimed the trio in unison.

As the little brood skipped from row to row, the men shook hands and went their separate ways.

Jed didn't have that much to put in his pack, but did take a few
pieces of his carving set in case he had a lot of time to wait. He
filled his canteen, sharpened his knife, made sure there were some
matches in his tin, and packed his moccasins. He was sure Jacob
had a reason for that. He tossed in some dried venison in case he
didn't get a chance to share in Hanna's provisions for Frank's trip.

At Birdie's, he checked on the animals he had hung to dry. He had
carved two short pieces of branches to a sharp point on one end
and then took another branch and made a cross piece by tying the
three together with spruce roots. Once the animals were dry, he
hung them from the cross bar.

Just then Birdie came out with Benjie in his cradleboard and
leaned him against what was left of the tree hit by lightening.

"Mr. Jed. I didn't expect you back so early. Ruth will be here later
with some things for you."

"I have something to do before she gets here," said Jed as he
took the cross piece with animals over to the cradleboard. He
pushed the two pointed ends into the ground on either side of
Benjie so the figures hung just where he could bat at them with his
fingertips, making them sway in the morning breeze. Benjie was
delighted and talked to them with baby giggles.

Martha came out chewing on a chunk of corn bread. "Can I make
them move, Mr. Jed? Can I wiggle them for Benjie?" She laughed
out loud as she made Benjie squeal.

Birdie clapped her hands in delight.

"I'm going to be away for a day or two. Is there anything you
need before I go?"

She shook her head 'no' as Ruth came across the clearing. She had
Jed's shirt over her arm. It was wonderful. Jed held it up to himself
and felt the soft hide and ran his hand along the fringe.

"Thank you. It's perfect."

"There's more Mr. Jed," said Ruth as she put her hand in the
basket bag around her neck. Out came a hat made from scraps
from the shirt and sewn in patchwork with sinew. It had a tall
crown and a wide brim that hung down just a mite.

Now it was Jed's turn to clap in glee. He plopped it on his head
and it was perfect. He grabbed Ruth and gave her a great big hug.

"Better be careful Mr. Jed," laughed Birdie. "Bear might see you and toss you like a log."

Jed began to flush.

"Wait just a minute. I have something, too." Birdie went into her shanty and brought Jed a handsome pouch. It had been made from the same hide with a tie to go around his waist. She had beaded the flap with a whimsical bird with a dark head like a chickadee. There was a tie to hold it securely closed so he could carry small items in it.

Jed headed toward her with a thank you. She jumped back. "Don't hug me like that Mr. Jed. You will break me in two."

Benjie gave out a wail. "Looks like my son is feeling left out. Would one of you take him inside for me?"

When Birdie put Benjie in his Da's arms she told him to be careful on his trip and went back to her work with Ruth sorting beans.

"I'll miss you little man," Jed whispered to Benjie, cradling him as they walked around the small room. "I need to try to let your Mum know that you are safe. I have no doubt that you will be well cared for. If something happens and I don't make it back, you need to know how much I love you. You are my world."

Jed took the small cameo from his pocket and with a narrow piece of soft deer hide, tied it around Benjie's wrist. The child was now asleep, content in his father's arms. Jed placed him gently in his hammock, kissed him on the forehead and walked softly into the day that was now bright with sunshine.

He gave a slight nod to Birdie and headed toward Jacob's shanty to finish up his pack.

"Where you going Uncle Jed?" asked Joe as they all surrounded him.

"Why do you ask?"

"You have your boots on," answered Pete.

They don't miss a thing! "I need to go into the forest to check out a few things for Jacob."

"Can we go? Can we go?" pleaded Sean.

"Not this time fellows. I'm going to be gone a day or two. Besides, Nuga is walking down to the river. You'd better hurry and catch up."

The three started to scamper down the slope when Sean turned and ran back up and hugged Jed as hard as he could around his leg. Jed picked him up and swung him around and gently put him back so he could catch up with his Nuga. He gave her a slight wave and she returned a knowing nod and led the children away.

In the shanty, he took off his hand-me-down shirt and put it in the pack and slipped on the new tunic. It fit like a glove. He wrapped the pouch around his waist and dropped a few small coins into it from the spruce gum box and then put that back in his hiding place. *Just as good as Nuga's,* he thought. He took a couple of molasses cookies from the top of the stove for his pack, grabbed a chunk of sourdough bread, flipped on his new hat, and walked out the door to make his way as quickly as possible down to the meadow where he had first met the boys, went beyond to keep out of sight from the path, and waited.

 He felt right at home sitting among the trees and listening to all the sounds of the creatures. In his walk he had found a nice clean chunk of pine and began to shape it into a thick rectangle and then began to hollow it. As the midday sun began to turn toward the west he was surprised to hear fiddling heading his way. *Good, Lord—he enters and exits with fanfare!*

Soon Frank and Zeke could be seen coming down the path. The fiddle had been secured on the mule's back. Jed was leaning against a large tree and as Frank passed, he nodded and said, "Afternoon."

Frank returned the greeting and walked several feet beyond, stopped and turned back and looked at the bearded stranger in slouch hat and handsome shirt. "Jed?"

Jed just stood staring and then flashed his big smile.

Frank bent over and smacked his hands on his knees and laughed out loud. Zeke was not pleased and dug in his hooves, not planning on moving another inch. "Tom Smith," he shouted. "Not even your dear Mum would recognize you."

Jed walked over and gave a piece of molasses cookie to Zeke, which seemed to bring him back in favor. He slapped Frank on the back and the two partners with obedient beast walked toward their spot to rendevous with Jacob.

15 The Chickadee

Jed realized why he had brought his moccasins. He could not have made his way this close to the Wingate manor in his boots without putting one of the workers on notice. He was amazed by his new prowess in stealth. He guessed his spying on turkeys was paying off. Their guards could hear the slightest breaking of a twig and call out the alarm, sending the flock in speedy retreat, like little soldiers in parade formation.

Jed could see the back of the house from his vantage point, but huddled down in the dusk to wait until nightfall before attempting the next step in his plan.

He and Frank had spent the night at the homestead of other immigrants from Ireland. They were a lovely family with three small children who seemed not to have the high energy of Frank's three. Hanna had sent some extra items to share with the family and they all enjoyed a hearty meal followed with gales of laughter over stories of their journeys to the new world.

As dawn broke, Frank made sure Zeke was secure in his pen, then carried his canoe to the Aroostook to continue his journey to the St John then south to do his negotiations for supplies. His canoe was like a typical Micmac vessel. The bottom was flat and sides curved up at the center, which was better for carrying a larger load. The morning mist was lifting off the water as Jed watched him disappear in the early morning light. Then he settled on a slope at riverside with a tin of good, hot, strong Irish tea and began his vigil for Jacob.

As the sun rose high enough to break over the pines, Jed bided his time whittling on the block of pine and began to make some designs on the sides. In time a pinpoint on the river came closer and turned into the image of Jacob making his way swiftly toward him. As soon as possible, Jed reached out and guided the canoe up the slope and practically lifted his friend onto land, he was so eager to hear how things had gone in town.

So far, so good. At first light, Dan and Jacob had met at riverside and planned to reconnect at the same spot two hours later.

Jed quickly told Jacob the short message he wanted passed to Mary. Jacob grinned from ear to ear at the instructions, slapped his friend on the back, quickly retreated back to the canoe and made haste on the river to meet farmer Thorpe.

Then started the longest few hours of his life. Jed whittled, carved and searched the woods until he found another piece of wood he would need to complete his project. All his busy work never took him out of sight of his meeting place. He enjoyed the freedom to be by the river. As the sun reached its apex, the lady of the house brought him more tea and some biscuits and molasses. Then his pacing took him to the well to refill his canteen and check his pack. He took some dried venison and put it in his pouch and tied his canteen on his belt along with his knife. Then he went back to his carving, pieces of pine flying in all directions in his frustration. Just when he felt his head would burst, he saw Jacob quickly approaching.

"Get in!" Jacob hollered as the canoe touched the slope.

Jed turned to wave thanks, but the family was not to be seen. He'd have to ask Frank to speak for him.

"I'll fill you in as we move," Jacob added as Jed tossed in his pack and they set off.

"Dan went into the general store at mid-morning as planned. He took his time looking at different gear and new items. Then he went to the fabrics and checked out the lace and trims. He had a definite idea of what Emma wanted. She had even drawn some rough sketches. This gave him more time to leisurely look through. Eventually, though, it began to get a little obvious that he was dragging his feet on this purchase, so he was about to give up when Mrs. Wingate wandered in and went straight to the counter. He was anxious for a moment, but then Miss Mary came in with her usual bouncy step, greeting all with a 'good day'"

"And then?"

"Hold on. I need to get closer to the shore so we can find a secluded place to drop you off. Take off those boots and swap them for your moccasins in the pack."

"Go on," Jed pleaded as he began to unlace.

"Mary finally looked his way and he tipped his hat and said, 'Good morning Miss.' She was pleased to see him and asked how Emma was feeling. He gave her a quick update and asked her to see if what he had picked out was close to Emma's wishes. She looked at her mother, who just smiled and nodded at Dan. Mary thought Dan had picked the perfect trim. He thanked her and told her it was going to be a beautiful day, so the evening should be wonderful to listen for the song of the chickadee."

Jed thought his heart was going to burst through his new shirt.

"She looked at him quizzically for just a moment, then blanched and dropped her basket. He reached down and handed it back to her with a nod and a smile. She laid her hand on her chest and thanked him. Her mother asked if she was all right and she answered she had just a bit of discomfort and probably had eaten something wrong at breakfast. Her mother chided her for always eating too fast. Dan then tipped his hat at both women, caught Mary's eye one more time and went to the counter to purchase the trim."

Jed felt close to tears with relief.

"Now it is up to you," Jacob said, as he steered his craft into a shallow cove just above the junction of the two rivers. "You will need to walk through the forest to the plantation ."

Jed knew just where he was as he knew every inch of this land. He and Addie had spent time playing and wading in this little private pool.

He had been silent through the journey and now whispered, "It just might work. It just might."

Jacob gave a slight noncommittal nod.

"Jacob, my friend, if something should happen and I don't come back to this place tonight—"

Jacob interrupted the thought. "I will raise him as my own son. He will never be at a loss for care. His Nuga will make sure of that."

"Thank you." Jed left his pack in the care of his friend and with moccasins in hand, slipped into the water and made the short wade to shore.

"I'll slip back into this spot at dusk and will wait until dawn if need be. There will be a bright moon tonight that will both help and hinder us. You look like a one of those Vermont mountain men, but I'd rather you be a Micmac tonight."

Jed smiled, showing his mouthful of big white teeth. He slipped on his moccasins, gave Jacob a quick wave and disappeared in no time into the forest.

He was slouched against the trunk of a familiar old oak tree, staying in the shadows until it was dark enough to act. He was concerned about being seen by one of the riff-raff that Wingate hired to patrol his property. They would act quickly if he were caught and report the catch to the boss when the prey had been eliminated. No questions asked. He wasn't at all afraid of the guard dog, for if anything, Brutus would cover him with sloppy kisses if he found him. The dog was Addie's shadow and had many times been the excuse for her to be away. After all, he needed lots of exercise. He had often played a lot of their games with them. No, the dog would not harm Jed even though he would tear into any intruder who dared come near his mistress or his home.

Jed loved watching the sun set, but on this night he was very impatient with that beautiful glow. He watched the trees he loved so much turn pink and since the moon was nearly full, he could still see the birches bathed in moonlight.

"Well Jedediah Thomas," he whispered to him self, "they must have cleaned up after dinner by now. It is now or never."

He stood straight next to the tree and whistled as loud as he could, "Chick-a-dee, chick-a-dee-dee, chick-a-dee-dee-dee! He waited a few minutes and repeated, "Chick-a-dee-dee-dee!"

He saw the lantern in the back hall flicker to life. He could clearly see Mary as she stepped out the door to the back stoop. "Just getting a breath of fresh air, Mother," she said through the door.

Mary took a deep breath and stretched her arms as in relief from another stress-filled day. She had worked in a daze through the silver polishing, mending and incessant chattering of her older sister. At times her brain had shouted out —would this day ever end? She wanted to run to the woodshed, but knew she might be watched. She was always watched. Especially since Addie had been wrenched from her loves and sent off in disgrace, never to be allowed to come home.

Mary picked a bit at the herb garden growing along the side of the shed. She and Addie always worked this small plot with all kinds of plants to add a bit of spice to their cooking, especially for the tea. As she weeded a bit at the end of the row, she turned her back on the house and whispered, "Jed."

"I'm in here Mary," came the voice from the small area in back, at the corner of the stacked wood.

Her hands began to tremble as she picked up a stray small log and went around the corner to put it back. She was startled to see a tall bearded stranger, certainly not the clean–shaven, handsome young man with tousled hair.

"It's really me, Mary. I'm safe and so is my son."

She dropped the piece of wood and jumped into his arms sobbing. She was much tinier than Jed remembered, not much bigger than Birdie. He thought she must have been suffering terribly at the loss of Adelaide.

"Why are you here, Jed? If father sees you he will have you killed on the spot and get away with it. He will tell everyone he thought you were an intruder and that he was protecting his family."

"I had to chance it. You need to somehow let Addie know that we are safe and the boy is thriving. It is best you know not where, but our son is part of a very caring family and is surrounded with love. I won't be coming this way again, but I'll try to send you messages about his life."

"I'll do it somehow. I promise. She is very frail, Jed. Each letter that comes from my aunt is sad. The trip to England so soon after giving birth took its toll on her health, and mentally she seems to be pining her life away. This news would help, I know it. What's his name?"

Jed flushed a bit, but the darkness hid it. "I did something that may have been foolish, as I don't want your father to have a way to find him. But thinking of Addie and how she would want revenge for his taking away her son, I named him Benjamin Wingate Smythe."

Mary nearly fell over. "Father would absolutely have a stroke if the world knew of the child." She giggled. "Would that I could let her know that. Benjamin Wingate Smythe!"

"I hope that happens in time. Right now, I know it would be too dangerous for him for everyone to know. Frankly, I do not trust your father. Those who care for my son know him only as Benjie."

"Father would hate that, too. To think someone would take his aristocratic Benjamin and make it common. Benjie. I love it" She giggled again.

"Where are you Mary?" came the voice of her older sister from the back door.

"Be right there. Just straightening a few sticks in the shed."

"For heaven's sake, let the yard help do that. You are beginning to act more like Addie every day. Get back to your ladylike chores."

That statement tickled both of them in the shed and they did their best to stifle their laughs.

"You'd better go, Mary. I don't want you caught up any more than necessary."

She reached up and gave him a huge hug and kissed him on the cheek. "Please give that hug and kiss to Benjie."

"As soon as I get back to him."

"Please, stay right here for a few minutes. I won't be long. There is something I want you to give to Benjie. I want him to know his Mum and his Auntie Mary."

Mary fairly skipped back to the house.

Jed started to get a bit nervous. He hoped she would come back soon, for the longer he stayed, the greater the chance he would be caught, and he was so close to putting this behind him.

The back door slammed and he could see Mary through the cracks in the logs. Her gait was so lively and he could hear her humming a tune as she carried a small wicker basket. Just as she reached the corner of the shed, they both could were startled by the distinct odor of Mr. Wingate's strong cigars. Sure enough, he was heading toward them on the path from the front of the house.

From the basket Mary took a small package wrapped in a remnant of red silk fabric and tied with a piece of ribbon and a sprig of lavender. She pressed it quickly into Jed's hands and whispered, "Teach him that we love him."

Jed pressed himself as tightly as he could up against the wall in the cramped corner of the open back of the shed. The space barely covered him. The toes of his moccasins could be seen. His brimmed hat was held tightly to his chest under his crossed arms.

Mary took one more look into Jed's eyes and squeezed his arm. For the first time, he saw in the moonlight that her eyes were the same blue as Addie's and Benjie's.

"What in the world are you still doing out here?" her father bellowed at Mary.

Jed's stomach turned over at the sound of Wingate's voice. He wanted so much to strike out but he knew he must think of Benjie and not give Wingate a hint that the boy was still alive.

Mary quickly turned and bent over the spray of herbs at the corner of the shed. "I came back out to gather a bit of rosemary to flavor our eggs in the morning. And I was favoring a bit of mint for my nightly tea," she added, trying to move forward in the garden.

Wingate stepped forward past Mary and leaned against the corner of the shed. The heel of his fancy boots just missed Jed's toe. He took a long drag on his cigar and the smoke wafted into the pile of wood.

Jed had a hard time not choking or coughing aloud. In his mind he thought *tonight I am Micmac. I am one with my surroundings.* His heart was beating so hard, he was sure it could be heard.

Mr. Wingate dropped his cigar and crushed the remains into the ground, once again just missing the colorful chickadee on the toe of the m'cusin.

A bead of sweat fell from the tip of Jed's nose and he was sure it sounded like a cannon going off when it hit the ground.

Wingate reached into the darkness and straightened a log that looked ready to fall off the pile.

"Come father. Let me make you some tea, too. I put some scones in to bake when I came out and they must be about ready. And mother churned fresh butter this afternoon!"

Showing the closest he could come to smiling, Wingate ground the cigar butt one more time and started off with his daughter.

They were just starting up the steps, when Mr. Wingate turned and rushed back to the shed.

Mary chased him. "What is it, father?"

"I heard something moving in the shed. Where's that damn dog?"

Mary felt faint but when they looked in the corner, it was empty.

Jed had run as quietly as he could from the shed and then dove and rolled into the brush. He was lying there, trying not to laugh, as Brutus licked his face.

"It must have been some birds, father. While I was getting some air, I could hear many thrashing in the bushes." She looked wistfully at the surrounding forest and whispered, "God speed Jed and Benjie." She wiped away a tear, followed her father into the house, and put out the lantern.

Jed traveled as quickly as possible while staying quiet and unobtrusive. He passed the remains of his home and picked up a piece of the charred door, on which he had carved a likeness of his home on the moors.

In the moonlight, he could see very little. He crossed the fields over which he had fled with Benjie and could still hear the curses that had followed him. When he came to the path leading away from the river where he and the baby had spent the night against the tree, he veered the other way and walked to the pool where his friend was waiting.

He must have done well, as he did not break Jacob's meditation with nature around him. It was a few minutes before Jacob noticed Jed standing quietly beside the pool, deep in his own memories of this place.

"Well?" asked Jacob, being a man of few words.

"Very well," replied Jed.

He took off his moccasins and waded out to the canoe so Jacob would not have to paddle it near any of the rocks close to the shore. He pulled his long body into place.

"It is time to let go off the past, my friend. Take me home so we can truly grab hold of the future."

16   Summer Glow

Late summer - 1825

The summer of 1825 flew by. Days turned to weeks and weeks
to one month and then another. Usually the hard work of taking
care of the crops and getting provisions ready for the winter
was pure drudgery, but this year was like no other. There was a
promise in the air. Jacob told the family that he was going out
on his own as a camp cook, Frank was going to supervise an ax
crew, and Jedediah was going to help them find good harvest
grounds and work with the landing crew. They were going to
work independently in hopes of bringing in a lot more money for
the family. This raised the self-esteem of each man, woman, and
child and in turn brought everyone closer together in their goal
of establishing a permanent settlement.   Even cleaning the bean-
hole ashes seemed much more important.

When Jacob finally brought them all in on the plans to establish
a wangan to service their small crew as well as other independent
workers who might pass by, the pride was palpable. Their Jacob
was going to be a businessman, and in time they might all own
a piece of land of their own. On that night, the drums came out
and Frank played his fiddle with even more zest than ever. Anyone
passing on the river must have wondered just what this tribe of
savages was up to as they danced around the fire, chanting in joy.

All the pieces of the puzzle started to fall in place once Jed was
able to turn his back on the Wingate Plantation. When he and
Jacob pulled the canoe up onto the slope at the landing, they had
just a few days to fill in Nuga and Hanna and set more plans on
paper.

Four days after they returned, Frank made his usual entrance leading Zeke, burdened with the biggest load his sons had ever seen. Even Zeke had a lighter step. That night Frank was to make his report; Jacob and Jed held their collective breath until they heard the results of his trip.

Nuga sat on her usual pile of blankets, while the three men sat around the fire hole in the small wigwam.

"Well, Francis. Just what do you have for us?" she asked.

"It's amazing Nuga, what gates can be opened with a gold half-sovereign. It bought us a down payment at three different dealers—one for clothing and shoes; one for equipment like ax heads, spikes, knives and matches; and one for the food provisions for Jacob."

"You mean, they just said yes without further investigation?" Jacob pondered.

"I've known these men for years. Working for them on the docks gave me a lot of recognition as a straight shooter. And committing to pay cash on delivery of each load went a long way to seal the deals."

"What about the larger coins? How will they be broken into manageable amounts?" wondered Jed.

"They have set up a bank of sorts on the docks. It is where monies can be deposited for the draw of the dealers with a note. It is well-protected and has become the lifeline for many. St. John is becoming quite the little city, the majority being Irish."

"Then your blarney must be the touch we need," laughed Jed.

Nuga wondered, "How will we get the two remaining gold sovereigns to the bank safely? You know the knowledge that valuable coins are coming down river is going to cause some of the riff-raff to come after it."

"As usual, you are a woman wise beyond all others," said Frank. "Very few will know when we are going to move it and who is going to carry it. They will be watching me like a hawk. Jed still cannot travel safely that way. It is going to have to take some planning."

"How much time do we have before the next shipment?" asked Nuga.

"At least three weeks, and then once a week until we get all the supplies up to the Thorpe farm. It will be close, but we should be able to finish before the ice begins to form. Let us worry about that, Nuga. We'll keep the coins safe."

"Just let me know when you need them."

"By the way Jedediah, these are your packages with some coins left over. Once you slip into these duds, your transformation to Thomas Smith should be complete."

Jed hugged the bundle with great glee. The thought of new shirts, pants and such made him almost giddy.

"Let's go. It's late and morning will come soon enough. Every day we have is going to be filled to the brim," urged Jacob.

Once back at Jacob's shanty, there was some tossing and turning, but mercifully the sleep that comes from hard physical work won over the fretting in Jed's mind.

Sipping his morning tea, Jed actually became anxious when his two rabbit companions didn't say good day. He started looking in the grass and under the shanty.

Jacob came out and stretched. "You lose something, Jedediah?"

Sheepishly he answered, "No, not really."

"Wouldn't be two furry critters that live in the sweet grass?"

"Jacob. You didn't."

Jacob didn't belly laugh often, but it was an exceptional moment. "Not to worry about your little friends. My nephews would have strung me up in the big pine if I'd set a trap for the rabbits. Come with me."

If anyone had been going by on the river, they would have wondered what in the world was going on to make two strapping men tiptoe through the sweet grass.

Suddenly Jacob stopped and moved the grass just a bit and pointed to where Jed should look. There lay one of the rabbits, with three small fur balls nursing as if there were no tomorrow. Jed had to stifle his laugh. Certainly the creatures knew they were not in danger. Papa Bunny was probably staring at them from another patch. Why you old softy. I would never have guessed you would pass up a chance to make rabbit stew. Your will must have worked hard against your cooking instincts."

"Look, Uncle Jacob!" shouted Sean." Here comes Philippe
with Auntie Amy." The three-part greeting party headed for the
landing, where a small bateau was approaching the slope. This
type of flat-bottomed boat was perfect for the shallow waters of
the river this time of year and was great for cargo.

"Of course he would not be seen paddling a canoe," Frank
grumbled as he came out to see what the ruckus was. "Can't even
handle his own bateau. Needs an oarsman."

"Frank, go get Amy out of the boat and help her up to Nuga's.
And stay there yourself. The last thing we need is for you to get
in a fight with her son," snapped Jacob. "Jedediah, you'd better
keep to the shadows. Don't think Philippe has ever seen you, as
he hardly goes near the lumber crews, but let's be safe. He is a
Wingate hanger-on."

Jed went up and sat near the back of Birdie's place and picked up
his whittling. He kept an eye on Benjie, who was nestled in his
outside hammock. The cradleboard no longer held him.

"Aunt Amy, what brings you up to our area? We usually only see
you at the trading post."

Philippe replied for his mother. "She has it in her head that we
need to stock a few more items for the ladies, like trims and fancy
buttons. Brought some samples to show them. I think it is just
plain foolish up in this area. What in the world do the women in
the forest area need of decoration?"

Amy shot back, "Have you ever opened your eyes and seen the
beautiful beading your sister does? Do you think that only the
fancy ladies you try to impress like pretty clothes? I want some
ideas from Birdie and Hanna."

Ignoring his mother, Philippe shouted, "You know my father.
Anything for his Amy. We're taking her to St. John to look at
more samples so she can place an order for the store. Will pick up
some lumbering supplies with the season coming up."

Frank did all he could to maintain his composure. He went over
and lifted Amy from the boat and then steadied her as she walked
to Nuga's. Jed swore he could see smoke coming out of his ears.

Jacob started to turn and Philippe shouted, "Don't you walk away
from me, cousin! I want to know what is going on here!"

"And you are raving about what?"

Philippe jumped out of the bateau and wagged his finger at Jacob as he walked toward him. "What's going on up here?"

"Figures you wouldn't bring your mother up here out of the kindness of your heart."

"I mean it. I heard that Frank was in St. John and had opened an account with three major dealers. How did you manage that?"

"Frankly, Philippe, that is none of your damn business."

"If you are involving my grandmother in some kind of illegal proposition, then it is my business."

"Since when have you given a twit about Nuga's welfare? Where were you when the spring storm went through here and nearly destroyed her wigwam? Did you check on her then? You are just trying to put your nose in where it doesn't belong. And what about your sister and Martha? Give them a single thought?"

Philippe totally ignored the questions. "My father would care what you're up to. He'll want to know why you think you can do business with St. John and not with us."

"You moron. We came to you with a proposition that would have given you and Uncle Henri the opportunity to make money on interest. It would have been easier on our finances. No. You couldn't get that fancy hairdo of yours out of your ass."

Jed almost cut his finger on that one. He was working on some intricate floral designs. Not a good time to mess it up.

"Where did you get your hands on a half-sovereign? Where do you think you are going to get the rest of the funding?"

"Don't lose sleep over it, Philippe. We managed to find ourselves some businessmen who could see a good opportunity. Obviously you couldn't see an opportunity if it bit you in the rear."

Philippe was red in the face by now. "You won't get any wangan business. My customers won't buy anywhere but at the trading post."

"Just think. If they break an ax handle out in the wilderness, they'll have some place close to replace it without losing days and pay waiting to get back to your place."

"You son of a—"

"Watch it. We have the same grandmother. Or have you totally

forgotten you have Micmac blood running through your veins just
like the rest of us?"

Just as it looked like Philippe was about to take a swing, his
mother, Nuga, Birdie, and Hanna started walking down the bank.
Amy gave each of the women a hug and thanked them for their
help. They thanked her for starting to stock notions that they had
such a hard time finding.

Philippe jumped into the bateau, leaving his mother stranded on
the bank. Jacob picked her up, gave her a kiss on the cheek and
put her in the boat that would take her to St. John.

"Come again, Aunt Amy, when you can stay longer. We miss you
up here," said Jacob as he handed her the little basket of samples.

As they pushed off, Amy hollered, "Don't forget, we need more
baskets and quill work, Birdie. I'll see that you get a bigger share
of the proceeds."

Philippe just rolled his eyes.

Jed thought he hadn't been this entertained in a long time.

"What was that about?" asked Frank.

"I've no need for more fireworks. I'll tell you when we all settle
down." Jacob picked up his canoe and practically tossed it into
the river.

"Must have been something if you need a canoe ride to calm you
down."

Jacob shouted back from the water. "Jedediah. Tomorrow we
go up to the Thorpe farm with the first of the supplies and sort
out the terrain before we have to start picking up an order each
week."

Jed stood and saluted from the bank.

"Mr. Jed, come quick," said Martha, with a wave from her shanty.

Thinking something might have happened to Benjie, Jed ran to her
faster than he thought he knew how.

Benjie's blanket was on the floor and he was lying on his back.

"Watch, Mr. Jed." Martha sat on the floor to the left and shook
Benjie's rattlebox, catching his eye. He reached for it with his

right arm and she pulled it further away. He tried even harder and suddenly he rolled himself over.

Birdie clapped her hands in glee from her bench at the table.

Jed found himself doing the same. He thought, *did my Da feel this much pride the first time I turned over?* He swooped Benjie up in his arms and spun in circles. "That's my big boy. Thank you for coming to get me, Martha."

She gave him a great big smile, hugging her doll, which was dressed in a bright red silk dress Birdie had made from the remnant Mary had wrapped around Benjie's gift.

The doll's dress was decorated with the prettiest white glass beads. "Yes indeed," he said to Birdie. "I'd say that the women in these parts know a lot about trim."

This really pleased her.

"Hey Jed. Where's my partner at the bean hole?" shouted Bear. He had been hunting and trapping. His boys had dried a great amount of venison and brought back several large pieces of fresh meat, plus some nice hides and pelts. "There will be a feast tonight."

It was Jed's turn to get a bear hug. Each time he saw Bear, he swore he was bigger, if that were possible. It was an easy task to lift the bean kettle with Bear on the other end.

Bear continued, "I passed Jacob on the river. Heard he had a few words with my baby brother. Looks like you guys put one over on him. Congratulations. I don't want to know how you managed to get the big guys in St. John to open accounts, but I'm sure glad you didn't work with Philippe."

"No brotherly love there?"

"He has no use for the rest of the family. Don't know why he considers us less than he. Too bad, for he'll never know the closeness of the rest of us. He may be fooling my Pop with his ways, but he's nothing but a money-hungry thief. I've heard my mother cry too many tears over that bum. You won't have to worry about the security of your son and the rest of the family while you're busting your hide to make this piece of land work for us. As long as I have a breath of air, I'll protect them from any of the rats on the river."

Frank had been right. Such a feast there was that night, with corn
roasted in the husk, early apples, and bowls of blueberries—some
cooked into a sauce with maple syrup and poured over biscuits.
Ruth had found a nice patch of raspberries and they were sweet as
honey. Jacob had put aside his planning and jumped into cooking.
He'd spent the rest of the day in Hanna's kitchen, baking six big,
crusty pies—three blueberry and three raspberry. He hardly ever
had the luxury of fresh berries in the camps. He just made lemon
pies once in awhile.

Jed could not get himself to enjoy fresh venison steak; he
preferred jerky. No blood there. He left a bit early. Once Benjie
was bedded down, he packed for a couple of days upstream. He'd
have to spend the early morning loading supplies into the canoes.

On the small table next to his cot sat the wonderful gift that had
been wrapped in Mary's red silk—two marvelous miniature oil
portraits set in a double rosewood frame. On the left was Mary,
wearing a brilliant blue blouse. She had a tender smile and every
hair properly in place. On the right, a remarkable image of Addie
grinned impishly at Jed. The likeness took his breath away every
time he looked at it. She was dressed in a white top with small
yellow roses embroidered across the yoke. Her long hair was
swept away from her face with a yellow ribbon. The artist had
correctly captured the wisps of flaxen hair that were forever
escaping the ribbon and dropping into her face. The thought of
her sitting still long enough to embroider those roses made him
smile. That she had sat long enough for the artist to do his magic,
he found hard to believe.

The ribbon Addie was wearing in the picture was the same one
that Mary had tied around this gift she had given to Jed for Benjie.
Birdie had fashioned the ribbon into a bow for Jed, and he had
put it on top of the frame. This was the last thing he saw each
night as he blew out his candle and the first thing he saw in the
morning when dawn broke. He planned to take it to Birdie in the
morning so she could put it on her high shelf for safe-keeping until
he returned. He had learned a long time ago that the forest and
the river held dangerous surprises and never to take return trips
for granted.

17   The Forest Primeval

There was a light fog on the river that morning. The previous day
had been warm but the night cool, so it would take some time for
the haze to fully lift. Jed decided to take the paintings up to Birdie
early so he could concentrate on loading the canoes later. He knew
Benjie might be nursing, but over time the embarrassment he had
felt at first had turned to knowing it was a loving, natural part of
Benjie's life. As for Birdie, she had always known that. He tapped
on the door and entered slowly. The baby was changed and
dressed for the day in a little tunic shirt, wrapped in his blanket
and lying in his hammock.

"You're up before the birds today, Mr. Jed."

"I am wondering if you ever go to bed. How do you rest?"

Martha was still sound asleep in the corner with her doll lying
beside her. They had matching cotton sleeping-shirts. She had a
cot like her mother's and told everyone that she was a big girl
now. Birdie spoke softly from her seat at the table, which was
covered with projects. "I get plenty of rest, Mr. Jed. I'm just a
fitful sleeper."

"Is he back to sleep?"

"No. Just watching his animals. At night, we hang them above his
hammock on a line from the rafter."

Jed walked over and Benjie's hands went up in excitement. He
picked up his son and brought him closer to the little bunny and
spun it around, bringing out a little laugh. "Now that Birdie has
blueberries, I'll be able to carve you a bluebird."

"The dye pot is already full Mr. Jed."

"You hear that Benjie? Da will take care of it." Jed held up the frame. "Look here, little boy. This is your Mum and this is your Auntie Mary. They love you so much. Your Mum is so beautiful and you have eyes just like her."

Birdie walked over and took a peek. "Such pretty ladies."

"Da has to go away for a little bit and I'm leaving this here with you. Birdie will keep it safe."

Birdie took it and put it on her treasure shelf above her cot, along with an old cornhusk doll, a well-used man's pouch, a dance rattle and reading book. Jed knew these must all hold special memories for her. She also had put the cameo there for safe-keeping.

"I'll show it to him every day and tell him about his Mum and Auntie Mary."

Jed gave his son a hug and laid him down. "You are such a lucky little boy. With Birdie, Martha, Nuga, Hanna, and all the others, you will be so loved."

Jed could see the morning was getting a bit brighter, so he gave Birdie a little nod and headed for the river.

He met Jacob coming from his morning walk around the perimeter of the settlement. "How could you do your inspection in the dark?" chided Jed.

"I was doing just fine until I stumbled over that pile of fieldstones you are collecting. What are your thoughts on them?"

"I could see by your little path that you have decided just where the boundaries lie around this growing little village. Don't you think it's about time to start using the fieldstones from clearing the gardens to show others what we will claim?"

"Indians with fences," chuckled Jacob. "That will raise many eyebrows. I'll have the boys add to your pile whenever they come across good-size stones."

"We'll make a proper British landowner out of you yet," said Jed as he ducked, knowing a slap could be coming.

Jed picked up one canoe. "We'll use the flat-bottom ones for these trips. They are not as fast, but are more stable and hold a lot more cargo. This trip we need to take up everything we'll need to start setting up the camp and the wangan. We'll stuff any little bit of extra space with cooking equipment."

"Can I take my pack and bedroll?" teased Jed. "You know, while your cousin was ranting and raving with his questions, he nearly tripped over all the answers."

The supplies ready for transport were lying in piles on the edge of the river, covered with just enough greens to give them a bit of protection, but they certainly were not hidden.

Jacob agreed. "He should have been able to see these supplies were not to stock a wangan, but to set up a camp. Let's keep him guessing."

Jed thought his friend was a magician the way he managed to put so many goods into such a small space. "You sure we'll not scrape bottom? The canoes are sitting so low in the water."

"We Micmac know how to build a canoe. These two take a burden like Zeke does. We'll do fine, even after we add our bulk. Now grab your things. I want to be out of sight before the rest of the family wakes up."

The men scampered up to Jacob's shanty, where each picked up a bundle of food and their packs and returned quickly, stopping only to make sure the canteens were filled with fresh water.

Each canoe had one seat across the middle. Jed put his pack and bedroll under it and found just enough room to squeeze in his long legs. He made a mental assumption that this trip was not going to be the most comfortable. He did have confidence in his maneuvering ability with the paddle and knew Jacob must feel the same or these precious supplies would not be entrusted to him on the water. He had been taught well. The only extra equipment Jacob carried in his canoe was his bow and quiver on one shoulder and a long-barreled rifle next to him on the seat. Jed hoped that was one piece he did not have to use.

The two canoes were quickly out of sight around the curve of the river, heading inland toward the Thorpe farm. Negotiating the water was tricky in the hazy early light. The river always settled to a shallow gentle flow at that time of year. It was hard to remember that just four months before it had been raging with the power and depth to carry thousands of logs toward the mills. It would not be long before the chill took hold, the river iced up and the cycle began again.

As the sun broke through the trees, the water sparkled like diamonds as a gentle breeze roughed up the surface. Jacob pointed

to the left shore, where a family of four deer was drinking. The
buck and doe stared at the intruders while the young twins paid
no attention. My, how Jed loved this time of day and hoped that
Jacob would keep the rifle and bow right where they were. Then
Jacob pointed to the right and Jed saw his first traditional Micmac
settlement. There were about a dozen wigwams like Nuga's, a
baby could be heard crying in the background, a communal fire
had just been set and two women were filling kettles with water.
On the landing were five traditional Micmac canoes with flat
bottoms like the ones Jed and Jacob were using, but with the curve
up on the sides in the center. An older woman walked toward
the fire with a bundle of brush. She was wearing a pointed,
brightly decorated hat much like the one in Nuga's wigwam. A
man in tunic and leggings stood up and waved at Jacob. There
was a small vegetable garden to one side, but no other signs of
permanence. Jed thought of many questions to ask when he had
a chance. The aroma of the smoke from the new fire made Jed
realize how hungry he was. He dipped his hand into his food
basket and was delighted to pull out a large chunk of blueberry
cake. Hanna must have packed it, because her brother certainly
hadn't had time to bake since he'd made those wonderful pies.

Songbirds began their morning wake-up calls and Jed realized he
already missed Benjie and that he couldn't wait to teach him about
the wonders of this incredible countryside.

By late morning Jed was beginning to get his bearings. They
passed the boulder in the water that had tripped up his driver and
thrown him off his log to his death. That meant Wilson's corner
was about a mile up and Salmon Brook less than a mile beyond
that. The death of that young man still haunted Jed.

By the time the sun reached its peak, the day had become very
warm and Jed pulled off his deerskin shirt and wore only a
lightweight cotton shirt, which was long-sleeved to protect against
the mosquitoes. The mosquitoes didn't bother Jed as much as the
black flies did in May; for some reason they loved to chew on his
fair English skin. He marveled that Jacob hardly noticed them.
Guess his hide was tougher.

A short, shrill whistle from Jacob brought Jed from his thoughts
and rhythmic paddling.

"Pull in over there." Jacob pointed to a small clearing on the
right, where Jed could just make out a canoe pulled on the bank

under the brush. "We'll bring them in far enough to unload and then move them higher up the bank."

After slowly and carefully guiding his vessel as far as he dare go up the slope, Jed stood and tried to get his bearings. He saw a narrow but well-worn path leading up into the forest and beyond. "Is this the Thorpe land?"

"This is his landing. Someday we can make it bigger, but right now we want to keep our presence quiet."

"This is close to where I buried Wilson," Jed said in amazement. "This land has some wonderful stands of pine. Wingate always wanted me to survey much farther up, perhaps with the idea of working back toward the St. John. What if he sends his crew in here?"

"Not to worry. Dan has talked to him about it. He told Wingate he doesn't want any large companies to work his timber; the big blowhard is not pleased, but understands the legality of the grant. Wingate could face problems. Dan says several Yankee loggers are claiming wood tracts farther inland and are forming posses to make sure the Canadians keep out."

"This is going to blow up some day, isn't it? How in the world did we get in this fix? I always thought the Aroostook Valley was part of New Brunswick."

"In 1783 a treaty ended the American Revolution but the boundary between British controlled New Brunswick and the District of Maine was not that clear. This didn't cause a lot of concern as Maine was part of Massachusetts and Massachusetts had a good working partnership with England. Things got sticky, though, when Maine became a state in 1820 and a lot of Canadian families were already on this side of the St. John River. Maine felt that was part of their state. There have been disputes over the land ever since. Dan Thorpe got his grant from the Commonwealth of Massachusetts just before Maine received statehood, and so far it has held, as Massachusetts held fifty percent of public land and since this was new territory, this was public."

"Well, that's a history lesson that has never turned up in any book I read in England."

"Not surprised. The history on this river has not yet been settled."

While they were talking, Jacob had casually started a small fire and hung the teakettle. He knew they would need a meal before they unloaded and found safe storage for the supplies. He was hoping they could walk and survey some of the property before sunset.

Jed had not known jerky could taste so good, especially with molasses bread and hot strong tea. The morning had sapped his strength more than he'd realized.

"Jacob, I thought that might be you when I saw the wisp of smoke above the pines," came a bellowing voice from up the path.

Startled, Jed nearly dropped his tea.

"Guess no one can sneak up you," said Jacob as he went up to shake the man's hand.

As the two men came toward him, Jed adjusted the brim on his hat and stood to greet them.

"Tom, this is Dan Thorpe."

Jed reached out his hand and was surprised by the strength in the grip of this stout, middle-aged man with slightly graying hair that fell to his shoulders. He was shorter than Jed by several inches, but what he lacked in height was more than made up by his gusto. By the roughness of his hand, it was evident he was not afraid of hard work.

"So, this is your mysterious partner," said Dan, peering up under Jed's hat.

"It's about time you met Tom Smith. He comes to us from England."

"Won't hold that against you," laughed Dan. His Irish eyes twinkled from his round, ruddy face. He put two of his fingers to his mouth and let out a short, sharp whistle.

Down the path came three boys, each with freckles and a mop of red hair. They were in the early to middle teen years.

Jed thought, *do all Irishmen sire boys in groups of three?*

"Jacob, tell the boys where you want to store the supplies and let them unload for you. Then we can get your two canoes out of sight."

Jacob set to walking up the path. He had spotted two large

boulders with a natural gully between them. He wanted the supplies stacked there, covered with boughs to protect them from the elements and hide them from casually prying eyes.

"Thanks Dan. We were hoping to make the best of what is left of the day to survey the riverfront and find a suitable spot to set camp." Because they hoped to be working this parcel for many seasons, the camp would be fairly permanent and needed to be situated close to midline between boundaries and have easy access to the farm and to the river.

Jed wanted to get a good look at the timber so he could plan to harvest the logs in a way that would guarantee preserving the forest. He was not one to strip the terrain and take the most timber by destroying the land.

The two men put on their heavy boots and tucked away the moccasins in the packs. This was a working walk, not one for hunting. As they moved west, away from the farmland, the forest became so dense that not much sunshine made it through the canopy. The ground was soggy underfoot and there was an odor of decay. It was obvious that it had never been harvested, so it still was a lumberman's swamp.

Jed found a large tree, which had most likely been felled by a lightening bolt, in a small clearing. He sat on the side of the large carcass, surveying the landscape in the warmth of the sun. He finally spoke to Jacob. "This is primeval. The pines are magnificent old growth and there are enough varied groves to offer many secondary products."

"I had no idea what a wonderful lot this was," marveled Jacob.

"Do you know what size?"

"Dan said near 150 acres, including the area up from the river that he has cleared for crops."

"My Da would quickly say near 60 hectares," Jed whispered.

Jacob nearly showed glee. "That should keep us busy for awhile."

"Jacob, with careful management this could keep a crew our size in business for many years. Wingate has many woodlots, but I have never seen one with as much potential as this one."

"What do you think about the cutting?"

"I'd say we should start right here, clearing some of the largest

trees. This will let in more light for the smaller ones, allowing
them more room to grow and setting up a second harvest."

Jacob said, "Spend the daylight planning the best area to cut this
coming winter. I'll walk back toward the farm and look for a good
place to build the camp house. I would like to build a separate
section where the men can eat and we can store the dry goods. I'll
most likely do most of the cooking outside or under a lean–to, as
that is what I am used to."

"Imagine, a camp that does not need to be moved constantly.
We'll have no problem picking the best of the crews if they know
they'll have a bench and table for eating away from the stink of
the bunkhouse. And, who would pass up the cooking of Jake?"
Jed took his turn to whack Jacob on the back.

For once, Jed was appreciative of the training Wingate provided
him as a walking boss. He pulled out his notebook and began to
figure board feet. Much of Wingate's timber was taken quite a
distance from the river's edge, as the growth near the water had
been cut and it would be several years before the saplings would
be big enough. Here the harvest would be bountiful closer to the
landing. No wonder Wingate wanted to get his hands on it. Jed
didn't want to stop his figuring, but with dusk approaching he had
to head back to find Jacob. *Now for a good pitch in the water this
spring.*

It looked like Jacob had been just as busy and successful as Jed.
He had marked out a level piece of ground up the slope a bit
and east of the path up to the farm. This would give them easy
access to the river while they brought up the supplies. It would
be easy for the crew to come in by canoe before the river froze
and it would place the wangan in an accessible place for outside
lumbermen to stop to buy supplies. Jacob planned to build a
permanent wigwam for his wangan; other landowners needed to
constantly move their supplies by raft.

The men did not have to speak. They knew just by looking at each
other and shaking hands that they must work hard not to waste
this opportunity. They also instinctively knew that there would be
danger and they would have to be wary.

"When did you have time to do that?" Jed wondered as he
pointed to two large, dressed turkeys hanging from a nearby
branch.

Jacob just grinned and shrugged.

"Don't tell me you sneaked up on them in them boots?"

Jacob again grinned. "Just thought we should leave a little something for Mrs. Thorpe. They should make a big enough stew to fill up even her brood."

"We'll need to get them up there before dark."

"Dan's boys will be down soon to get instructions on what needs to be cut to begin the camp house. They'll take the turkeys. I've got tea brewing at the campfire and it will be dried venison and molasses cake for us."

"Better than steak."

"I want to head back at dawn so we can plan the next stores to bring up."

"We also need to figure out how to get those coins safely to St. John. All of this depends on that step."

At that the men went about their business, deep in their own thoughts. No talking necessary.

St. John Account

Things were not as jolly when the partners returned to the settlement. It seems that earlier that morning, Philippe had been snooping around. He had sent his father to St. John to be with his mother while she shopped and placed orders for the trading post. He was still grumbling about the waste of money. More than that, he could not make sense out of what was going on at the settlement.

He went up to the wigwam and called out for Nuga. He was quite demanding about the whereabouts of Jacob and the stranger he had been hearing about. He had tried to convince his grandmother that letting an unknown stay there was dangerous; how did she know he wasn't some kind of thief? He was probably a penniless bum who would steal whatever money was saved for the wangan.

Nuga had a hard time not to laugh in his face.

Then when Philippe caught sight of the supplies along the river waiting for transport, he was furious. These items were not for a wangan. They were for setting up a camp. "What in the world is going on around here? Who are you working for? I know Jacob quit on Mr. Wingate; who's he setting up camp for?"

"We work for no one but ourselves."

"You're trying to tell me that this unorganized bunch of half-breeds has put together the wherewithal to set up a logging company?" Philippe spat. "That's precious. What a laugh this will be among the land barons."

Hanna came running over to the wigwam. "What are you up to, cousin?"

"I could say the same."

"I'd say it is obvious what we are up to. We are working very hard with Jacob's leadership to find a way to give our families a better life."

"That's rich. Just where are the likes of odd- jobbers like you going to get enough money to open a camp, and do you really think that any landowner will let you harvest his land?"

Nuga stood between them. "I'd say that since you turned your back on your family, whatever we do is none of your business. And just because you have your mother's fair skin and color, you grandson, are also part Micmac."

Ignoring the latter, Philippe feigned caring. "It is my business if you are being swindled by some ne'er-do-well."

"I've seen your dealings with the trappers and those trading at the post. Swindling seems to be something you know a lot about!" Hanna shouted.

Philippe started toward her, "You bitch. How dare you talk to me like that."

Suddenly Nuga let go with a slap across his face that could be heard across the yard. By now Birdie and Ruth and the children were standing around them.

Ruth shouted to one of her boys, "Go get your father. He is stretching some hides in the smoke house."

Philippe rubbed his hand on his cheek and looked amazed that his grandmother would do such a thing. "Don't bother getting Bear. I'm leaving, but I'm going to watch the whole bunch of you like a hawk."

Birdie put her hand on her brother's arm. "Why can't you be happy for us? We've worked so hard to save for this."

"You don't have a business mind among you. You need funds in the union in St. John. Do you have a clue how expensive it is to fund a camp?"

Nuga looked him straight in the eye. "Nothing that you need to worry about, Philippe. You made the choice not to back us. Our success or failure is up to us."

"Word will get around that you may have new-found money. There are men on the river who will never let Jacob, Bear or Frank get to St. John with enough money to open an account. You're playing with fire."

"Not to worry, Philippe. Go back to putting together your own fortune. We don't need you."

Just then Bear came running out of the woods. "What the hell is going on here, brother?"

Philippe tossed his hands in the air. "I'm leaving. Something is going on and I'm going to get to the bottom of it."

Bear made a move toward him and Philippe stumbled down the slope to his waiting canoe. One of his trappers was waiting. He pushed off and paddled away.

"Damn, brother. You still haven't learned how to paddle your own canoe?" Bear's laugh set off the whole group, who found the scene funny. All, that is, but Sean. He was softly crying.

"What's the matter, little guy?" said Bear, as he picked him up and held him on his shoulder.

Sean sobbed. "Is Philippe going to take away Jacob's wangan?"

"No way, Sean. Your papa, Uncle Jacob and Uncle Jed will take care of it. They will find a way to make it work. Just you wait and see."

And wait they did. The threesome sat by the river skipping stones on the calm water. When the two canoes began to appear around the curve, they let out whoops as good as any warrior.

"Uncle Jacob!" came the chorus. "Philippe was mean to Mama. He's going to try to take the wangan away from you."

Just then Frank came back from checking the potato crop. "What do you mean he was mean to your mother?"

"Philippe called her a bitch. What's a bitch papa?" This from Joe - the quiet one.

Frank started to turn bright red, so Nuga made her way to the river's edge as fast as she could without taking a tumble.

Just then Jed and Jacob pulled their canoes on shore.

"Give me a hand, Jacob," Nuga pleaded. As it was obvious she was not going to be able to stop Frank from going after Philippe, she quickly filled in Jacob and Jed.

Frank ran up to the back of his cottage. Bear's boys had been working on some new paddles for the canoes; he grabbed one and headed back down to the landing.

In a flash, Jacob intercepted him. "Don't do it, Frank. We've come too far. If you touch him, he'll have that gang of roughnecks that hangs around the post rough you up. If you get laid up or worse, who is going to work with the St. John vendors and dock workers to get our supplies?"

"I have to let that asshole know that even though he is family, he has no right talking to his grandmother and my wife that way. I'm just going to talk with him."

"There is no way you are going to be able to control that famous Irish temper."

"And there's no way you are going to stop me, Jacob. I don't want to get physical with you. Trust me. I won't jeopardize our plan. If anything, I want to jam it down his throat that we are going it alone and it is his loss for not jumping in."

"It's more likely you'll jam your fist down his throat."

Just then Birdie came down from her shack. She had little Martha by the hand and carried a large handled harvest basket in the other hand. Martha carried a smaller gathering basket. Birdie's basket was filled with small birch boxes highly decorated with quills, small sewing baskets that had covers with bows on top made from thin ash, and a few pairs of beaded moccasins. Martha's basket was filled with beaded wool wallets and an assortment of miniature sweet grass baskets.

"Martha and I will go with Frank. I promised mother that I would bring more items to the trading post and she should be back from St. John by now. I'm looking forward to picking up some of the new lace."

Jacob shook his head. "Not sure that would be wise, Birdie. How could you keep a handle on his temper?"

"I'm sure Frank won't make a fuss in front of Martha. Right, Frank?"

He took a moment and looked down into the intense eyes of this wisp of a lady. Then he looked at Jacob, who shrugged and at Nuga, who smiled and nodded.

Birdie looked at Jed, who had remained quiet as a church mouse through all the turmoil. "Benjie has nursed. I don't think you would mind sitting with him for a while as he naps in his hammock."

Jed smiled from ear to ear.

Birdie looked at Nuga. "Perhaps you could take Benjie to the wigwam later. There is some hard bread he could suck on if I get back later than thought."

Nuga walked over and gave Birdie a hug with a thank you, then ran her hand through Martha's hair. Martha smiled adoringly at her great-grandmother. Then Nuga said to Frank, "I'll let Hanna know the story if your three scamps don't beat me to it.

At that, the threesome, who had been standing silently through their father's fussing, ran off toward the gardens.

Frank picked up Martha and placed her in the canoe that Jed had just pulled up on shore. Before he slid the vessel in all the way, he helped Birdie in, gave it a shove, and hopped in himself. He turned and mouthed "I'll be good" to Nuga and yelled to his partners to meet at Nuga's when he returned. Then he set to paddling the mile or so to the trading post while Martha waved enthusiastically until they had rounded the bend.

It was a quiet day. Everyone was busy with all the work necessary to prepare for another winter. Even though Jed's pile of fieldstones was growing each day, he relished the time he was able to spend with Benjie. He settled down on the blankets in the corner of the shack and took a half-finished bird from his pocket. Wings began to form as if by magic as he whittled. It was not long before Jed was able to run a piece of sinew through a hole in the back of the neck so the rest of the body would balance the head. Birdie's dye pots were on her table and Jed dunked the bird in the blue stain from the berries, adding a light coat with each dip. Pleased with the result, he took it outside and hung it on a low branch to dry.

"I see you have hatched another," said Jacob as he came around the corner.

"This will complete his wild friends for now. I needed to wait for the blueberries to ripen."

Jacob gave the little bird a slight tap with his finger and laughed as it swung in circles. "Is the boy sleeping? I haven't seen him for awhile."

"Come take a look."

Jacob bent quietly over the hammock and whispered, "He certainly would not fit comfortably inside your shirt now."

"Did I tell you he rolls over by himself?"

"Perhaps a thousand times."

Just then Benjie stretched and that strong right arm of his came free of his wrap. Then he freed a leg and Jacob said, "He's going to be a tall one like his Da."

Jed placed a light cover back over his son and the two men walked quietly back outside.

"I'm going to start loading my canoe with the next group of items for the camp." Jacob continued, "When Frank brings your canoe back, you can do the same. I'll sort things out for you. I want to start back up to Dan's at dawn."

"What about the major order? We need to start getting materials up there soon. We have about two months to get everything up there and stock the camp.

"Frank tells me that he and Nuga are working out a plan, and believe me, she is not going to release those coins if there is any possibility of their being lost."

"How long can he wait before that account has to be opened?"

"From what I understand, the vendors can start drawing two business days after deposit and papers are signed."

For the first time Jed felt a huge knot forming in his stomach. He took a big breath and told himself to shake it off and get on with it.

The sound of the rifle shot going off fractured the peace of the afternoon. Both Jed and Jacob were startled enough to jump. Benjie also did not like it and started to wail.

Nuga came from the wigwam, "What's that about?"

Just then Bear came out of the woods behind the bean hole. "You better keep the children close. We just saw a pretty good-sized black bear knocking down a beehive. I took a shot but it only scared him. Not sure if he will come back. We are going to try to salvage some of the honey and hope he stays away. Tell Birdie I'm taking this pot off the table."

"Better make sure she has no secret potion in there," laughed Jed.

Bear held it upside down and gave it a shake, waved, and headed back.

Nuga comforted the baby and carried him out. "I'll take him to the wigwam. I'm showing two of Ruth's young nieces how to strip ash for baskets so they can start weaving. I'm sure they will be more than happy to amuse Benjie at the same time."

"Thanks Nuga," Jacob said. "Jed and I will warn the women at the garden. The trio will most likely be with them."

Hanna, Ruth, and her sister-in-law were hoeing between the rows of potatoes and nearly burying the lush plants in mounds of soil so they would produce more of the root vegetable.

"Where are the boys?"

Hanna answered Jacob with a nod toward the woods. "They got hot in this wonderful sun, so I let them go for a swim. What's the problem?"

"Bear spotted a black bear, so all of you keep to the field so you can't startle him. Bears don't like to be around men any more than we like bumping into them. Just keep close."

Hanna looked worried.

Jed and Jacob ran toward the beaver pond, calling back to the women, "We'll find them."

They could hear the trio long before they saw them.

"That noise should keep any bear away," laughed Jed.

"It's the walk back through the woods that is more of a worry."

Three little naked brown bodies were climbing on a downed tree that had fallen into the pond. When they hit the water they swam like flying fish toward the dam.

Jacob let out a whistle and Jed thought they all would go under with the sudden stop.

Up came Jacob's finger. "What did I tell you about going close to the dam?"

Answers came from all directions. "It is dangerous." "We don't want the beaver to go away." "The beaver's dam gives us the pond." "The beavers protect our trout stream." "We only trap extra beavers so the others can make more families." "Beavers give us things to trade."

"Whew," said Jed. "They sure know their lessons."

"Too bad they tend to forget the biggest. The dam is dangerous and tangled and grows each year."

"Sorry, Uncle Jacob."

"Get out and shake yourselves off. Then find your clothes and go back to weeding. There is a black bear in the woods, so stay close to your mother."

"Can we go find him?"

"I'll get my bow and arrows."

"He doesn't scare me."

"Yah, but if I get angry you better get scared. Don't forget your moccasins," growled Jacob.

Those three little bottoms made haste.

And so the rest of the day went.

Frank, Birdie and Martha were back in the late afternoon. By then Jed had added the bluebird to Benjie's hanging collection and Martha was delighted.

After a delicious evening meal with lots of fresh vegetables and applesauce, the men headed over to Nuga's to get Frank's report. This time Ruth came and stayed with the boys so Hanna could go, too. The boys were sure to settle quickly as they were still under the effect of Jacob's magic finger.

Back at Nuga's, Jacob remarked, "You look none the worse for wear, Frank. How does Philippe look?"

"No physical wear but he will never call any member of his family a bitch again. When Aunt Amy heard about that, she gave him a tongue lashing that brought him more to his knees than I ever could have. It was such a pleasure to watch."

"My, I wish I had gone," Hanna whispered wistfully. "Did you show Jacob and Jedediah the sewing trims Birdie brought you, Nuga?"

The men gave a "who cares" look at each other.

"Not yet, but I will with pleasure." Nuga picked up one of Birdie's sewing baskets and took off the bow-trimmed top to display some laces and ribbons. She reached under the materials and brought out a small flat package carefully wrapped in deerskin to keep it well protected.

Frank took it from her and opened the wrap, which covered a

small flat ledger. He opened it and read aloud: "Account name –
Buck and Company, est. 1825. Signature of person authorized
for deposits and drafts – Francis Sean Ryan with secondary
authorized signature – Hanna Buck Ryan. Deposit Balance -
$702.84." He handed the book to Jed and then to Jacob.

"What the hell!" exclaimed Jacob.

Up came Nuga's finger.

"So that's where it comes from," laughed Jed, who added, "please
explain how you did this."

They all looked at Nuga. "When Amy came that day to show
us some of the samples of trim and to ask Birdie, Hanna and me
for help with what she should order for the post, I asked for her
help. We explained what we were doing and how we had found
someone else to fund us, since Philippe had refused. She was
delighted; she was pretty upset with the way Philippe was acting.
so she was more than willing."

"But how?" pleaded Jacob.

"Hanna drafted a letter to the union at the waterfront, giving
them all the particulars for the company. She and Frank signed
it. Then she wrote a note, which they both signed and dated,
authorizing Amy Croteau to set it up on our behalf. I gave her
the coins and we made up the package. Amy and Henri are very
well-respected by the vendors in St. John, so when she told Uncle
Henri she wanted to get a bit of fresh air by walking down by
the waterfront, he thought nothing of it and in truth it gave him
a chance for a pint or two at the pub. When Amy walked into
the merchants' union and asked for the manager, he immediately
invited her into his office. He had one of his clerks weigh the
coins, figure the amount, and set up the account with no questions
asked. Amy is our heroine."

"But how did she get it out of here without Philippe noticing?"
asked Jed.

"I should have known you would pick that up," answered Nuga.
"When they left, Frank helped Amy down the slope and into the
boat. Obviously, Philippe didn't. It was then that Frank handed
her the basket of samples."

"It was in the basket!" both men exclaimed.

"You haven't heard the best," jumped in Frank. "This morning, dear Philippe without question gave me the perfect reason to go over to the trading post. Birdie picked it up right away so asked to go along with her crafts."

"She brought it back with her order of trims," Jacob said with light in his eyes.

"Don't get ahead of the story. When Amy gave it to me on the sly and had finished her rant with Philippe, I looked him in his sorry eyes and told him, 'by the way—we already have a merchant's account in St. John, so don't bother having the loonies on the river looking for any money from us.' Philippe turned bright red and shouted, 'You lie, you Irish bastard.' "I never knew Amy could move across a room so fast. She looked at him with her hands on her hips and he cowered. Then I took the ledger, and being careful to cover any signatures while exposing the balance, waved it in front of his eyes."

"What about Aunt Amy," asked Jacob. "Did she want him to know that she did it just to rub it in?"

"No. Even better. She said, 'Let him stew. It will drive him crazy trying to figure out how you did it. Serves him right, the way he has been acting.'"

"I think we better put the ledger in the safe place, grandmother," said Hanna.

The men were astonished when Nuga took her grandmother's ceremonial pointed hat from the hanging bar across the wigwam. She put her hand up into the point and pulled down the inner fabric. There was an opening in the lining where the outline of the pouch of coins for the settlement and the payroll could be seen. She placed the book in the lining, pushed the fabric back in place and put the hat back on the rack.

By now Jacob was laughing so hard, tears were making dark water spots on his deerskin pants.

Jed, still the businessman asked, "How soon before we can use the funds?"

Frank answered, "Since Amy started the account yesterday and tomorrow is the second business day, I can take Zeke and start out in the morning for the first load."

At that Jed let out his own whoop as good as any warrior.

19   Buck and Company

Fall 1825

Summer rapidly slipped into early fall.

Jed and Jacob made two trips a week up to the Thorpe property.
There they helped build a camp house from logs felled to clear the
land for the camp. Nails would have been very heavy to transport
in a canoe, so hardly a nail was used.   Pegs were fashioned from
pieces of the same trees. Taking the supplies up as the canoes
were packed brought no special attention from others on the river
who were also beginning to get things ready for logging camp.
The partners wanted no large and wealthy company trying to
put a crimp in their plans. They wanted to get firmly established
before anyone caught on. Even the Micmac families living on the
route thought they were most likely working for one of the big
companies or helping some settlers farther inland.

Zeke and his master clearly carved the trail between Jacob's
settlement and the curve in the Aroostook where it turned east
toward the junction. It was heavy and tedious work, but because
the trail was created, no big shipments gave away the building
of a new company. Frank didn't even carry his fiddle with him to
mark his coming and going, which freed up space for merchandise
on Zeke's back, such as a sack of wool socks. Frank's friend, who
boarded Zeke, earned a bit of money for his family because he
helped so many times.

Frank's garden produced a great crop for its size. As Dan Thorpe
had found, potatoes did very well in the soil in the Aroostook
Valley, and they decided that they would double the clearing for
planting potatoes in the next growing season. The small crop of
yellow-eye beans did well even though quite a few of the seedlings

had been lost in the spring storm. The teen-aged boys in the group helped with the clearing. Frank discovered he could not work as long and as hard as he once had, so he started training young Peter to help clear brush and stones.

When he could, Jed taught some of the boys how to stack fieldstones and the border fence began to wind its way along Jacob's path. The trio enjoyed finding ways to fit the pieces together, especially little Sean, who found small stones to fill in the gaps.

The air was full of anticipation. There was hope of the future—one of permanence, rather than a nomadic life based on the seasons. People pushed themselves a bit harder and some were able to give a few more coins to Nuga for the community fund.

By this time Benjie loved sitting on his father's lap rather than cuddling in his arms. He chuckled with glee when his Da bounced him on his knee and played horsey.

One early morning when they had no load to take up river, Jacob took the trio turkey hunting. He also dragged Jed along as promised. One of Sean's tries at the bow set the arrow off straight in the air and it landed by Jed's feet, just barely missing the brim of his hat, so he took to slipping behind the nearest tree whenever the boys took aim. Peter did bring home his first turkey and Hanna made a very special meal to celebrate. She roasted the bird on a spit in the fireplace rather than putting it in the stew kettle. Uncle Jacob even made an apple pie with maple sugar.

Jacob got one canoe made. Jed was amazed at the steaming and bending of cedar ribs. Carefully cut sheets of birch bark were stretched over the frame and the pieces were laced with stripped spruce roots. Jacob made cuts in a spruce tree and then collected the resin that oozed out. He heated the resin and spread it on the seams of the canoe to make a waterproof seal. Jed had seen men find a leak, chew on some spruce gum to soften it, then make a patch for the leak using the gum, but Jacob always carried a small pot of resin in the canoe so he could stop and soften it in hot water to make a more permanent patch. Rather than trading the canoe for goods, Philippe offered a fair price so he could resell it. Perhaps Aunt Amy was keeping a closer eye on things. Jacob gave most of the money to his sister, as Frank had not been able to make any money at the docks to leave with Hanna for the winter.

When a chill began to fall in the mornings, duties began to change. Care for the garden turned to careful harvest, drying beans, storing potatoes and squash, picking apples to be stored and crabapples for drying.

Jacob knew that he had to start the final stage at the camp and recruited Bear and his older boys to work there for a few days. He knew that of all of them, Bear had the best skills for building a sturdy wigwam, and he needed two put on the Thorpe property. One wigwam would be good–sized, for storing his wangan supplies where they could be easily seen and not in jumbled piles as they often were in temporary camp stores. The other wigwam would be for Jed and himself and would also be used for their office.

Jed had never watched a wigwam being built, but he soon realized he would be of no help, so he kept out of the way. Bear's boys cut long saplings, and their Dad placed them in holes around the perimeter of where the wigwam was to sit. Before his eyes the skeleton of the shelter was forming.

"I'm going to check the land east of here. Haven't seen much of that timber yet."

Jacob nodded without missing a beat in bending, forming, and tying the frame of the wigwam.

Jed meandered just above shoreline. He could see where some of the trees in this area had been harvested, perhaps to supply wood for the Thorpe farm. It was quite pleasant and very different from the swamp forest to the west. He spotted a large boulder a bit higher on the river bank and sat in the late morning sun.

Suddenly he was overwhelmed and in the quiet of the place, all that had happened over the past months filled his soul and he wept.

Addie—sweet Addie. I'm so sorry. I wish I knew how you were doing. I wish I could comfort you in my arms. You'd love this area. I can see you running along the edge of the river trying to catch butterflies. I can see Benjie playing in the yard of the home I would build for you right here. Oh, Addie it is perfect.

Jed stood and stretched and watched a flock of geese heading south. He loved to see their 'V' formation. "Hey, fellows!" he shouted to the sky. "If I could fly, I'd head to the warm weather too when the nip shows in the air." Then he whispered, "Addie I'm looking at the sun. The same sun you can see. Are you looking at it too?"

In London, Muriel Wingate carried the tea tray up the curved stairway to the second floor bedroom of her niece. Muriel's home was lovely and she smiled at her reflection in the polished shine on the mahogany banister. The small chandelier over the foyer below sparkled as if cut by a diamond master. Muriel enjoyed being the spinster of the family. She could enjoy her treasures and fuss as much as she wanted. Marriage did not take her fancy, especially since most of her suitors were of the same ilk as her brother Benjamin. There was no way she would put up with his ways and would probably end up in jail after hitting him with a rolling pin.

She tapped gently on the door and then slipped into the dark room. The heavy velvet drapes were closed, but a sliver of sunlight splayed across the pale face of the frail girl curled in the tapestry-covered chair. She never looked up. She seemed mesmerized by a loose thread in her shawl.

"Adelaide, it is a lovely afternoon. Let me open the blinds just a bit." Muriel spread the drapes just enough to lighten the room so she could place the tray on the antique oriental table. "Please, dear. You must try to eat. I made the currant scones you like so much. The tea is nice and hot and I brought extra sugar cubes." She placed the delicate hand-painted plate on the table in front of Addie next to the matching bone china cup and poured the tea over three sugar cubes. "Try just a bit Adelaide. I have a surprise for you. A letter came today from Mary. Will you read it or shall I open it and read it to you?"

Addie gave a dismissive wave of her hand.

Muriel held the cup to Addie's lips and coaxed her to take a sip. "I'll sit here by the window, dear, and read this to you while you nibble on your scone."

Muriel used a slender silver letter opener that had a single-stemmed rose engraved on the blade. "You must smell this Adelaide. Mary put a bit of dried lavender in the letter."

August 17, 1825

Dearest Sister,

How I miss you. The summer has not been the same without your joyous enthusiasm of each and every flower. No one has used your butterfly net. It is still on the hook in the back entry. Mother also misses you terribly. She does not say it out loud, but I can see from the sadness in her eyes. Our "dear" sister has not changed

*a bit and talks incessantly. You and I never did find a way to stop
her chattering, but I do pretend when I look at her that you did
manage to stitch up her lips while she slept.*

Muriel thought she could see the slightest smile on Addie's face.
She did see her take a nibble of scone.

*Father is the same. I don't know how mother puts up with his
ways. Somehow, I feel that Aunt Muriel would not abide it.
Perhaps that is the reason he seldom makes the journey to visit
London.*

This brought a smile to Muriel's round chubby face.

*I had a wonderful experience a fortnight ago. I know you would
enjoy hearing about it. I had a visit from the chickadee.*

It took just a moment for Addie to respond and sit a bit straighter
and pay closer attention to her aunt.

*Remember when we found the nest on the ground this spring and
there was one newly hatched baby still in it? We put the nest back
in the tree in hopes that its parents would come back. The only
one we ever saw after that was the father so we worried about
baby's survival. Well suddenly one night I heard the call of the
chickadee. I know it was the same father, for I remember he had
a funny tuft on the side of his head. And answering him was a
young one. They certainly survived and the father is taking good
care of his son. I thought you would enjoy that story. I know it
made me feel a lot better.*

*Please try to get stronger by eating as best as you can. I pray for
your recovery.*

I send love from all who love you.

Your sister, Mary

*PS – I heard one of the yardmen talking about the young
chickadee. He said it makes such noise and gets so puffed up that
he surely must be named Benjamin Wingate. – Wouldn't father
have a fit!*

Muriel thought she heard her niece giggle. She handed her the
letter and was pleased to see she had eaten a good portion of one
scone and had had a few sips of tea. "You are tired, aren't you
dear?"

Addie nodded yes.

Muriel moved the table with the tray so she could help Addie
up and back to the feather bed. Addie did not want to let go of
the letter, so Muriel covered her gently with the quilt and kissed
her on the forehead. "Tonight we'll try a bit of soup. I have been
stewing a chicken. Do you want me to close the drapes again?"
Muriel was surprised when Addie nodded 'no' and said that she
wanted to see the sunny day.

If her aunt had looked more closely, she would have seen the tear
slowly working its way down her hollow cheek. This was not a
tear of sadness, but one of joy. She held the lavender close to her
and slipped into sleep.

Leaning against the boulder on the Aroostook River Jed felt a rush
of warm air. He looked for a reason, but the sky was a brilliant
blue and no wind was in the trees. *I must have dozed off and
dreamt it. What a perfect spot to find some peace.*

Over the next few days, Jed watched the camp sprout from the
ground like well-planted seeds. The two wigwams amazed him.
Jacob told him that the birch bark covering made it as snug as any
settler's stick-built shanty. The log house had five double bunks
with a small fire pit in the middle and a smoke hole that could be
covered in case of rain or snow. Deacons' benches made from half
logs lined the wall. A pole hung down the middle over the fire pit
so the men could dry their wet woolies. There would be a kettle
for tea hung there and the men could store their tin cups on a
narrow shelf built over the benches.

As Jacob had planned, a separate room with a table and benches
to hold up to a dozen men was built just off the bunkroom. On
the side, was a counter with shelves above and storage bins below.
Not many camps had this kind of room where the men could
spread out a bit, as the other camps were temporary, to be moved
as the crew cut through the timber. Next to the door that led out
the front would be one of the most important pieces of equipment.
Dan planned to let them use his grindstone so they would
not have the expense of buying one to start out. If he needed
something sharpened he would have his boys do it at the camp.
The crew would need to keep their axes and knives sharp at all
times. Frank had managed to pick up some glass and they placed
a window next to the door. Capturing some light would make the
winter days less dreary.

This would be the last trip before they moved up there and did the final preparations. Everything had to be ready before ice started to form.

After Bear and the boys went home, Jed and Jacob went up to the farm. It was the first time Jed had seen what Dan had built over the past few years. Mrs. Thorpe was a wonderful hostess and made them a meal to remember. She was nearing the end of her pregnancy, so Jed wondered how she managed to tend to her men – Dan and their boys. Dan reported that two other families from New Brunswick had moved up and had built their first shanties. They were squatting next to his land in hopes of making a claim. This first winter would be hard, but it would be nice to have two women nearby to help Emma with the birth.

Word was starting to spread and some men had asked Dan when he would start hiring. He gave the list to Jed. Talking with them would be one of his first duties. Jed felt that once they knew Jake was the cook, there would be no problem finding a good crew.

As soon as he touched shore, Jed made haste in going to Birdie's. The trio was waiting for them and they brought the canoe up the slope and took his pack and bedroll to Jacob's shack. All of a sudden Jed realized that when he next left, it could be six months before he saw Benjie again. In an emergency he could snowshoe back, but it would take him away from his work with the crew. He didn't know if he were ready for this.

Martha saw him first and came running to him and jumped into his arms. She was such a different little girl from the one who had been so shy the previous spring. She gave him the biggest hug. "Come and see Benjie. He misses his Da."

That didn't help his new apprehension.

It wasn't long before the reflection of colorful fall leaves created a masterpiece on the river. Jed so wanted the beauty to be captured in his mind's eye, that he spent any free moment he had surveying the shore from a quiet perch. He marveled at how the vision changed according to the whims of the sun and clouds. The evergreens only accentuated the reds of the maples. The golds formed settings as in fine jewelry.

The briskness in the air brought an increasing briskness of activity. Before the partners left the settlement, they wanted to make sure all the dwellings were ready for the harshness of the winter. They put more straw and mud in the crevasses of the shanties and

made sure the roofs were whole. The birch bark was checked on
Nuga's wigwam and some seams were patched and blankets were
attached to the inner walls. Jed helped Birdie hang quilted pieces
of scraps on the walls where she and the children slept. Firewood
was carefully stacked near each home with some piled inside to
keep dry and to be replenished daily for the next day. Birdie's
small metal stove was cleaned well and a large carrying basket was
filled with tinder. All the families were tending to the same. Jacob
would not be using his shanty again until spring, but he made
some preparations in case someone needed shelter. His place was
used to store extra dried foods and prepared hides so the women
could work on clothing and moccasins during the cold days. He
spent any time he squeezed out working on Hanna's home with
Frank. Hanna and the women were working long hours getting in
the harvest and making sure each home had its share.

A great bonfire and celebration came the night the harvest was
complete. Everyone was home at the same time and Jed could see
how the large the population was. Ruth was growing bigger each
day and they had just found out one of her sisters was pregnant
again. Jed selfishly hoped that Ruth's baby was not another Little
Bear so she wouldn't need help in nursing. He felt that Birdie was
Benjie's angel.

In the crisp air of the autumn evening, Frank's fiddle was joyous.
The drums echoed the heartbeat of the festival. Some brought out
their traditional clothing and danced around the fire with rattles
of pebble-filled horns. The rhythm was hypnotic and pulled Jed's
soul into the elation of accomplishment.

The bean kettle was pulled and the table loaded with food from
all to be shared by all. The finale was baskets of Jacob's biscuits,
to be drizzled with honey donated by the black bear.

Two days later, the three partners loaded their canoes with food
staples. Each carried a barrel of flour, for it was not possible
for one canoe to take it all. Bear was borrowing a small bateau
to transport the barrels of molasses, salt pork and salted cod in
another day or two. It took a lot of planning to divide the weight
of the goods. Now they had to be careful that none was lost to a
spill in the river.

The night before they left, Jed spent a good deal of time with
Benjie, making him laugh until his bright blue eyes twinkled. "I
need to do this for our future, little man. Even though I won't be

here, Birdie will hold you close and Martha will make you laugh. Someday you'll understand that I will never leave your heart and you are always in mine."

He stayed until the baby and Martha were fast asleep and then gave Birdie a pack that had gifts for Benjie and Martha for Christmas. He had finished the chunk of wood he had worked on while he waited for Jacob to come get him to see Mary. It was a lovely covered box with flowers carved on it that Martha could use for her doll's clothes and was much like his mother's handkerchief box. For Benjie, he had carved a miniature mule that looked like Zeke. Also he carved an ox and a log sleigh with runners. He gave Birdie a few more coins and told her to buy herself a piece of fabric with all the trims she wanted. She protested but he said, "Merry Christmas."

"I'll put these in a safe place, Jedediah. They will be so happy."

Jed walked slowly toward Jacob's with a heavy heart and a tear on his cheek.

In the morning Buck and Company was ready to move on to the next step. Bear came down and shook their hands. "I'll take care of the families with my life. I'll take turns with my two boys going out on the hunt for game while they are slowed by the snow and easy to track."

Just as they were ready to paddle away, Nuga came walking down the slope. In her arms was Benjie all wrapped up in his blanket. She took his little arm and helped him wave 'bye to his Da. His two feet hung out and he was wearing the tiniest pair of moccasins Jed had ever seen. His growing cowlick stood straight in the air and around his forehead was a worn soft leather band, decorated with quills and topped by a marvelous turkey feather.

20 Timber!

TIMBER! The warning rang out through that parcel of old forest for the first time. The stately pine swayed a bit as if on a drunk, tried to keep its balance and finally lost its stance. Down it came with a roar, as it fell through limbs from other trees, which seemed to try to catch it. A cloud of leaves that had not given up to the change of seasons finally fell like rain. The thud of the great carcass shook the ground. A cheer went up from the small crew that had won the battle with the goliath.

A lot of preparation was needed to lead up to that first cut. The partners had spent the last few weeks rushing to beat the first snowfall and then found themselves ready with not much snow at all. The fallen giant would need to be stripped of its limbs by the chopper's ax and divided into logs. Then Dan's oxen would skid them closer to the river.

When the partners first got to camp, the excitement was palpable. They made themselves take a night to sit down and write a list of chores that needed completing, in order to prevent duplication of effort and the chance of omissions.

"We'll have to get the grindstone down from the farm," said Frank. "My men need to sharpen their axes daily to take down these monsters."

Jed found himself taking notes in three columns. The grindstone was put in Frank's column, along with making a list of choppers who were looking for work.

Jacob spoke up. "I need to find a cookee who can dig a good bean hole. I'm going to talk with Dan to see if any of his boys or one of the neighbors might want the job, to pick up a little money. He can help me sort out and price the goods for the wangan, stock the kitchen, and build the lean-to for the cook fire and reflector oven."

"So noted," said Jed. "I'm going to pinpoint a good piece on the riverside to build skidders so we can store the logs for easy access when the river goes out next spring. Also, I've been working on a design for our company mark. I was thinking of a large 'B' and small 'c'. If Dan can manage it, he can forge the design onto a hammerhead for marking the bark on the logs. We'll need to have it registered at the mills before the drive reaches them in the spring.

"Never thought of it," exclaimed Jacob. "I've been so busy thinking of marking store goods that it slipped my mind that we need a mark for our own product."

"Must admit, the Brit has a good business mind," laughed Frank.

"Glad one of us does. Hate to do all this work and lose the logs to some river pirate."

Frank said, "You'd better stick to counting beans and leading a good crew to us with your cooking."

Then practical Jed broke in. "We all had better stick to getting this list we made so we have a plan. I've never run a big business, but I have run my sheep herd and know that you can't let them take the lead. You've got to be in charge—no ifs, ands, or buts. If not, you may find yourself getting a butt from a ram."

"No wonder Wingate wanted you out of England and on the St. John," Frank jumped in. "His loss. Our gain."

"That's the closest you're going to come to major praise from an Irishman," laughed Jacob. "Better enjoy it, for his red-faced temper comes much easier."

Slowly the three columns filled with enough projects for ten people. But they were fired enough with excitement that they probably could have done the work of twenty.

Dan and his boys had spread the word that he was going to work his timber and was looking for experienced choppers and landing crew to pull the timber to the riverside. They let it be known that the camp was planned so there wouldn't be a lot of moving around, they would have a separate room for eating and socializing and that Jake had left the Wingate crew and would be the cook. The partners wanted to give the appearance that Dan was in charge of the harvest, for they were not sure a crew would work for an Indian boss. They needed to prove themselves as a company and that would take time.

Proving themselves was going to take a lot more work, but they had arrived at step one —finally watching the first pine felled by Buck and Company.

Sweet Addie, how I wish you could see this. You would be so proud that we managed to get this far. I so wish you were home with Benjie, waiting to hear the story. If only I hadn't taken a couple of extra days to protect your father's harvest. If only.

"Jed, how can your mind be so far away? All I want to do is run and scream but I'm sure the crew would wonder why the savage cook is so excited and why is he not tending to supper," Jacob said, trying to stop his smile from totally overtaking his face.

"Someday, my friend. Someday, we'll remember the felling of this giant was the first day of the success of Buck and Company and we will shout to the world that this wonderful little business belongs to a Micmac chief, a fiddling Irishman and me, a British shepherd. I just wish Addie could know about this."

"I had a feeling your mind was in England."

"I would have married her in an instant. Why didn't he give us the chance to be happy? I would have made her a good husband."

"At the expense of his reputation? When do you suppose Land Baron Wingate ever thought of anyone else but his own inflated ego?"

Jed sighed. "I believe that at one time, the only other he may have thought of was my Mum."

"Ye gads, you could have been a Wingate?"

"Heaven forbid. From what I could glean from between the lines, he courted my Mum, but she quickly figured out his ambition. Wingate senior was very shrewd and would buy up any piece of land available and his son didn't fall far from the crabapple tree. Mum saw that she would be his trophy and she'd have none of that malarkey. She was a strong, intelligent, mostly self-educated woman. My Da and Wingate were buddies, but my Da had to start working his parents' land at a young age. The more the Wingate fortune grew, the less dirt ever touched the boots of junior."

"And when your mother married your father?"

"Benjamin was very spiteful. He did whatever he could to keep my parents in their place. If a piece of land came up and my Da wanted to grow our place, he would come in with a bid more than my father could match. I'm not saying I had a pauper's life, but extra money was scarce and we lived day-by-day with hard work and frugal habits."

"Nothing wrong with that," chuckled Jacob.

"I believe it now, but it was not easy as a child."

"If there were such hard feelings between him and your father, why did Benjamin offer you this opportunity to get to the new world?"

"I was so excited about the ocean voyage to New Brunswick, I hardly thought about anything but leaving. Now I wish I had spent a few more hours talking with my folks. I didn't start thinking about his motives until I had to fill many lonely hours at sea."

"And what conclusions did you come to?"

"At first, when I saw him look at my Mum, I thought he might be giving me an opportunity because he was still sweet on her. Then I thought he might be doing it as spite again, showing them that they could not do this for me. Then I imagined that perhaps since he had all girls, he could bring me into the business like a son. After all, I was Abigail's child. What a daydream," spat Jed.

"When did you realize the truth? That he wanted to use your talents to further his goals as a landowner? Nothing else."

"It didn't take long. Mrs. Wingate would want to have me up to the mansion for dinner and to visit with the girls. He would have none of it. I was the hired help and I was supposed to keep my status. The best thing he ever did for me was to let me build my cabin. That was such a special place."

"Until he burned it down. Can you ever forgive him?"

"Perhaps for that; it was property. But I will never forgive him for sending Addie away and putting our son in such danger. And now I understand that Addie's life is so fragile, she may never recover."

"What do you think he would have done if he had found out how much you two meant to each other?"

"I would have been tossed out and he would have made sure we never saw each other. Every minute we had together, we cherished."

Up came Jacob's 'pay attention' finger. "You certainly did more than cherish each other."

Jed could feel the flush growing in his face. "Jacob, she is such a free spirit. The only thing that ever put a damper on our love was the constant worry that her father would catch wind of it and send me packing. He already rules his women with an iron fist and he would have clamped down even further, which would have been unfair to her mother and sisters, especially Mary."

TIMBER!

The two men quickly turned their attention to the forest in time to see another giant lose its foothold and crash to the ground with a thunderous roar.

"They've done it again!" shouted Jed. "Congratulations, partner. I think you'd better put on your cook's apron and see that this crew has a feast tonight."

And so it was. Dan's youngest helped pull the bean kettle, which was swimming in salt pork. Jacob outdid himself with sourdough biscuits and pots of honey. They still had a supply of fresh apples, which were piled high in pies, and the tea was hot and strong. It was the first night that Frank played his fiddle and it was quite a sight to see those robust men dancing a jig. They felt that Buck and Company could take on the world.

21   The First Harvest

Winter of 1825-1826

The lack of snow did not last long, for soon after the first tree was felled, snow started falling at a rate far greater than the average. Keeping the trails clear from the farm to the landing to the camp and the timber took tremendous effort, but the crew was up to the challenge.

The piles of logs began to grow on the skidders and with that, confidence grew that it would be a good drive, once the water rose. It took Jed no time at all to mark the "Bc" on the logs with the hammer Dan had forged in his fledgling blacksmith shop. He was beginning to get very good at the skills and was teaching them to his oldest son. That would also bring in extra money for the farm, especially when more settlers began to migrate to the area.

The word spread through the other camps that Jake had supplies for sale. His wangan began to have customers, even though some were just curious about a small company having such a thing; especially run by a Micmac. He had made some clever buys and red wool socks were a favorite. Independent cutters were pleased to find they could buy ax handles; saving days of trekking by snowshoe and losing days of pay. It was obvious that some of the buyers were there just to see what kind of competition Jake would be for the larger companies that for years had charged outrageous fees. It also became obvious that some, perhaps from the Wingate store, were not happy to lose business, especially when they heard that their own workers were sneaking off to buy from Jake in order to get fair prices.

Coming around the wigwam, Jacob hollered, "What the hell!"

"What's going on?" yelled Frank. He had just finished sharpening his ax for the new day. The rest of his men had done their sharpening the night before and were already gone to the next stand of trees Jed had chosen for chopping. Jacob had made sourdough pancakes for breakfast and sent them off well-fueled.

"Some bastard tried to cut his way into the wangan. Looks like he used a large knife to make a hole in the bark. Lucky for us, he picked an area where many heavy boxes were stored up against the inner wall. This side of the wigwam is out of view from my place and I'm sure the window on the camp house was frosted over."

"Does Jed know?"

"He started out before dawn to check the road from the cutting area. He had one of the men work late last night spraying water on the incline to the river so the sled could glide more easily on the icy surface."

"He must have seen the number of logs my guys cleaned up yesterday. The crew is working well together and the branches just flew. I wasn't sure of these odd-jobbers when I took them on, but I hope they stay through the winter. Maybe more pancakes would help," Frank chided.

Jacob just waved him off with a grunt. "If you see Jed, tell him I need to talk. In the meantime, I'm going to heat up some resin so I can make a patch."

He was carrying the heated resin pot from the cooking lean-to when Jed came running up the path. Obviously he was not happy.

Jed was breathless from his sprint from the landing. "Who would do that?"

"Some scumbags. I have my ideas, but no way to prove it. From the tracks there were two of them."

"Want me to track them?"

"We can't take the time for that. These storms have set us back already. We have to work every bit of daylight we can get. We have to do everything we can to at least break even. Losing money the first season would really set us back on our plans."

"I'm going up to the tree line to watch some of the felling. Haven't really done that," confessed Jed.

"Where is the red wool shirt we bought you?"

Jed shrugged. "Why in the world would I want to wear that? I'm not an axman; that seems to be their uniform. I'm not the uniform type."

"Have you ever wondered why they all wear red wool? Or has that coincidence never crossed that British brain?"

"I just figured they were the cheapest to buy."

"Far from it," answered Jacob. "If you were a chopper and there were more than one of you working on different trees, would you not want to be able to see each other? We've had more than one man crushed by being in the way of a falling grand conifer. Most of them were not wearing their red; they had taken the red off because they were warm and were working in their white wool undershirt. Not the best color for working in the snow if you want to be noticed. That buckskin would blend in, too."

"Should have known there was a reason other than using up a surplus of red wool. Think I better fill my canteen before I head out."

Jacob went to work on a patch for the wigwam. He had a few pieces of birch bark with him so did not have to strip a tree, which is harder in the winter. He needed to work fast or he'd have to heat the spruce resin again. Out of the corner of his eye he caught the sight of Jed heading toward the forest dressed in his floppy hat, bright red wool shirt and even a pair of red socks that came up to his knees above his heavy boots. Angry as he was over the damage, he could not help but smile.

Jed had not seen Frank at work as a chopper. His ability with the ax was amazing. One of his crew was assisting and soon would be a head chopper himself. Two other crew members quickly cut away the branches and prepared the log for the sled. Then one of them secured it to the load, which was nearing capacity.

Jed gave Frank a wave. "Think we can get the sled to the landing before sunset? That would give us a great start for tomorrow."

Frank gave him a thumbs-up.

"I'll have the oxen ready and up to you in the next hour."

Another thumbs–up, hardly missing a whack with the ax. Frank had notched the other side of the tree to give it a direction for

falling. Jed saw the pine begin to sway and after what he had
heard from Jacob, made haste toward the river.

TIMBER! Once again the ground roared in protest as the tree hit
it with enormous energy.

At the riverside, Jed sent his two crewmen to the hovel to ready
the oxen. "As soon as the team is ready, take them up to Frank.
The sled is full. Bring it down right away."

Jed turned his attention to the piles of logs already in the
skidders, waiting for the water to rise. *Not bad for a new crew.
I don't think the Wingate gang ever paid this much attention to
preparation.* While he was waiting, Jed started catching up on his
bark-marking. His mind wandered to his carvings. On Sundays
and storm days, he had been working on spruce gum boxes for
both Birdie and Nuga. They were medium–sized, but still had
plenty of area for his delicate carvings. For Birdie he had done the
edges in the pattern of her favorite lace trim, the back was carved
to replicate her quill embroidery, and on the front he was working
on a little girl with her doll. For Nuga he had carved the edges to
mimic the Micmac symbols he had seen on her grandmother's hat.
The back showed an intricately worked replica of her wigwam,
right down to the lacing on the birch bark. He was stumped as
to what to put on the front, but hoped that as he marked his way
through the pile of logs, he'd get some inspiration.

"Watch out, Tom. They are coming fast on this ice." The shout
came from the front of the sled, where the men were working
as hard they could—one with the team, the other with the hand
brake. Frank was hanging onto the back and working the brake.
Oxen are much stronger than horses, but they are not as able to
hold back a load.

It took a minute for Jed to realize they were calling out to him, for
he still was not accustomed to the hired men calling him Tom. He
dropped the hammer and ran to the right of the landing path just
as a strap came loose and one the logs fell free when the sled hit a
bump. Instinctively he dove for a fairly large boulder near the edge
of the river and pulled his long frame as tightly as possible against
the base. The log hit the boulder with a sickening thud, chips of
bark and shards of wood flying in all directions. It bounced off
the top of the rock as if it were playing leapfrog and landed on the
frozen surface of the Aroostook with such force that the forward
end pierced the ice as if it were a knife going through butter.

Jed did not dare to move. He thought he heard a loud ringing in his head, but it turned out to be Frank whistling the distress call. One chunk of the log had landed on his ankle, which was beginning to burn. For a minute he felt as though he could not breathe, but he found himself with a mouthful of woodchips. He could hear the men working with the pair of oxen, finally slowing them. *Please don't run over the stacked logs. I need to put more wood chips at the bottom of the run. That's what I need. More wood chips to slow the sled.* Then he drifted off to hearing nothing. He did not know that one of the shattered chunks had grazed the back of his head.

Jacob came running down the path like a frightened white tailed deer, the ties of his apron flying behind him. In the rear was Dan Thorpe, red-faced and gasping. "What happened?" yelled Jacob.

Frank was still settling the oxen. One of the men was shifting the logs with his pike and the other pointed at the boulder. "Jake, check on Tom. One of the logs went wild."

At first look, Jacob sucked in a deep breath. A scalp injury tends to bleed a lot and the sight was not pretty. Then at the other end, a piece of wood had punctured Jed's leg just above the boot. With the red socks, it was hard to see that it was bleeding, at first. The chunk of wood was sticking out of the wound like a miniature of the log stuck in the ice. Jacob saw the log and said to Dan," Lucky it was that bit that hit him and not the big one."

Jacob took off his apron and wrapped it around Jed's head and slowly turned him over. "Don't take the wood out of his leg yet. We have to make sure we get it all."

Jed did not stir. Jacob grabbed a handful of snow and rubbed it over his forehead. "Come on Jedediah. Don't shut down on me. Come on back. Think of your son."

Dan took a look at the man he knew as Tom and then at Jacob, who seemed not to remember what he'd said. "I'll go and get the boys and the toboggan. We'll take him up to the farm. Emma will know what to do."

"She's about ready to have her baby. That's too much for her."

"And you?" Dan asked. "This crew runs on their stomach. You know that. How are you going to be able to take care of Tom and keep the camp running? You will need to boss the landing now, too. I'll help Emma. The boys can handle what needs doing around the farm. Besides, he may not be hurt as badly as he looks right now."

Jed began to stir.

"Come on big fellow. Open those baby blues," coaxed Jacob.

"What happened?" The words came slowly to Jed.

"You had a dispute with a wayward log. He got in his licks before you tossed him in the river."

"Huh?"

"Don't try to figure it out just yet. We need to see just how bad you are."

"It feels like my head has split in two."

"Let's hope not. You know, if you weren't such a tall drink of water, you might have had a better chance. There was no way you could get the length of yourself totally protected by the boulder."

"What boulder?"

Dan shook his head. "I'd better get going for that toboggan."

"Don't you mean taba'gan?" chided Jacob.

"You and your Micmac words."

"If you white men are going to steal them, you should learn how to say them."

Dan just shook his head. "You hang on, Tom. We're going to get you fixed up. You should have better luck than Humpty Dumpty."

Humpty Dumpty? I wasn't sitting on a wall.

When they put him on the toboggan, Jed opened his eyes and looked at Jacob. "Little good this damn red shirt did."

"Never saw a log with eyes, Jed."

"Too bad I wasn't chased by one of Frank's potatoes; they're full of them."

Jacob stood up with a sparkle in his eyes. "Take him away boys. He's going to be just fine."

And with his "let's-get-back-to-it" attitude, Jed amazed everyone with his recovery. With great patience, Emma had slowly backed out the errant shard from Jed's leg. He had been well-fortified with some of Dan's Irish whiskey, so he withstood it well. She'd bandaged the wound tightly and before anyone expected, he was hobbling around the farmhouse, pitching in with whatever chores he spotted. Dan did put his foot down on seeing him do dishes, but Jed planned that if he were still there after the baby's birth, he would do every dish. Once his head was cleaned up, a nasty scrape was exposed, but that started healing quickly.

Jed couldn't remember when he had ever slept in a real bed. He had had a straw mat in the loft at the farm, a narrow straw tick-covered pad on the cot at his cabin, and just a blanket under him on a cot at Jacob's. Waking up in a wide rope bed with soft mattress and handmade quilt was pure luxury. He made himself a promise that when he built his next cabin he was going to have a real bed and so was Benjie.

He was given the small bedroom just off the kitchen that belonged to Dan's oldest boy, whom they called Red. Red had great shocks of bright red hair that hung around his round freckled face. There was no way he could deny his Irish blood. During Jed's recovery, Red was staying in the wigwam with Jacob. This worked well, because Red had to be available early to help with the breakfast and had to stay late to set the bean kettle; that was one thing that began to draw more men to apply for jobs. Dear Nuga had done a good job of passing the bean techniques to her grandson. He, in turn, was using the recipe to the delight of the woodsmen.

Jed stretched his wiry body in the comfort of his bed. He wondered why it was still so dark, as his body clock felt it was time to get up and stir the pot of beans he had set to bake the previous night in the corner of the Dutch oven in the fireplace. *Mum, I bet you would have such fun seeing me learning to cook, especially something like dry beans.* Dan was getting used to having beans for a meal, and in his far-thinking mind could see that his yellow-eyes could become another cash crop, especially if other crews began to ask their cook why they were fed only pickled beef and salted pork.

Jed lit the candle on the bedside table to take a look out of the tiny window and realized the glass was covered with snow. He pulled on his trousers and slipped into his moccasins. Limping into the kitchen, he saw Dan trying to pull open the door. As Dan pulled on the handle, Jed put the broomstick into the narrow crack to help pry the door open. Suddenly it let go and snow started to tumble into the kitchen.

"Good grief, Dan. There must be over three feet of new stuff out there. The path will be nearly as tall as the roof. No wonder I couldn't see out the window, with the drifting. I heard the wind howling, but this is still a surprise. I'm glad Red is already at the camp. The crew will not be out in this right away and the dining table will be a busy spot."

Dan hollered for the two boys in the loft to get the shovels in the back shed. They tumbled down, still in their nightshirts, and with bare feet. Dan had made shovels out of thin oak boards. They were heavy but did a good job of forcing the snow back outdoors where it belonged. Jed got the fire going in the fireplace and put a couple of sticks in the small metal stove on the sitting side of the room. Then he put the teakettle on the stove to steep. Soon the frigid air was forced back out of the house.

Since Mrs. Thorpe had not come out yet, Jed set to work putting out some molasses bread and plates of beans for Dan and the boys; then he started a pot of cut oatmeal. He knew it would be hard work getting to the side barn. Dan had a few laying hens at the back of the shelter, two milking cows, and a pair of workhorses. They would need to be fed and watered so a path would have to be made to the well and extra pails brought into the barn and the house. Dan had used an empty oxen stall to store some extra hay. The barrels of oats were against the wall by the front door.

Dan and the boys bundled up, and fortified with breakfast and some good hot tea, headed out to clear the yard and tend to the animals. "Tom, please take Emma a cup of tea. She is not feeling up to par this morning. Perhaps you can get her to eat a bit of gruel. Jed felt a bit embarrassed to be going into the Thorpe's bedroom, but he gathered his nerve, tried to control his blush, and put together a tray with a cup of tea in one of Emma's mother's china cups; a bowl of oatmeal with a bit of cream and a sprinkle of maple sugar; and a small piece of molasses bread. He timidly tapped on her door and heard a soft "enter." He was not prepared for what he saw.

Mrs. Thorpe was sitting in her nightdress on the side of the bed. She was doubled over. "Tom," she whispered. "Get Dan! I think the baby has decided to come a bit earlier than planned."

Jed nearly dropped the tray. He forgot the pain in his leg, put down the dishes and fairly hopped as fast as he could out into the snow. "Dan. Mr. Thorpe. Dan," he shouted over the still-swirling wind. He breathlessly hopped toward the well and found the three, each with a yoke of two pails.

Dan was shocked to see the half-dressed hobbling Jed in the path. "What in the world?"

"The baby. The baby is coming."

"Can't be. Emma usually knows."

"She says it is a surprise."

Dan put his yoke down and ran to the house. The boys continued up with their pails. Jed tried to carry the other yoke but his leg would not take the load.

"Don't worry Mr. Tom, we'll get them," came the duet.

Coming back into the kitchen, Jed did what he always heard his Mum say when she helped out a neighbor. Start getting some water warm. He was never sure if it was for a purpose or to keep the men and boys busy. Not taking any chances, he put a large pot on the hanger in the fireplace and a smaller pot on the stove.

He could hear the Thorpes. "You can't send the boys, Danny. The snow is too deep and they never would be able to pull her back on the toboggan. "

"I won't leave you."

"Don't be a stubborn ass. She'll never be here in time to help me if you don't start now. It's not like I haven't done this before. I won't be alone. Tom will be here."

To this Jed just shivered.

Dan ran out and grabbed the snowshoes off the hook by the front door. While he was strapping them on, he shouted orders to the two boys who stood, dumfounded, by the fireplace. "Finish taking care of the animals. You'll need to milk the cow and don't forget to gather any eggs. After that, stay to your loft unless Mr. Tom needs your help with anything."

The boys nodded and scurried back toward the barn.

"I need to get over to the neighbor and bring back one of the ladies to help," Dan shouted over his shoulder as he ran out the door. "I'll try to be back within two hours."

Stunned, Jed didn't know which way to turn. He soon found out, as Mrs. Thorpe shouted from the bedroom, "Tom. I need your help."

"Yes, Mrs. Thorpe."

"Being in this situation, I think it is about time you called me Emma."

"Yes ma'am, Mrs. Thorpe. Emma it is."

During her next labor pain, Mrs. Thorpe actually laughed. "This little girl is in so much of a rush to be born. My boys were much lazier."

Emma Thorpe was surely a woman who knew how to take charge. She barked orders so fast that Jed had no time to stew.

"Have you started boiling water?"

"Yes, er–Emma."

"I knew you were a sharp young man."

"I have a pile of clean torn sheets on the dresser. Please bring them here and then you'll need to bring a bowl with hot water. Then get the kitchen shears and twine from the cupboard."

I've helped more than one ewe birth her lamb but never needed shears and twine. He pushed around jars of jelly and canned vegetables in the cupboard until he found the roll of twine and grabbed the shears off the nail by the table.

"Now put the scissors in the hot water."

Guess there was a reason.

"Now check on the boys and then keep me company."

The boys were huddled together in the loft playing cards. They were doing their best not to hear what was going on below them.

"Now," said Mrs. Thorpe. Sit in the rocker and tell me some stories, Tom. I hear you were a shepherd. What was that like?"

Funny. I don't remember telling Dan about that.

And so between bouts of pain, Jed kept her amused with tales about the sheep on the farm, how he would spend days alone with them, named most, and he had a funny story about each.

"Oh, my. Tom. Please put some more hot water over the scissors and get another wash pan."

Jed was concerned about the 'Oh, my.'

"I'm not going to be able to wait. You'll need to help me."
Mrs. Thorpe grabbed the rounds on the headboard of her bed
and began to push and holler things that probably would be
understood only in Dublin. "She's coming, Tom. You'll need to
guide her. NOW!"

All fear melted away and Jed went to work. Tossing back the
cover, he was not at all concerned about the blood but was totally
in awe of the little head that was beginning to appear.

"She's nearly here, Emma. I'll help her." With that, Emma pushed
as hard as she could and out slipped a tiny miracle, cradled in
Jed's hands.

"Is she here?"

"She sure is Emma. And so beautiful."

"Now you must cut a piece of twine and tie it close to the baby's
stomach and again a few inches above."

Jed did so without hesitation. This little life was his to help.

"Now you must take the scissors and cut the cord between the
ties."

This Jed was not prepared for. He took a deep breath and did as
he was told.

"Help herTom! Pick her up and pat her back. She hasn't cried."

Dear Lord, I had not thought of that.

Jed picked up the child and did what he had heard his Mum
talk about. He gave her a smack on her back. And then, again.
Suddenly the room was filled with the most glorious sound—a
little girl announcing her arrival to the world, and with great
gusto. He wrapped the baby in a piece of the sheet and gave her to
her mother.

Emma was crying with joy. "I knew it. I knew it was my Nettie"

"Nettie?"

"Yes. After my sweet grand-mamma. Please take a warm cloth
and wipe her beautiful face and wrap her in the piece of wool on
the dresser."

Jed did, with pleasure. He wrapped the little girl in the white wool with pink flowers. As he cuddled her, he was overwhelmed with memories of Addie and how she must have felt when she first held Benjie.

Just then Dan burst into the room with Mrs. Jenkins. "Goodness, Tom. You look right at home with that child."

"I have a child, Dan. He was just a couple of weeks older than this when I first held him." He handed the baby to the neighbor and knew that Mrs. Thorpe and sweet Nettie were in good hands.

Dan walked over and gave Jed a big bear hug. He had a tear in his eye.

"I have my girl, Danny. I have my Nettie," Emma gushed.

Dan went to his wife and kissed her on the forehead. With this, Dan turned to Jed. "Thank you with my whole heart, Jedediah."

Jed was totally taken back, yet relieved.

"Come, Jedediah. We need something a bit stronger than tea. Boys, come see your sister." And as swift as the winter wind, they were there.

The two men settled by the stove and Benjie's story was told.

22   Spring 1826

Spring 1826

The day Jed saw the geese flying north, he shouted "Welcome back." He knew once they started headed for their nesting grounds, spring would be right behind their tail feathers.

The rest of the winter had passed quickly with cutting, hauling, and stacking the harvest by the river. Jed never quite got the strength back in his leg; he needed to rest it longer, but he was still able to mark all the logs, get the bookkeeping up to date, and do Jacob's inventory in the wangan and kitchen. He helped do chores at the farm to free Dan to work the landing with Jacob. Jed loved working at the farm so he could see Emma and little Nettie, even though it made him miss Benjie all the more.

After Jacob caught someone sneaking up on the wangan again, Dan lent him his shotgun until Jacob could get one of his own for the camp. Neither partner liked the idea of the gun but they took turns guarding the big wigwam during the night.

The snow started to settle, and walking the camp became easier without the snowshoes. The river showed no sign of going out, but the warmer days gave hope of it happening.

One night as Jed stood sentry at the supplies, he heard rustling in the branches, then saw a couple of shapes that evidently thought they were invisible. *Good grief. They would never make good Micmacs.* He aimed just slightly over their heads and let off a round from the shotgun, hitting a limb just above them, which fell in pieces around the two. The one in the back freed him self from the debris and ran toward the river. The second started in that direction when suddenly Jacob leapt from the shadows and

held him to the ground, one leg on each side of his body and his
knees on the intruder's arms. He pulled out his large hunting knife
and held it above the frightened man's head. Then he whipped it
downward and in one slash cut the raccoon tail off the trespasser's
hat.

By then Jed was standing next to him with the gun pointed at the
prowler. It was the first time he had seen the savage of the Indian
within Jacob's eyes.

"Next time," Jacob spat, "I'll take your scalp instead. You can
count on it."

He grabbed the terrified man by the front of his shirt and lifted
him to his feet, holding him with one hand while pointing his
finger at his nose. "You tell your boss, Mr. Benjamin Wingate, that
he is welcome to buy at our wangan any time he is in need. Cash
in hand. Other than that, tell him to keep his riff-raff in check.
We know who you are now, so don't take any chances around our
camp. Our axmen are very accurate. They could flatten you with
the blade or an entire tree before you knew what hit you. Now get
and don't come back."

Released, the ashen-faced intruder ran backward toward the
woods until he tripped over a stump. He picked himself up and
hopped away like one of Jacob's rabbits.

Spring quietly started to creep closer. Of course, that also meant
that mud season crept in as its partner. It was soon evident that
whatever logs were not pulled out, weren't to be harvested that
season. An ox can skid a large tree with snow, ice and even frozen
ground, but mud makes for a different story. So it was make-
or-break for the choppers and they worked as many hours as
daylight allowed.

Sunday had always been a day of rest, but the men were not
trapped in the camp house. They could be seen working on their
whittling while sitting in the warming sun. The two from the
landing played cards on a makeshift table of stacked pieces of
firewood. The choppers did the same with the checkerboard.
Jed went a bit down river to his favorite spot by the big boulder.
Sitting there, he put the finishing touches on the gum boxes. He
finally decided to carve a majestic five-point buck on the front of
Nuga's. It seemed fitting.

Suddenly Jed heard voices behind him and was surprised to see

Bear and his boys tromping through the woods on their round Micmac snowshoes.

"Hey there," he shouted. "You won't be needing those shoes much longer. The snow is really packing."

The Croteau boys were startled by the voice behind the boulder. When he made his way up to them he got a true Bear hug.

"What's the limp all about? Did you lose a battle with a falling pine?"

"Close. But we'll catch up. Benjie okay?"

"He's a true little Micmac. Nuga is singing the old songs to him and has him beating on a little drum. Where will I find Jacob on this beautiful day? I'll bet in his apron, working on a Sunday dinner."

"Either that or counting if he is going to have enough red wool socks to get through the season. The wangan has been very successful, but we have stories about that, too."

"Pop, let's get going. This is heavy," complained the boys.

"What are you bringing us, Bear?"

"Why, your favorite, Jedediah. Some nice fresh venison."

Jed could feel his stomach turning.

"And the payroll for the crew," Bear whispered to Jed.

"She finally let go of it," Jed whispered back with a big smile.

With the fresh meat, Jacob put out quite a spread for the crew. He had managed the season with provisions to spare and no complaints from the crew about scrimping. Jacob knew that men with a full belly gave a full day's work. He had Jed take a good-sized piece of venison up to the farm so Mrs. Thorpe could make a stew for her family and then he cut up the rest to start a stew for the crew.

They bedded the boys in the wangan and Frank, Jed, and Bear met around the fire pit in Jacob's wigwam.

"Bear says that the river's edge has opened down by the settlement. He was surprised that we were still iced all the way," started Jacob. "That means it will be only a few days before it starts to open here."

Frank piped up, "Jed, are all the logs marked?"

"All those at the landing. None of those that are waiting to be brought down, and there are some still in the woods. It is going to be hard to bring the sled down unless we get a few cold nights or a bit more snow."

Frank added, "I talked with Dan. He is going to bring down the draft horse and the wagon. He thinks the ground is still hard enough for him to pull the wagon down. I'll have my crew load the wagon and the rest will have to stay in the woods. I had no idea it was going to warm up so fast or I would have ended the chopping a few days ago."

Jacob wanted to know if Jed could walk up to the woodlot.

"Of course. I'm not an invalid. Just have a bum leg right now."

"Don't get your woolies in a knot. Just wanted to know if you thought you could get our mark on the logs that haven't been brought down yet. Then they will be ready for the river when they get to the landing."

"Why the rush?"

"We've decided that we're going to ship you home as soon as the river edge lets Frank take out the canoe."

"No way."

"No arguing," said Frank. "I have to get to the sawmill at the junction to register our mark before any of the logs get there. Sure don't want them mistaken for another crew's take."

"Why do I have to go?"

"Forget that stubborn Brit attitude," said Jacob. "You will be of more use to us getting the records straight away from the confusion around here. Besides, I think it is time Benjie spent some time with his Da. It will soon be his first birthday."

"What about the drive?"

"Frank says one of his choppers is a good driver. He's seen him bringing in logs at the junction. His brother wants the job, and one of your landing crewmen is pretty mean with a pike, too. So I think we have a crew for getting our harvest out of here."

"What about their pay?"

"Always the businessman. I have enough money from the wangan to offer them a decent pay— half now and the rest when Frank feels the job is done. I've also offered them all a new set of calks for their boots. These are the newest available and much sharper than the old ones."

"When did you all figure out my plans?"

Frank laughed. "You have spent a lot of time birthing babies and keeping house."

"What?" Bear was all ears.

"Another one of those things that I have to tell you about," whispered Jed.

"Well, then. The quicker we get you back to the family, the better."

And so it was. Within a week the river had opened enough for Frank to paddle Jed home. Before he left, he spent some time with Emma and Nettie. He had made a little rattlebox with a bunny on it for Nettie. It was hard to find pebbles this time of year, but he'd put a few dry beans inside. Emma was delighted.

As they approached the growing little village, Frank handed the paddle to Jed and picked up his fiddle. "Better make this official," he said.

23   Aunt Mary

With spring in full bloom, the ice went out quickly and soon the Aroostook River ran wild, gnawing away at the shore, making the channels deeper and wider. Before long, logs would clot the surface with acrobatic river drivers herding them toward the mills at the junction; then on to the St. John River.

Dan took a few days to make his way to the store on the edge of the Wingate Plantation. Emma was so full of joy at the birth of her daughter that she decided she wanted more dainty materials and frilly decorations. Even though Aunt Amy had done a good job of stocking more cloth and trims at the trading post, it was still not a big enough assortment for Mrs. Thorpe. She wanted a wardrobe befitting her little Miss Nettie.

"You look a bit uncomfortable, Mr. Thorpe. Are you not in the wrong end of the store?" came a soft voice behind him.

Startled, he jumped out of his quandary and turned to see Miss Mary Wingate smiling broadly at him. She looked like a fresh bit of sunshine in her delicate peach dress with tatted collar. Standing with her was Mrs. Wingate, looking a bit more gaunt than he remembered.

"How nice to see two of the lovely Wingate ladies."

"And you, Mr. Thorpe. Are you not a bit early to the store?" questioned Mrs. Wingate. "We usually see you more when you're planning crops."

"Yes, 'tis true. But Emma and I are now the parents of the most beautiful little girl and it seems to be my duty to see that her mother has the wonderful fabrics she has always dreamt about while raising three rough-and-tumble boys."

"What wonderful news! A mother is blessed to have girls to teach social matters to and to show the way with the needle."

"I can see you have done an exemplary job, Mrs. Wingate," remarked Dan, causing a deep blush on Mary's cheeks.

To this she seemed wistful and suddenly a bit sad. "We do the best we can. There is nothing else to do."

She turned to go to the counter to order her supplies for the day when Mary spoke up. "Mother, may I take a few minutes to help Mr. Thorpe pick out some materials?"

"I think that would be wonderful, my dear."

"I would be most appreciative," sighed Dan. "I am in over my head."

Mary passed her basket to her mother, "I'll be with you soon."

She led Dan to the far end of the stacks of cloth and began to look through the shelves.

"Thank you, Mary. I never would have known where to start."

"This is such fun Mr. Thorpe. I have never had a reason to look through these sweet designs. Look at this pattern of tiny lambs with rosebuds and this one with baby rabbits and clover. I just love this sweet plaid of pink, yellow and green. And look! There are tiny buttons and lace of the same colors. Oh, and yes, you must have some soft flannel for sleep dresses."

"My—I don't think Mrs. Thorpe could be any more excited. Thank you."

"You must be in a rush to get back to your farm and family."

"I am eager to get home, but I have more things to order and the store keep won't have them all ready for me until morning. I'm going to stay at the boarding house and get a bit more sleep than has been possible the past few weeks."

As she turned to go, Mary paused and looked into Dan's eyes. "Tell, me Mr. Thorpe, with this lovely weather have you seen the chickadee?"

He was taken aback for a minute but replied, "Yes, Miss Mary. I believe I have."

"Perhaps I shall see you again before you leave in the morning. I would like to send a little something back to little Nettie."

"I plan to leave early, but surely our paths will cross here at the store. Good day Miss Mary." As he left, he tipped his hat to Mrs. Wingate.

A number of miles west, Jed was working on his fieldstone fence, since most of the patches of snow among the trees were losing their struggle against the warmer air. Because they had been clearing the land in order to create a larger area for crops, more rays of sun were able to sneak into the once impenetrable forest. Before the land was dry enough to prepare for planting, there was time to clean up the winter mess and work on projects that would take a smaller share of time later on. Once in awhile Jed sat on the bank of the river and watched the harvest of logs riding the pitch of water. He wondered how many of them were marked with his 'Bc.' Waiting for the final count of board feet was brutal. The future of Jacob's people and his Benjie was riding on the back of that timber.

Jacob was still cooking for the river men, so he moved his kitchen every night to be ahead of them. Frank had long since gone to the mill to register the Buck Company mark and keep an eye on the sorting. He certainly didn't want any of their harvest to go astray. Dan's boy Red was with Jacob as his cookee and his second boy was keeping watch over the wangan. Even as crews were making their way out of the woods, they stopped by in hopes of finding a good price on leftover goods.

Jed spent some time each day cleaning out Jacob's cabin and helping Birdie get hers in order after the cold winter. He had been eating with Birdie and the children, as he felt Hanna had enough to do with her three rapidly growing boys, while she waited for her husband and her brother to come home. This gave him precious time with Benjie who loved to stand, holding onto his Da's hands. It was getting close to his first birthday and Jed was beginning to realize that the Micmacs didn't dwell much on celebrating days of birth. Their culture celebrated significant events such as first steps, first turkey kill, and first deer hunt. Still, Jed was going to figure out how to get Benjie a cake like he had always had as a child. His Mum would bake one with little treasures inside, including a hidden coin.

One night he was particularly weary from taking the rocks from the pile the boys had made near the river and carrying them farther in along the back of Jacob's path. His leg, though much better, still began to drag at the end of the day. He would have to tell them to start another pile farther in when they cleared new land for the potatoes. As he drifted off on his cot, he looked around Jacob's place, imagining how he would design a place of his own.

Yes, Addie. I am going to build a home for Benjie. It will take awhile, but Dan is going to let me start my cabin on the spot near Wilson's curve where the big boulder stands high above the current. In a few years, Benjie and I will have our own permanent place. This one your father will not destroy.

Jed had a tear in his eye as a sliver of moonlight slipped through the small window and fell on Addie's painting. The little cameo was pinned to her yellow ribbon that lay atop the frame.

Early the next morning Dan Thorpe made his way to the general store. The slant of the spring sun bouncing off the small chop of waves on the river gave the appearance of a long gold necklace that spread as far as could be seen north and south. He thought Emma would find this glorious. As he approached the open porch in front of the building, he was surprised to see Miss Mary waiting for him on one of the outside benches. It was unusual, for she seemed to be alone. As the father of a new daughter, Dan finally understood why Mr. Wingate never allowed his daughters out without a chaperone.

"Good morning, Miss Mary. Is your mother not well?"

"She's fine. It takes her a bit longer to finish her errands now. She has been not quite herself for many months. She is across the way at the butcher, but I'm sure she's watching closely."

"Mary, will it help you to know that I know the story of little Benjamin?"

Relief seemed to soften Mary's features and her body relaxed. "Thank the good Lord, Mr. Thorpe. I feel as if I am perpetually choking on the knowledge of my nephew and my pain for my dear sister."

He could see a dainty tear slowly flowing down her cheek.

"Tell me, Mr. Thorpe. Have you seen the child?"

"No, Mary, but I know he is cared for very well by people who love him very much. I do see Jedediah quite a bit. Would you be shocked to know that he alone assisted Emma with the birth of our Nettie?"

Mary let out a gasp and then a giggle. "You know, at second thought I would never be surprised by what Jed is capable of. Look how he saved Addie's child."

"He is totally dedicated to his son."

"Before mother finishes her morning gossip across the street, I want you to have this basket. There is something in there for your sweet baby but under that is another package and a letter for Jed. Would you be able to get it to him in some way? I would be so grateful. I leave for Boston soon for a voyage back to London."

"I'll make it happen, Miss Mary, and as quickly as possible."

Just then Mrs. Wingate started across the muddy avenue, doing her best not to let her skirt drag in the muck.

"Good morning, Daniel."

"Ma'am."

"I just love to feel the newness in spring air, but am not pleased about the mire from the thaw."

"My Emma feels just the same. But soon the songbirds and violets will take the memories of winter away."

"Come, Mary. We have to get this chicken back to the kitchen. We need nothing in the store today."

Dan tipped his hat. "Thank you for the gift for Nettie."

Mrs. Thorpe interjected, "You're welcome. Mary also made you some sugar cookies; looks like she is feeding an army."

"Mother, that was supposed to be a surprise."

Dan smiled broadly. "She must have heard how my three sons eat. They are of that age now."

"Goodbye, Mr. Thorpe," Mary said nearly in a whisper, and as her mother turned, she mouthed 'thank you.'

By mid-morning, Dan had all his purchases packed carefully in his canoe. It had been quite a puzzle to figure out where each package could go in order to keep the load well-balanced. All was covered in hides to protect from any splashing water, as he would be paddling against the strong spring current. He carefully wrapped

Mary's basket in a separate hide and placed it just behind his legs. He had added a seat to his canoe, as he'd found sitting on his knees was no longer tolerable.

The river was treacherous not only because of the spring flow, but because of the multitude of logs beginning their trip, which would take many to the far ends of the world. He didn't usually ride the river while the drive was on, but he was glad he had bent to Emma's wishes for sewing materials, because without her coaxing, he never would have seen Mary before her Atlantic crossing. He figured that if he could make the northern-most curve of the Aroostook by late afternoon, he would find Jacob's night camp, stay there with Red and start south, then west in the early morning.

Going against the flow proved to be much more difficult than going with it had been. The best way to dodge a wayward log was to stick as close to the shore as possible, but he found himself jammed up against a rock and blocked by a log. He tried backing his way out and suddenly another log stacked behind him.

"God Lord, help me find a way out of this fix."

Suddenly a rope came from nowhere. "I'm not the Almighty, but I'll give a try at saving your sorry Irish ass."

"Jacob Buck. Never thought my prayer would be answered by a bloody savage, but as I heard once, beggars can't be choosers. God, am I glad to see you!"

"Hang on, Pop, we'll get you out!" shouted Red from the bank.

Then Dan realized Jacob was balancing precariously on the log and didn't have any calks on his boots.

"You crazy? That log can roll at any time."

"You saying I'm crazy? Look at you, trying to paddle upstream against a drive."

"Thought I could make it to your cook camp and then things would be clearer behind you, except for some strays."

"Did you forget that your timber is not the only harvest in the river? Wingate probably has ten times as much."

"Told you I don't know much about harvesting. That's your job."

"You got the canoe tied off, Red?"

"Yes, sir."

"Now tie off this one. I've got your Pop on the other end."

"What about my goods in the canoe?"

"We'll get that out after we get you on shore."

Jacob walked across the jumble of logs as if they were nailed together.

"Jedediah told me that you walked above the ground like a damn spirit."

"Now let's see if you can get that well-fed belly of yours across the same way."

Dan climbed slowly out of the canoe, took a step and the log started to roll.

"Pull quickly and hard, Red," yelled Jacob. "We don't want him to get caught between two of them; your Ma won't be happy about us bringing him home in pieces."

They landed Dan as if they were pulling in a whale, soaking wet but with nothing hurt except his pride. Next Jacob went back out and nudged the nose of the canoe up a bit and then the three men slowly pulled the narrow boat very slowly over the logs to shore. It made it with just one small tear in the birch bark, which Jacob could easily fix with some hot spruce resin.

"Our boys will be in soon for a meal, before sundown. They'll go back out to make sure things are moving at sunrise. Food's ready; let's get a head start on it."

While Red was cleaning up the pans and fixing firewood for morning, Jacob and Dan sat by the river with a cup of hot tea.

"What the hell were you thinking, Dan? What was so important that you couldn't have waited another day or two until the biggest swell of the logs passed? Better yet, why did you go to the junction in the first place?"

Dan explained about how Emma had wanted things for Nettie, so he'd made a list of the supplies he needed to get ready for planting. "And before you roll your eyes any more, I'm glad I went, because I saw Mary Wingate and it became more important that I get back quickly."

Dan told Jacob about Mary's letter for Jed and how important it

was for him to have it before she went back to England. "I was
going ask you who I should give it to."

"You take it yourself. And take Red home with you. I'm going to
be cooking only one more night. Tomorrow our river boys should
be at the mills and Frank will take over watching our harvest."

"I've never been to the settlement; I've only seen it as I passed."

"Then you know where to go. When you pull up to the landing
you will probably be met by Frank's three boys, who will be full
of questions. Just tell them you are a friend of Jacob and have
come to see their Uncle Jed. If they hesitate, ask to see Nuga. They
are very protective of Jed and his identity."

In the morning, Red somehow wiggled into a space in the canoe;
with him handling a paddle, it would be much easier to navigate.

"Remember, the Aroostook flows north in this area, so the current
won't be any easier. Keep safe."

The logs were scattered a bit farther apart, but they still stayed on
the edge and hoped there would not be another small jam.

"There's the trading post, Pop. Why do we have to get to that
side?"

"I have an important message to deliver a couple miles farther.
There's a good-sized gap coming. Once we start, paddle as hard as
you can."

The tom turkeys in the pines must have been laughing their
wattles off watching the stocky Irishman and his flaming-haired
son moving an Indian canoe against the spring current. An Indian
might have been able to do it, but the Irishmen were being a bit
foolhardy.

Safely hugging the shore past the post, Red let out a big sigh, then
turned to his Pop. "Ma is not going to be happy with your taking
a chance like that. Now it looks like you are going to take me to
that Indian place. She *really* won't like that."

"I have a feeling she'll agree with me completely on this one,
although I know it doesn't happen very often. See that landing just
before the stone wall? We are pulling in there."

Surprised, Red said, "Who ever heard of Indians with stone
fences?"

"Who are you? What do you want? Don't come in here. Stay away." All that and more bombarded Dan's ears as he pulled up to the slope. It was hard to keep the canoe in place—he needed to get in farther so they could pull up the nose.

"You must be Frank's boys," Dan shouted up at the stepping-stone youngsters.

"How do you know that?"

"I'm a friend of Jacob's and I need to see your Uncle Jedediah."

"Sean, go find him," Pete barked. "Joe, help me pull them up a bit. Don't you two get out."

"Tell him it is Dan Thorpe," Dan shouted to the quickly disappearing Sean.

To Dan, who was bouncing around in the canoe, it seemed like an eternity before he saw Jed running past a wigwam and then starting down the slope. It was obvious that he still had quite a limp.

Jed was totally surprised. "Why in the world are you risking life and limb by coming this way during the drive?"

"Frankly, I was beginning to ask myself the same."

"Help them out boys, and tell Birdie to put on a pot of tea."

"No. Can't stop. I want to get up to the farm while there is still plenty of sunlight, in case we need to dodge more logs." Dan had given Jed's share of the package to Red, who had to reach out to give the basket to Jed. "Give us a shove, boys."

"What's this about?" Jed shouted.

Dan gave shrug. "It's from Miss Mary."

Stunned, Jed gave a wave to his friend.

"What you got, Uncle Jed?"

"Can we see?"

"Time will tell, boys."

Jed dropped the basket off with Birdie to keep it safe, but he took the letter with him. He wanted to find a quiet place to read it.

Sitting on a log under an old growth tree near the river yet out of sight behind a bush, Jed opened Mary's letter.

My Dear Jedediah,

I will soon be traveling to London. My Aunt Muriel is getting more crippled with arthritis day by day and is having a hard time tending to our Addie. I am going to move in with her to care for her and for my sister. I must ask a favor that would mean the world to me. If at all possible, I would like to see Benjie, for I may never be this way again. Addie is still fading and if I can tell her I have seen him, it may help her. I understand she sits by the window listening to the songbirds and when she is feeling stronger, she knits sweaters and booties to be given to charity. The doctor feels that concentrating on the babies has kept her going all this time, but she is still anemic and no medical means has helped. I'm afraid that her future will be short.

I am going to tell Mother that you and Benjie are safe. I feel in my heart this will help her burden. I know that she will keep your secret and do her best to keep you secure. A week from this coming Monday, she and I will be taking our annual excursion along the river to look for early wild mushrooms. My sister will not be with us. Heavens—she might get her shoes dirty! She is too busy primping for social events to care what goes on in the kitchen. We will be at your special cove by late morning. It would mean so much if you could bring Benjie to us. I have no idea how far away you are and the difficulty.

If you don't get this letter in time or if you can't make it, I will certainly understand. Please know how much we care about you and how much I love my nephew.

I will give your Addie your love.

Fondly, Mary

Post Script – There is a birthday gift in the basket; I baked little Benjamin a cake like we used to have in England, with a coin and a few tiny trinkets inside. I hope this brings back many fond memories of your Mum. I know at times I am wistful about the sheep flocks. Also, I have baked some sugar cookies. Know you like these.

Jed's head was spinning. *I must figure this out. I must. Birdie and Nuga. They'll know what to do. I must take Benjie to see his grandmother and aunt.*

That next week, Benjie had his first birthday celebration just as his father once had. Hanna agreed to have everyone at her home.

Ben's guests were Nuga, Birdie, Martha, Hanna's boys, Ruth with
her newborn girl and Little Bear, who was far from little, even at
two years old. Benjie's Uncle Jacob had just come home from the
drive, which delighted the one-year-old. His Da had carved two
more animals to go with his growing herd of farm animals. Aunt
Mary had sent him a fuzzy toy lamb. There was good hot strong
tea and a weaker version for the children. They laughed and ate
sugar cookies and then shared the cake. Each of the children
found a small toy in their piece of cake, and Martha found the
coin in hers. Jed told the story of how Benjie's Aunt Mary had
sent the treats for them.

Sunday was a misty day and Zeke soon disappeared down the
path. Jed was leading the beast in order to miss any ruts that
could cause the animal to stumble, because on Zeke's back, along
with a few supplies, was Birdie holding Benjie close to her in a
sling. He was sure Frank's friend would let them take shelter in the
hovel, where Zeke would stay. They would pick up Frank's canoe
for the trip the next morning.

The river was like glass that morning. Jed paddled slowly near the
bank and Benjie was delighted in his first canoe ride. Birdie would
dip her hand in the water and playfully flick a bit of water at him
and he would squeal in delight. The logs on the river were few,
as most were near the St. John and the mills at the junction. Jed
would not have risked the journey with his son if it were not so.

When they got to the cove, everything was quiet, so they had a
bite to eat and Jed tried to tell Benjie about how his mother loved
this place. Then Jed jumped on shore and Birdie passed him his
son.

"I'll take the canoe just a bit down the river and will come back
to your whistle, Mr. Jed."

Sitting on a log, he bounced his son on his knee and held his
hands so he could do his own little toddler dance. Jed's mind
wandered to memories of the times he and Addie had spent there,
dreaming about being together forever. If only her father was not
so controlling. They knew he would send Jed away if he found
out. They had daydreamed about the time Jed could save enough
money to take Addie away to start a life of their own. What a
wonderful life they would have had with their son.

When Jed heard the ladies talking in the woods, he stood and held
Benjie tight to his chest.

"I can't believe it," Mrs. Wingate gasped when she saw Jed.

"I didn't tell Mother that you would try to be here. I didn't want her to be disappointed if it didn't happen. She knows the story now."

When both women saw the child with Addie's bright blue eyes and Jed's stand-up cowlick, they hugged each other and wept.

"Mrs. Wingate, sit here on the log." When she had settled, Jed placed the curious little boy on her lap. "Benjie, this is your grandmother."

Mrs. Wingate smiled through her tears and the child smiled back. "Jedediah, he is so much like his mother was at that age. I am so sorry. I am so sorry I was not stronger. Sweet Adelaide, what have I done?"

Mary put her arms around her mother's shoulders. "Mother, it isn't your fault. Neither of us could have stopped father."

"His day will come, Mary. His prideful ways will be his undoing. Someday, everyone will know that this child is Adelaide's and Jedediah's, I promise you that."

"Mother, may I hold him?" Mary picked up her nephew and hugged him closely and kissed his sweet forehead. "Jed, you have done such a wonderful job. He is so healthy and bright."

"I have a wonderful friend who has helped me. There are plans in the works that will secure his future and I promise he will be well-educated."

"We can't tarry long, Mother. It's past noon."

"I can't bear to let him go, but am so grateful I met him. I will have that sweet face with me forever," Mrs. Wingate sighed.

Mary handed over a cloth bag. "Jed, I brought him Addie's small spinning top, her ball in cup game and her slingshot. Yes, mother, she had a slingshot and was good with it."

Jed took the package and took a gift from his pouch. "Please give these to Addie. They were his first." He handed her the tiny pair of beaded moccasins.

Mary reached out and hugged Jed. "She will treasure them. Please pray that I find her well enough to understand." She handed the baby to his father.

Mrs. Wingate stood and hugged Jed and his son. "Your mother would be so proud to know how well you have protected her grandson. I also believe that Thomas Smythe himself would smile."

With tears flowing, the two ladies walked into the brush. When they looked back one more time, little Benjie was waving his right arm.

At Jed's whistle, Birdie came quickly into the cove. "You alright, Mr. Jed?"

"Couldn't be better."

Spring flew by. Things fell into their seasonable pace. Everyone knew his or her part in the whole. Peter worked steadily with his father in the garden and they doubled the size of the potato planting. They also increased the yellow-eye beans by three long rows. Jed helped drag out more than one kettle of beans made with last year's crop. Everyone thought their beans tasted a lot better than any they had ever had before. Pride was another thing that grew that year.

Buck and Company did not make huge money, but they did turn a profit, most of which was turned right back into the company. Frank was able to leave Hanna with enough to carry the family through the winter. The pot for the village was paid a full share and there were plans to build a strong landing, a new hovel for Zeke and to purchase a milking cow. Dan was pleased, as he made a goodly payment on his claim and more of the land was deeded to him. Both Jacob and Jed kept a minimal share—they wanted to double the stock in the wangan, so made sure they had a healthy balance at the account in St. John.

In late June Dan made another stop at the settlement; this time he got out of his canoe. The minute Jed saw him, his heart sank, for he knew what Dan's message must be if he personally sought him out.

"I'm so sorry friend, but your Adelaide lost her long battle with poor health. Mrs. Wingate sat down with me at the store and told me what I needed to tell you."

Jed balanced himself against a birch tree, then lowered himself to the ground with his head in his hands. Dan sat down beside him.

"Mary wrote that Adelaide was so pleased to see her that she perked up a bit and even managed a few short walks in the park with her sister. She slept with the gift you sent her. One evening when they were reading together, she felt faint and just made it back to her bed. The doctor said her heart finally succumbed and he knew not why it had kept on for so long."

"I know why," whispered Jed. "Her heart was nourished by her love for her son."

"And I would say for you also. Mrs. Wingate said to tell you that she has kept her promise. You and your son will have no more terror from her husband. She says that she was strong and told him not to touch either of you or she would go to the people around him and tell them what a crook he was. He put up a fight until she showed him the death notice she had put in the paper."

"There was a notice?"

"She said that when her eldest daughter Phoebe read it, she fainted dead away. When Mr. Wingate read it he nearly had a stroke and felt he would not be able to walk again with his head held up."

"What did she do?"

Dan gave him the notice Mrs. Wingate had sent from the paper. It told of Addie's death in London and a brief history of her life in England and on the Wingate Plantation.

When Jed read the last line he smiled broadly. "It is perfect. Addie would love it."

Also surviving is her beloved son, Benjamin Wingate Smythe.

24 A Letter to Mary

June 30, 1833

Dear Miss Mary,

Since your mother is returning to England, I will send this with her. It is funny of me but I am still leery of sending word of Ben by the mail. Just leftover fear from the past I suppose, but it is there.

We are about to leave on the next bit of our journey. We will be leaving our home with the Micmacs to live in the forest on the edge of Dan Thorpe's woodlot. I will tell you all about it to catch you up on our story since I sent the note enclosed with your mother's Christmas package to London.

First, however, I wish to extend my condolences on the sudden death of Mr. Wingate. I cannot lie about my feelings for the man, but he was your father. Addie fought against his dominance, but I feel she still had a special love for him.

You will be so proud when your mother arrives to be with you in London. She is far from the timid lady I saw near the cove when she met Ben. Holding her grandson was the catalyst that hardened the mettle in her behavior when it came to her family. She was never the same and they say your father was at a loss to understand until she put the announcement in the paper.

You see I write of Ben, not of Benjie. On his eighth birthday this spring, he stood straight in front of me with his hands on his hips and announced he is much too old to be called Benjie and from that very moment on, he would be known as Ben. Mary, I was laughing so hard on the inside, as he looked just like his Mum. When she put her foot down on anything, she stood there with her hands on her hips and spoke in the same manner.

We had a near tragedy this May. Ben and the three Ryan boys were fooling around near the beaver pond. It was a hide-and-seek game like we played in England, but with their own twist that when the seeker found someone, he had to chase and tag him. Ben was the seeker and when he found Sean lying under a rotting log, he lunged to tag him and Sean took off in a flash. I learned years ago how swift afoot an Indian can be. In his exuberance Sean started to run out on top of the beaver dam. He and Ben realized the danger as Jacob had spent many hours drilling it into their minds. They both stopped as if running into a black bear. Ben tumbled like a clown in the dirt, Sean lost his balance and tumbled into the pond. By now the two other boys were standing next to Ben, laughing at their brother as he thrashed about. Soon though, the glee turned to fright as they realized Sean wasn't able to keep his head above water.

In tandem, his brothers leaped into the pond and Ben crawled on his belly on top of the dam to get to the spot where Sean had fallen in. He reached down and grabbed Sean's hand and pulled as hard as he could but he couldn't pull him out. Joe yelled that his foot was tangled in some of the branches that stuck out from the dam. He and his brother kept diving to free him. Soon Peter realized that he could not free his brother's foot and swam to shore and let out the loudest whistle he could. Joe kept diving and pulling on the branch and Ben slipped into the water and did his very best to keep his friend's face above water. Sean in his panic grabbed Ben and began to pull him under, too.

In no time, Frank came running from the garden, Jacob bounded down the path from where he was setting the frame of a canoe, and met me, covered with soot from the bean hole. Peter was screaming that Sean was drowning. It was a mad scene. Jacob and Frank pulled their knives and dove in unison into the water. I crawled out on the dam and just below the surface I saw my son staring up at me in terror. I reached down, grabbed hold of his shirt collar and pulled him up, choking and gasping for air. All he could say was 'save Sean.'

Jacob cut the tangled branches and Frank broke the surface with his son and swam to shore with the limp boy in his arms. By now Hanna was there, screaming in a way I had never heard before. They laid the child on the bank, where his uncle started shaking him and hitting him on the back. After what seemed an eternity, he started coughing and began to breathe again, however weakly.

Over the next three days, his brothers and Ben refused to leave Sean's bedside, where he seemed to be sleeping like a baby. Jacob looked at the boys and knew no other words were needed about the dam. They were being harder on themselves than any adult could be.

On the fourth day Sean opened his eyes, looked at the boys, and asked Ben if he had caught and tagged him. Then he looked at his exhausted mother and complained about being hungry. He certainly had his guardian spirits working overtime.

I know you must have heard about the wedding, but through the eyes of your mother. We all had such fun with it; much to the expense of your sister. Ah, yes—Philippe and Phoebe. A match made somewhere, but I am sure not in heaven. Philippe was flying high for months with the fact that one of the Wingate daughters was returning his interest. You should have seen him get pumped up like a tom turkey in heat. I'm sure your mother never wrote you about the obvious ass-kissing when it came to your father.

Aunt Amy took to your mother from the first time they met at the trading post. She and Phoebe came up the river to spend the weekend with Philippe's family when they were about ready to announce the engagement. The two English women found they had so much in common, from friends in London and up in the North Country to favorite places to eat in the city. They talked of Addie's death as they became even closer and found it so funny that Philippe was yet to figure out that Jedediah Smythe and his son had been living right under his nose and that Jed was one of the partners in Buck and Co. And dear Phoebe had not yet figured out Philippe's ancestral line. It became a running joke between Aunt Amy and your mother and they sometimes giggled like schoolgirls when the couple paraded around Philippe's business establishment.

With your mother visiting Aunt Amy, it became possible for us to make plans for her to see Ben once in awhile. My, he loves his grandmother. Of course, his grandfather had no idea of the connection between the boy and his future son-in-law. And since he would not trouble himself to meet Philippe's family, he had no idea of the Micmac bloodline. He hung onto only the fact that this young man was fairly wealthy, owning his own store, and believed that at least one of his daughters was going to marry successfully.

*Mary, how I wish you could have been a bird in the tree
overlooking the flower garden in the manicured front lawn of the
mansion when the wedding took place. Your mother may not have
had a chance to tell you of that day at the end of May. I, about
split laughing when Nuga gave us the details. How Addie would
have loved it.*

*Of course Philippe's grandmother, brother, sister, and niece were
invited at the insistence of Aunt Amy. The guests from the social
set were seated on chairs on the lawn. The day was lovely and the
river glittered in the sunlight. All the spring flowers were in their
glory.*

*Just before the mother of the groom arrived, Cateline Dondo was
seated in full traditional Micmac dress wearing her grandmother's
tall pointed hat, along with her granddaughter Beatrice and her
great-granddaughter Martha wearing exquisitely beaded soft
deerskin tunics. Next came Aunt Amy in a traditional English tea
dress and wide-brimmed flowered hat, escorted by her son, the
gentle giant Bear, who was also in deerskin, but with a traditional
brilliant red wool coat with embroidered ceremonial sash.
Following was Uncle Henri in a gray tailored suit, but also with
a Micmac ceremonial sash. The fashionable ladies just twittered
behind their lace fans and then took a closer look at the handsome,
fair-haired, green-eyed groom and finally noticed his definite Indian
features. You could almost hear their collective thoughts. How
fitting—a half-breed savage and the aunt of a bastard.*

*The sugar topping on the cake, however, was your father's
look when he pompously started down the center aisle with his
daughter looking as regal as the queen. When he saw the honored
guests in the front row, he turned beet red and you could almost
feel the arrogance leak from his self-important body.*

*The only other thing that would have made it more perfect would
have been Ben as the ring bearer.*

*As for the bride and groom, they seemed totally unaffected and
enjoyed their day with noses held high.*

*Another peek into life at the trading post you would have loved
to tell Addie. About a week ago your mother visited Phoebe. They
were sitting on the front porch enjoying tea with Amy, when Ben
ran up to see his grandmother and stopped short in front of your
sister and said, "Hello Auntie Phoebe, I'm Ben." He offered her
a handshake and she dropped her cup with a crash. Your mother*

and Aunt Amy laughed out loud. He gave both ladies a kiss. Then I came on the porch, tipped my hat, smiled at her, and took Ben home. I swear she looked so white, one would think she had made up with laundry bluing.

Now the reasons for our moving on. I had always hoped to have a place of our own soon and I think at eight, Ben is ready for it.

Birdie is going to go live with Aunt Amy and Uncle Henri soon. Now that your mother is moving back to England, Phoebe and Philippe will be moving to the mansion; Nuga's grandson is getting his dream. The only problem is that it is quite an operation to support and since your father never laid claim to any of the woodlots when he could, it is not certain that the Wingate logging business will continue; Philippe will have to find places where he can send his crew. The landowners who dealt with your father with a handshake, most likely will not do the same for his son-in-law, particularly because of the way he did business with them in the past at the post. Wish them luck. Birdie will help her parents with the post and take over the management of day-to-day business. She will do great and Martha will be able to go to the nearby convent school.

Hanna has her hands full caring for three teenage boys. They remind me of how Dan's trio were when I first met them. They are helping their father add rooms to their home. It is no longer adequate and Frank has the bit of extra money now to allow for the changes. Hanna deserves it. She is such a lovely lady and a hard worker.

Nuga is not that well. She is quite frail and sometimes I can see in her failing eyes that she so wishes to join her much-loved Pierre. So, watching over my active boy for the winter is no longer possible for her.

This special group of people have kept Ben safe for all these years and treated me like one of their own. I shall always be grateful.

Dan Thorpe made the last payment on his claim after the harvest this spring. Buck and Co. will keep logging his land, as it is a good investment for all.

The company has built a permanent cabin for the wangan on the spot where the wigwam stood and it has supplies year-round. Jacob still likes to cook outside, but has allowed a cook stove room to be added to the dining room for the dead of winter. He

*will always be at the village of his people for the summer. It is still
a huge project in progress and we can only pray they can keep the
land when the border is settled.*

*Yes, we are still fighting over the Aroostook Valley. It is getting
worse Mary, for Yankees are moving into the Aroostook valley
and are trying to drive out all the Canadian settlers. If we are not
careful, there may be a war with Britain over the whole situation.
This year the king of the Netherlands worked on a boundary
settlement that New Brunswick accepted but Maine did not. I
have no idea why. Now it is all back to skirmishes and uncertainty
and I fear people will be hurt before it is over.*

*I have been building a cabin on the spot at the eastern edge of
Dan's land, near the big boulder by the river. Eventually I hope
to buy the piece of land from him, making a permanent place for
Ben to live. Ben and I will work on Dan's farm in the summer,
especially in the potato fields. When I go back to Buck and Co. in
the winter, Ben will stay with Emma during the day. She will hold
classes for Nettie, Ben and Little Bill. Did I tell you Bill Jackson
has moved his family to a piece of land just below us? He is also
hoping to get a deed as a settler whenever this conundrum is over.
He is back to bossing the crew at the landing.*

*I have rattled on so. By the time you get this, Ben and I should
be on our way up stream. We are leaving in late summer while
the river is very low. Since Dan's place is on the other side of the
Aroostook, I will ford the river at a narrow spot and carry Ben.
He still will not go in the canoe. We will carry provisions for a
couple of weeks and make our way by land to our new home.
One of Bear's boys will bring up our belongings. It will be nice
camping with him alone for that time. I told him we can leave the
valley and settle somewhere else, but he is adamant about staying
near the river. He says he loves the Aroostook River; he just hates
the water. I guess to his mind, that makes sense.*

*I do not know what our future will be, but as long as I am with
my son I will be content.*

*Keep well, Mary. I hear you have been seeing a wonderful man. I
know you will make the best decisions for your future happiness. I
will send news with Aunt Amy when it is possible, as it is sure she
and your mother will stay in touch.*

Fondly,

Jedediah

25   Spruce Gum

Fall 1833

The full moon of late summer lit up the forest with a special glow. Ben was rolled in his blanket under the lean-to he and his father had made of a woven branches covered with pine boughs. It was bright enough for Jed to relax with his carving. He was working on a small spruce gum box just the right size for Ben to carry in his pocket. He could see the hulking bodies of turkeys nestled high in the pines. The songbirds had long gone to bed to prepare for another dawn concert. Right now he heard the hoots of owls and the rustling in the bushes of night creatures on the prowl.

It had been a difficult morning, for it finally settled in Ben's mind that it could be a long time before he saw his friends again. Nuga hugged him close and he wept quietly. She dried his tears and gave him one of her loving smiles and whispered comforting words that only he could hear. It was as though they both knew this would be their last time together, at least on this earth.

At the river crossing, Ben clung to his father's neck and wrapped his legs around his waist. Ben was wearing his pack and Jed decided he would go back and get the rest of the supplies once Ben was safely on the other side. First they waded to a narrow island in the center of the river and then crossed to the mainland. This strip of land was totally under water during high water in the spring. Ben was trembling when they reached shore and Jed realized he truly had no idea how much the water terrified the boy.

When Jed finished bringing his pack and food across, Ben was sitting quietly in the noon sun, staring at the clouds.

"Look, Da. That one looks just like the toy lamb Aunt Mary gave me."

"He'd better be on the lookout, because that cloud coming over the pines looks like the head of a fox. I'd say your little lamb had better start running." At that Jed grabbed his son and started tickling him until Ben was laughing out loud, forcing his tension to melt away.

When the first rays of sunshine hit him in the eyes, Jed was amazed to realize he had slept so well. He panicked for a second when he didn't find Ben lying next to him, but quickly saw that the small fire pit had been lit and tea was already boiling. Ben had laid out a cloth and had put out some molasses bread Hanna had packed for them with some chunks of maple sugar and early small apples.

"You'll make someone a great cookee someday," Jed laughed as he walked to the river's edge to splash some cool water on his face. He brought back a damp cloth for Ben to use to wipe the remnants of sleep from his eyes. Somehow, his son seemed to have grown from a child to a brawny boy overnight.

The trek toward their cabin was leisurely. Ben was full of questions and his father was more than ready to take the time to answer them. Ben observed that trees were as different as people. They walked through shrubs and tried to name the wild flowers. They discussed what was edible and what to stay away from, especially when it came to mushrooms. Ben had some lessons for his Da too, from the stories he had heard from Nuga. Jed pointed out that moss grew thicker on the north side of a tree and what to look for at the top of healthy hemlocks, for the tip always points to the East. Good information if one should get disoriented on a cloudy day or when the sun could not make its way through the canopy of dense growth.

"Here. This is what I have been looking for. Look at the tips of the branches of this spruce. It is time you learned how to collect your own spruce gum."

Ben was not that keen on the gum when he had first tried it a couple years before. He nearly spat it out when Jed gave him the nodule off the spruce tree, but his father told him to stick with it. At first it tasted terrible and it broke up into tiny granules almost like sand. But with patience it softened in his mouth and the pine flavor became pleasant. He wished it would stay that way, but after awhile it hardened up again and he'd have to spit it out. Once he had gotten used to it, he looked forward to it and didn't even mind if there was a bit of bark trapped in it, for it was easily spat out when the gum got to the good chewing stage.

"How does the tree make the gum, Da?"

"Well, the resin is in the tree and when the tree is nicked in some way; say from a woodpecker, it seeps out and forms a ball. Look at this tree, though. The limbs were broken when another tree fell against it and the gum is seeping from the tips of the branches. This is the best. It is clean, for it hasn't run against the bark."

"How can I pick it?"

"I'll lift you up on my shoulder so you can get the highest pieces; they are the best."

"Look Da, this one is as big as a robin's egg. Wow!"

"When it dries some, it will break up into nice pieces for your gum box."

When he was back on the ground, he wondered, "What gum box, Da?"

Jed showed him the one he had been carving. It was a bit bigger than his rattlebox. Jed had carved "B" on one side and two bunnies with clover on the other. When the top slid open, it was the perfect size to carry pieces of the spruce gum. The boy was thrilled.

"Listen," said Jed.

They could hear the gobbles of turkeys somewhere around them.

"Can we watch them?"

"You'll need to show me just how much Uncle Jacob has taught you about not making any noise."

"Da. I'm wearing my m'kusin. I can be quiet as a mouse."

They put their packs and supplies up in the crotch of an oak tree to keep them away from four-legged scavengers and did their best Micmac stealth walk toward the noise. Jed raised his hand and they hid behind a downed log. It wasn't long before the parade of big birds came into view. There were many broods of hens with young chicks, and scattered between them were yearlings. Toms didn't usually run with the flock at that time of year unless they were young ones. They must have found some seeds or fruit, for they scattered a bit to feed. Two of the older hens stood guard on either end of the group. They stood very still, moving their heads from side to side, looking for anything out of the way, and listening intently for the hint of intruders. They would feed when they stopped again and another pair took their turn as sentries.

Suddenly the guards let out a distinct call and the birds ran into the woods, quickly lining up in a procession, and fleeing out of sight. Jed was always impressed with how fast the clumsy looking birds could run. If necessary, they spread their wings and lifted their bulk into the trees.

"What scared them Da?" whispered Ben. "It couldn't have been us."

Jed held his finger to his lips, as there was the sound of talking heading their way, moving through the forest as if following the path of the turkeys.

"Damn. I swear I saw some of them going this way," came an unfamiliar voice. "I could just taste a stew made with one of them critters and the potatoes and carrots we snatched from the farm behind us."

"We need to push that Irishman out of here. That land should be for Maine settlers, not Brits from New Brunswick."

The third man bellowed, "Don't worry. We're going to make things rough on the Canadians that think this river is theirs. Bullshit. I'll do whatever it takes."

"Some of the fellows farther up river have formed a Yankee posse and are raising Cain. If we keep making their lives miserable, they may pack up and scoot."

"We're already driving them Indians out of here. The governor is sending them to reservations like the new one in Bangor. They say the ones that set camp on the Aroostook are going to be rounded up and sent off to the coast or over the border to New Brunswick and Nova Scotia."

Ben audibly gasped.

"You hear that?"

"I didn't hear anything. Perhaps it's just one of those turkeys you imagined."

"How they going to get the savages to leave their hunting grounds?"

"A few years back, the governor decided they're not that bright and the state needs to care for them just like children. He's promising them a place to live, work to support their families and schools for the children. Seems like they're falling for it. Just what I need, having my state acting like a father to some idiots."

"I saw that the bunch of Micmacs that always camped just down from here didn't show up this spring."

"Most likely some settler has made a claim on the land and they had no place to set their wigwams. Talk about being stupid."

"Never met an Indian that had half a brain."

Jed grabbed his son and put his hand over his mouth. He looked like he was ready to take on the whole bunch.

"Let's see if we can meet up with that posse and find out what they have in mind. I don't care that these settlers have made claims. Far as I'm concerned, they are all squatters on land belonging to Maine. We need the government to use stronger persuasion to push them back over the border where they belong."

"Yah. And how about them Canadian lumberjacks? It's about time they stop taking the trees that belong to us. They need to keep to their side of the boundary too."

"That's the problem. No one knows just where the border is."

"When it's settled, this land will belong to the Yanks, just you wait and see. Then we'll see if the state of Maine recognizes their claims. If it were up to me, they'd all be sent packing."

"I heard farmer Thorpe back there has paid off the state for his land."

"So what!"

"Let's get the hell out of here. I want to shake that apple tree on the way back. Looks like some of them are just asking to be snatched."

When the men were out of earshot, Jed let go of Ben, who looked up him with tears swimming in his blue eyes.

"Da, Nuga lives in a wigwam. Are they going to send her away?"

"Not if we can help it. Jacob is working hard to settle his family where they won't have to go anywhere. That's why he works so much."

"You too, Da."

Jed hugged his son close and whispered, "Come on, we need to find a good place to set a shelter for another night. I'm getting hungry. How about some jerky and some lumberjack cookies."

The next morning, Jed was the first awake. The previous day's adventure had worn the boy out. Many birds had joined the dawn chorus and the rays of sun through the swaying branches were dancing to the song. Dried apples were puffing up in water warming over the fire next to the teakettle. There was a bit of molasses cake left. Jed put a couple of warm apples in Ben's tin cup and sprinkled on some maple sugar. He took the cup and placed it near the sleeping boy, and as soon as the warm aroma wafted near his nose, Ben's eyes popped open comically.

Jed laughed out loud, "Come on sleepy head, we're close to our new home and I want to get settled before the day ends."

Ben's day started with a yawn and a grunt, but soon his peppy self appeared.

They hiked closer to the river to make sure they didn't get off course. "We are getting near to the place I call Wilson's corner. Our cabin is not far away now. Look for a large boulder that sits on top of the riverbank." The path was more defined there and the walking was easier.

"Look, Da. Is that it?"

It was still a bit rough-hewn, but the cabin was a wonderful sight. Jed had sewn some flower seeds from Emma's garden at the base of the boulder and thought about how much Addie would have loved the display of color.

"Come on, Ben. Let me show you our home. We have a lot more work to do, but I think you'll like what I've done so far."

Jumping up on the stoop, Ben yelled, "Look Da, it has a porch like at the trading post. Aunt Amy has a chair on hers. Will we have a chair some day? Maybe one that rocks?"

"One thing at a time. We'll put that on our list of things to do. Come see inside."

Ben could not believe his eyes. There was a nice-sized room with a fireplace on the back wall and a sideboard to the left. Next was a table perfect for two, with a bench on either side. Between that and the front wall was a small window. Along the front was another bench up to the front door. Over the bench were pegs holding Jed's bow and quiver and a pair of round snowshoes. Over the pegs was a rifle. Ben had never seen this father with a gun. On the other side of the door was a larger window letting in lots of sunshine. The wall on the right had two doors and between them was a small metal stove. To the right of the fireplace was another door.

"Is there a loft, Da? There's no ladder. Will I sleep on the floor in the corner like at Birdie's?"

"Come here, Ben," Jed said as he pushed aside a colorful Indian blanket that covered the first door.

Ben squealed with delight. "Da, there's a real bed. Is it mine? Is it mine?"

The room was small but light and airy from a window high on the center of the back wall. To the right was a bed a bit bigger than a cot with a rope mattress and a quilt of Mrs. Thorpe's fabric scraps. Under the window was a side table with candle. The left walls had some pegs and a shelf. "No loft for you, Ben."

"Do you have a bed too, Da?"

"Come see." On the other side of the stove was another bedroom built much the same but quite a bit wider. The rope bed was more man-sized with a wool blanket. The table by the bed had a lantern and to the left was a bench at a table that most certainly was used as a desk, for it was covered with books, ledgers, papers and pens. Above that was a shelf holding Jed's spruce gum box and the paintings of Addie and Mary. His pegs were by the door.

Ben bubbled with excitement. "What's the other door by the fireplace?"

Opening the door in the main room, Ben saw a storage room with shelves of food and tools and in the center a door to the outside.

"Da, we have a back door? Like Uncle Henri? Are we rich, Da?"

Jed laughed out loud. "I don't think Uncle Henri, or especially Philippe, ever put this much work into a dwelling. I've been working on this for years, just waiting for this day to come. Mr. Thorpe was nice enough to let us use this piece of land."

"Hey, anyone in there?" came the booming voice.

Ben ran out on the porch. "Uncle Jacob! See our cabin. Isn't it the best ever?"

Then he ran outside and jumped into Jacobs arms, leaned his head back, stared into his eyes and said, "Uncle Jacob. Are you stupid?"

Jacob was taken aback. "I hope not. Where did you get that idea?"

"I heard some men say that Indians only have half a brain. Is that true?"

Jacob didn't know what to say and looked over at Jed, who was rolling his eyes.

Jed shrugged his shoulders. "I'll explain when I get a minute. Believe me, you are far from stupid, but from what we heard, I'd say we have a few two-legged animals around here that really do have half a brain."

"How about some help bringing up your belongings, young man?"

The three of them headed toward the landing at the farm. Jed asked, "Why did you come up with our goods? I thought one of Bear's boys was going to come."

"You've been gone for two nights and I found I missed you already, and besides, I have some figures for you to look over."

Dan Thorpe and Red were pulling up their canoe when Jed, Ben, and Jacob got to the landing. "Well, look who's here. My, you've grown, young man. You were just starting to toddle around the last time I saw you. Mrs. Thorpe can't wait to meet you, and my daughter Nettie is a bit curious about her new schoolmate."

Ben put out his hand to shake. "Did you know there are some half-brained men stealing your apples?"

"Huh?"

Jed put his arm on his friend's shoulder. "I'll catch you up."

"But, Da, we need to stop them and tell them to stay away from the farm. We don't want anyone to be sent to the reservation. Can we tell them to go away?"

"How about you and Red take these sacks up to the cabin and I'll talk to Mr. Thorpe and Uncle Jacob about it."

"Well, I think we should give them a talking to before they go join up with the posse."

By then both men were more than curious, so Jed took time to explain what they had heard in the forest.

"Actually," Dan said, "I think your boy has the right idea."

"He could be right," Jacob agreed. "Now would be the time to stop this problem so they don't think they can get away with any funny business."

Just then the boys came back down the path. "Da, can we go find them now and give them what for?"

"He is nothing else but persistent. I like your attitude, young man," said Dan with a tousle of Ben's hair.

Looks like he is really home.

Jacob said, "It won't do any harm to take a walk up into the orchard and take a look. Let's go, Ben."

It was obvious to the group that someone had been messing around the apple trees. The grass was trampled and there were cores and half-eaten fruit on the ground.

"You smell a campfire?" said Jed.

"Guess all those years with my people did sharpen your senses."

"Do you suppose they're so sure of themselves that they hung around for awhile?" asked Red.

"Told you they were stupid," Ben whispered so they could not hear him.

Jacob shushed everyone and pointed in the direction of the smoke. They crept quietly toward the spot, and for the first time Dan and his son understood the benefit of moccasins and thought they might want some.

Peeking through the brush on the edge of a small clearing in the forest, they could see one of the intruders tending the teapot while chewing on some hardtack.

Jacob crept up behind him. Jed whispered, "Told you he could walk an inch above the ground."J

Suddenly Jacob grabbed the man around the neck and pushed him to the ground on his stomach. By the time the rest of the group got to him, Jacob had the man's head back and his hunting knife at his throat. The intruder was terrified enough not to open his mouth.

"Where is the rest of your gang?" growled Jed.

"Tracking a turkey for our meal."

"By the time they get close, the whole flock will be up in the trees looking down and laughing at them in their turkey way," said Ben, on his hands and knees and staring into the man's eyes.

"I think we need to show him what happens to anyone who trespasses, especially on my land," said Dan. "Red, go get that piece of logging chain that I saw under the apple tree."

Jacob pulled the man to his feet and turned him around so he could see who was dealing with. He put the point of the knife to his throat. "Not a word. Do you understand?"

It was obvious the intruder was weak in the knees and not about to disobey.

"Here you go, Pop." Red handed the heavy chain to his father.

"Now, let's find the proper tree. Be happy this is a chain and not a noose," explained Dan.

"Over here," said Jed, pointing to a broad oak.

"Perfect," agreed Jacob, dragging the hapless bully to the tree.

They wrapped the chain around him twice, holding the man tightly to the tree. "Now we need something to secure it."

Jed pulled his father's watch fob from his pocket, took a small key from it, and then pulled a brass lock from his pocket. The lock was clearly marked with the Roman numeral III. "I'm sure this will do." He held the chain together and used the key to make sure it was securely locked."

"Looks good," said Dan.

Suddenly they could hear the clamor of the other men as they made quite a racket coming back through the woods. They were closer than expected.

"Ben, you go into the brush and keep hidden," ordered Jed.

"Take the key and let's get out of here," Red stated with urgency.

"Damn, it won't come out. It has a bend and has jammed in. I can't move it," explained Jed.

"You two get out of here as fast as you can," Jacob ordered Dan and Red. "It will be easier for Jed and me to sneak out after we pick up Ben."

"I forgot how much the Brit has picked up the way of the Micmac," said Dan. He grabbed his son and they ran back toward the farm.

"Try it again."

"Won't budge."

"Let's get out of here. It would have been better with no key but at least they'll get the point."

Jed gave the key one more try and then threw up his hands and went off to find a safe place to hide with Jacob.

They ran into the forest for a bit and then clamored up a pine tree so they could see the opening in the woods where the man was struggling in the chain. "Help!" he yelled, when he was sure the Indian was gone. His partners thrashed through the woods and were there in no time.

In the tree, Jed let out with the song of the chickadee, but Ben didn't answer. "Where is he," whispered the worried father. He called out again. "Chick-a-dee-dee-dee."

The group was coming into the clearing. "Help. Get me out of his thing."

"Chick-a-dee-dee-dee," Jed tried again.

Then to his relief came the answer, "chick-a-dee-dee," very close to them.

Jacob pointed in the brush behind them. Jed reached down from the tree and grabbed Ben by the hand and quickly yanked him up into the tree, where they all huddled together like three tom turkeys.

They were far enough away that they could not hear what all were saying, but they could see the group shaking the chain and looking around on the ground.

"How come they aren't using the key, Da?" whispered Ben.

"Good question."

They could see the men still yanking on the chain while one was digging through the old leaves that were around the tree.

"Looks like the key is gone."

"But how," whispered Jed.

"Maybe it fell out while he was jiggling the chain trying to get free," said Ben.

"That would be perfect," answered his father.

Jacob pointed out that one of the men was trying to break the chain with his ax. "That will take hours," said Jacob with a big grin on his face. "They won't be bothering us for awhile once they're out of this fix. I know that for sure. Who would want to face that crazy, stupid Indian again?"

Ben giggled.

The three slowly slithered back down the tree and started back to the farm with hardly a sound. Every once in awhile they could hear one man or the other yell - "Damn. Bloody chain!"

After reporting to Dan, who bent over in laughter, Ben and his Da walked back to their new home. It was not long before the boy was in his real bed, after taking time for a molasses lumberjack and a big cup of water from the well Jed had dug just outside the back door.

When Jed came to tuck Ben in, the boy asked his father. "Do you suppose that a pack rat found the key?"

"I suppose that could be. I haven't seen one here, but remember them back on the farm when I was a boy. Yes, I suppose that's possible."

"I think so too." Ben drifted off to sleep, smiling with a vision of a little, slightly bent brass key lying in a nest somewhere in the forest.

26 Nuga

Summer 1834

The year after Jed and Ben moved into their cabin seemed to go by in a flash, although there were a lot of little problems to work out that first winter. The well wasn't deep enough and froze in mid–season, so it wasn't fun carrying buckets every day from Dan's farm. An errant pine branch that fell during an ice storm smacked the window in Ben's bedroom. It couldn't hold the weight of the ice and sounded like it shrieked when it tore from the body of the tree. They did the best they could to cover the window, but it was always very cold in the room. Ben said he didn't mind, as his quilt was his warmest wrap ever. He bundled up tight each night and pretended he was in a cocoon, from which he would emerge in the spring as a large moth able to fly all over the forest.

The first school sessions with Mrs. Thorpe were not Ben's favorite, for they were much more formal than the wonderful lessons Nuga had. Emma was a stickler. She liked letters and numbers to be just so and because he had a creative, free-thinking mind, Ben struggled with the discipline she required. Over and above that, he just hated Nettie; she was such a know-it-all. After all, Ben was the oldest but she never did what he said. Since Little Bill was the youngest, they both gave Ben a hard time. Yes indeed, Emma had her hands full, but loved every minute of it. Another family was moving just east of Little Bill's family, and they had another girl, who was eight. *Great,* thought Ben. *As if one isn't enough.* He liked being nine.

During the lumber harvest, Nettie and Bill loved to go to the river to run and slide on the ice. Ben wouldn't do it and said he didn't care if the ice was 10 feet thick. How they laughed at him for being such a sissy. He was a daredevil around the choppers though, and more than once Jed had to punish him for being too close to one of the giant trees when it was felled. After awhile he was not permitted to even go into the chopping area.

Mrs. Thorpe couldn't show favoritism, but just loved Ben's quick mind. She made sure there was extra paper so he could draw pictures while the other two finished up the lesson. She tried to keep ahead of him, but it was not easy.

The spring of 1834 brought pure terror to Ben's heart. He had never seen the river go out with such fury. Nuga had kept all the children from river's edge when the logs started coming down the Aroostook, but hearing the rapids churning in the river just below his cabin, made him wrap himself even tighter in his cocoon and pretend he was safe on the floor at Birdie's. After awhile he allowed himself to watch the workers from his perch out of harm's way on top of his big boulder. He pretended to be king of the mountain, but cringed when a driver lost his footing on a spinning log and ended up in the water. He loved the river, but gained even more fear and respect for the water.

Ben was too small to be a cookee, but did act as a shanty boy for Jacob, doing dishes and straightening the dining area whenever he was free from his lessons. On Sunday he worked in the wangan counting socks and opening boxes of new merchandise to display for customers. He had a natural knack for organization and the wigwam had never been as orderly. Some Sunday afternoons, the neighbors got together for a picnic lunch near the landing. It was such a nice open area and they waved at other Canadian families that went by in canoes.

In summer, father and son worked at the farm. Ben preferred to be tending the animals, but he did do his bit in the potato fields. Nettie always had to stay in the house learning girl things, but in the evening they played games and always ended up in a fight. Mrs. Thorpe was never pleased that they made more mending for her. Nettie hating practicing with the sewing needle and was jealous when Ben and Jed would go for walks in the forest to watch the birds or visit Bill's family. Once in awhile Ben brought back a bouquet of wildflowers for her mother and a small bunch for her. Ben didn't care much for the new little girl down the way. Her name was Gertrude and she always seemed to be a mess from working in the potato fields. She was a plain old cry baby and was no fun at all when he teased her by calling her Dirty Gertie.

Late that summer, Bear came up river to deliver the sad news that Nuga had died peacefully the night before. Jed told Ben after he and Nettie came back from an afternoon of blueberry picking. The boy wept quietly but did not take it as hard as his father had thought he might.

"Da," he explained. "Nuga told me that she was soon going to be with Grandpa Pierre. She was happy about it, Da, and told me not to be sad. She told me that someday she would see me again and until then her love would always be here in my heart, and her words in my head."

Jed gave him a hug. "Nuga taught you well."

"Will there be a ceremony tonight?"

"Yes. That is why Bear went right back. There will be a dance tonight and tomorrow a service at the convent, and then she will be buried in the church yard."

"I want to go."

"There is no way we can hike there in time."

"I want to go in the canoe."

Shocked, Jed made sure the boy meant it.

They set off right away. The river was low and like glass, yet Ben kept his eyes shut as tight as he could and hung on to both sides of the canoe with a death grip.

Jed told Ben about his first ride in the canoe and how Birdie had splashed him with water and he had loved it.

"Da, I was just a baby and only half-brained and stupid."

Feeling an opening to explore his son's thinking, he asked, "Why does the water scare you so, Ben?"

"When I was trying to help Sean keep his head above the water at the dam, he pulled me under with him. I could see you looking down at me. You were so clear, just like there was a piece of glass between us."

"That frightened me, too."

"I could see you talking but couldn't hear you. I tried to scream but couldn't breathe and felt you were disappearing and I would never see you again."

"I'm so sorry, son. I pulled you up as quickly as I could."

"I just hate the water, Da!"

"But everything worked out. Both you and Sean are fine."

"I'm afraid you won't be able to pull me through that watery pane if it happens again. I just know the darkness will win."

With a glimmer of understanding, Jed paddled as smoothly as possible past the now-visible fieldstone fence, toward the landing.

The reunion with Jacob's family was bittersweet. They were so happy to see Jed and Ben, but the loss of Nuga was palpable.

That night around the fire, Frank did not play the fiddle. The drums sounded with a slow mournful beat while Nuga's loved ones danced with a steady pace. The only other sound was the shells and small bells around their necks or ankles. All the traditions of generations past coursed through their veins and the ancient spirit of Glooscap permeated the air. Anyone on the river would have seen the solemnity in the circle, but might have wondered about the very tall white man in a fringed tunic keeping step with the boy wearing a single turkey feather in his headband. The beat of the drums were muffled when Jacob, in full Micmac garb and many feathers in his headdress, stepped near the fire and raised a sorrowful cry with words Ben and Jed had never heard before. The woeful sound echoed through the tall pines and bounced off the other side of the river. Then everything stopped and the only sound was of the breeze rustling though the trees. Even the animals of the night were paying their respects. Jacob tossed some pinecones on the fire and they crackled, making sparks that Ben thought flew so high that they must have reached heaven. After many minutes of silence, Jacob raised his arms and let out a piercing cry and the group came to life, dancing to the drums at a much faster beat. The bells rang out louder and Frank joined with his fiddle and the little village on the river bend awoke with new life.

The rest of the night was spent telling stories of Nuga. Most were inspirational, but many were funny tales that delighted those who had not heard them before and stirred wonderful memories in those who had.

Early the next morning, Hanna and Ruth made a wonderful breakfast feast for their visitors. Jed decided that he and Ben would not go to the Christian burial at the convent graveyard, for they did not want to bring any discomfort to Aunt Amy and Uncle Henri—it was hoped that Philippe would come to honor his nou'gou'mitj and if Phoebe came with him it could be stressful with Ben there. Ben and Jed had said their goodbyes to Nuga with those who meant the most to her. And besides, they would be burying her body in the graveyard; her spirit was already with Pierre, her mother and her grandparents.

When the pair pushed off from the familiar landing, they waved to all, but knew it would never be the same. Birdie would go back to the post and Martha was not at all the little girl who had played so many hours with Benjie. She was nearly thirteen now and very sure of herself; Jed thought she might break many a heart. Jacob's family had nearly doubled and there were many they did not know at all. Frank's boys were tall and would be strapping like their Pa. Jed smiled with memories of Sean riding on his foot.

They would see Bear and his young men on and off at the lumber camp. Only Hanna had tears on her cheeks; seeing Ben growing so tall brought back memories of the starving little Benjie with a blue ribbon around his ankle. She was holding Ruth's newest toddler in her arms and hugging her tight.

As Jed paddled around the curve, Ben picked up the other paddle and stroked in rhythm with his father. There was still fear in his eyes, but he whispered, "I'll try Nuga. You are the strength in my heart and I will try for you."

27   Cry of Grief

Spring 1838

The river broke early and the drive was off well before Ben's thirteenth birthday. Jed had his bookwork and payroll done for the season and was able to do Jacob's inventory while he was at the junction with Frank, receiving the final figures of the harvest. It was much too muddy at the farm to be able to work in the fields. The sudden thaw had filled the small creeks. Even the Salmon River was running over its banks and the boggy marsh near it looked more like one of the Great Lakes. Jed spent the pleasant days getting a good start on cleaning the camp house and kitchen while Ben was at school at the Thorpe's.

The previous summer Dan and his boys, Ben, and Jed, with some help from Bear's boys, had built a room off the kitchen at the farm so Emma would have a bigger space for her schoolroom. How she loved having tables and benches for the children without having to clear out her kitchen every day. Dan had managed to find a good-sized piece of slate for a chalkboard and bought a small woodstove to take the chill off during the dead of winter. When they built the room, Jed designed it so there would be extra windows to let in more natural light for doing paperwork, arranging them to make the most of the fleeting sunshine. With the settler population growing on the river's edge, the class numbered seven—the six-year-old twin sisters of Little Bill, a nine-year-old boy who had just moved in, ten-year-old Gertie , eleven-year-olds Bill and Nettie, and twelve-year-old Ben. Of all her chores as a pioneer woman in the growing frontier along the Aroostook River, Emma most loved to teach. As word spread of her work, lumberers left books for her that they themselves had never read. The little library grew more each year at the end of the

season, when Jacob and Jed gave a bit of their earnings to help
with the costs of keeping up the schoolroom.

The Thorpe farm had grown to quite a few acres because of land
that was cleared at each planting. As he had hoped, over and
above what Dan needed for his family, he also had quite a crop to
sell at the trading post and on the docks at St. John.

Buck and Company continued to thrive. Keeping production
steady with well-planned organization, the small logging company
met most of its goals. Dan met all his taxes to the state of Maine
and had managed to pick up a few more acres from settlers who
had given up their claims. Frank took lessons from Dan, and with
his extra earnings he turned the little garden at Jacob's village into
a plot that not only fed his people, but provided a good deal of
income to put toward the needs of the community in general. His
son Peter was eighteen and had spent the previous two harvests
as an axman for his Pa. It had not pleased Hanna, but the young
man was building his own cabin and was sweet on one of Ruth's
nieces. Jed's investment, with the blessing of Addie in his heart,
had increased many-fold. He kept working on his cabin for his
son. Four rockers were on the front porch so the two could watch
the river and share the love for their home with visitors. Their
new well was so deep, it should never freeze. Come summer, the
flowers and bushes around the boulder were breathtaking as seen
from the Aroostook. Jacob's dream of having his own company
store had gone well beyond his imagination; his wangan was very
popular among woodsmen for the quality of the goods and the
fair prices. He still lived sparsely in his little shack. for material
things didn't matter to him. He put any extra cash right back into
his village, trying to make it as ready as possible for the day when
the border was settled, in the hope that it would be accepted as a
true village and the land would not be lost.

The company had run into more than one snag, but they all had
worked to pull them straight. The previous year they had made
the mistake of hiring the brother of one of their steady workers.
After he was hired they found that for the first time, they were
having a drinking problem among the workers. For a while, they
weren't able to figure out how the alcohol was getting in, but
eventually they found a small animal cave where the new man had
hidden a barrel with bottles of the drink, which Jacob had not
allowed. The last thing Jacob wanted in his camp was alcohol,
after witnessing his father's problems. He didn't want to be
reminded of how his father had walked away from his family and

how he had always wondered what might have happened to him when he was in a drunken stupor.

The biggest challenge over the four years Buck and Company had been in business was the constant worry about the ever-increasing acts of vandalism by the red-shirted Yankees, who were looking for ways to trouble Canadian lumberers, and the Canadian blue-nose lumberjacks, who tried to pester any Yank in their way. Many times, Buck and Company found themselves the victim of both groups. Who were they, anyway? And would the border dispute ever allow the people in the area a true identity?

"Da! Da! Come see! Hurry!" came the shouts from the front of the barn.

Jed jumped out of his reverie. He had been thinking about everything that had been going on and the warm sun had lulled him into a trance. *Now what?*

He ran up to the barn, trying to miss as many mud puddles as possible.

"Da, look. One of the cows had babies last night. There are two of them, Da!"

Jed ran into the dim light of the shed to see two little ones on wobbly legs, trying to get to the right spot to nurse.

"Look, Mr. Jed. Aren't they just the cutest?" said Nettie, barely containing her excitement.

"There're not cute for pity's sake. They're cows. Leave it to you to think they're cute." Ben gave her an exasperated look.

"Well, I think they are pretty cute myself, Nettie," smiled Jed. "And twins, too. How about that."

"How come Mr. Thorpe didn't tell us they were coming so we could watch?" asked Ben.

"Yah, how come?" repeated Nettie.

"Well, that is grown-up work, in case the mother needs help."

"Like you had to help Mrs. Thorpe when Nettie was born?"

Nettie turned bright red and punched Ben on the arm.

Jed just smiled, thinking this was one case where there was nothing he could say.

"My father says the other cow is going to have a calf, too. Do you think it will be soon, Mr. Jed?"

"Well, from the looks of things, I'd say very soon. Come on. Let's give the new family some privacy."

On the way into the yard, they bumped into Dan.

"Looks like your little herd is growing again," said Jed.

"Yep. I'd say the other one will calf sometime tonight."

Nettie and Ben went running off, whispering to each other.

"What you suppose they're up to now?" pondered Dan.

"One can only imagine."

"I sure hope we get some more days like today to dry up this mud. It would be great to get an early start on preparing the fields."

"Ben. Time to go and start supper. You'll see Nettie in the morning."

The two had another go at the whispering before breaking away, while the two dads just looked at each other with a shrug.

Ben could barely contain himself in his little room; excitement kept away any visit from the sandman. The light from the nearly full moon fell through the window onto the shelf that held his growing collection of books. Whenever Aunt Amy found an interesting new book on her shopping trips to St. John, she brought it back and sent it up to Ben with Bear or one of her grandsons.

Finally Ben heard his father's nightly snoring serenade and knew he would be asleep until dawn. He slipped on his clothes and work boots. He would rather wear his moccasins, but they would not be practical with all the mud. He crept out the door and headed up the hill toward the pile of firewood on the back side of the barn.

"Nettie," he whispered. No answer so he whispered a bit louder, "Nettie."

"Sshhh," came the reply from behind the woodpile. "Come quickly. My father just lit the lantern in the kitchen and will be here soon. Can't you hear the crying from the barn?"

Ben heard a long moan from the mother cow that was obviously in pain. "I couldn't hear that from the river."

"Hurry, we need to climb into the hay before he gets here."

The children started up the tall and very rickety ladder nailed on the back side of the barn near the door. They slithered through the hayloft door and into the dry hay just as Dan came in the front door below. They had a perfect spot to observe the goings–on, especially after Dan lit a couple more lanterns.

When Nettie saw the pre-birth mess, she started to let out an "eewww," but was quickly silenced by a glare from Ben.

"Say there lady, looks like you are doing a pretty good job on your own," said Dan as he stroked the cow's rump. "Won't be long now."

The eyes of Ben and Nettie nearly bugged out when they saw the nose of the calf and one of the hooves, as if in a sack that they could see through, hanging out of the backend of the cow. It just hung there for a while and then the mother started grunting. She had been down but now was up on all fours doing the work of pushing her baby out. Then in a gush the little one slid out—legs, head, body, legs. The calf was encased in her sack; when she slid to the ground, a big gush of blood and birth fluids came out. At this Nettie gasped and looked ready to gag, so Ben wrapped his arm around her and put his hand over her mouth, holding her close until the scene was over and the mother was licking the baby clean and pushing her to her feet. As the friends stared in wonder, the calf began to suckle the first of the milk meant for the newborn.

"Good job lady," said Dan, covering the afterbirth with hay so the calf wouldn't slip in her attempt to remain on her feet. "I'll let you be with your little girl and clean things up better in the morning."

With that Dan blew out the barn lanterns and started back to the house with the kitchen lantern. There was a good deal of moonlight coming through the hay loft door, so the couple could see the cow nursing and cleaning her baby.

Ben took his hand away from Nettie's mouth and felt the tears on her cheeks. "It's okay. Da would say that we saw one of God's miracles." He released his arm around her but she snuggled back in, for she was not ready to leave the security of his embrace.

When she was ready, Nettie backed up toward the ladder and without a word, the two climbed down, hugged each other one more time and headed in opposite directions to get back into bed before both homes started a new day.

There was quite a buzz at the barn when Ben walked up to the farm the next morning. He had been practicing being surprised but there was no need, for Jacob was there and he truly was surprised. He ran as if to hug him, but suddenly stopped and held out his hand. Jacob just laughed and grabbed the boy and gave him a bear hug.

"Look Ben," shouted Nettie. "We have another calf. Come see."

"Really?" said Ben with a hidden wink at Nettie.

Jacob looked pretty serious after the children left.

"What's up?" asked Jed. "You Indians may walk on air but *you* would never make a good poker player."

"Let's go up to the kitchen for a cup of tea," offered Dan. "Emma will be starting classes so our conversation will be shut off from the little ears."

"It's getting very messy. I no longer have any idea how this dispute is going to end," reported Jacob as he sipped from the steaming mug.

"What did you hear?" Jed urged.

"Remember when that census-taker came by from the Maine capital last year?"

"Yah," said Dan. "He was getting an idea of who would be getting a special tax refund from Maine due to problems with bookkeeping with the settlers."

"Well, looks like the government in New Brunswick saw it as a bribe to the settlers so they would favor the Yanks."

"That's ridiculous," whispered Jed in disbelief.

"That's not the worst. The governor in New Brunswick has sent a message to Maine that if they keep acting like they belong along the Aroostook River, he will bring military action. They are whispering on the waterfront that England is going to relocate some of their army regulars from the West Indies to New Brunswick to guard the St. John and all tributaries of the Aroostook River that flow that way."

Dan jumped in. "I can feel how tense some of the merchants are when I go down to the junction. I heard down there that the Brits are thinking about building a road inland along the northern bank of the Aroostook."

"Maybe that's why Maine is getting so jumpy. I bumped into a few lumbermen from Bangor," said Jacob. "They heard a rumor that the Maine Legislators are ready to announce they are being invaded by a foreign power and ask the federal government for troops to help them protect the state."

"What are you going to tell your family?" asked Jed.

"Right now, nothing. I don't want them getting discouraged about the unsure future of this area. They are doing a grand job of building up our village. I'm heading there now to make sure no one makes any problems."

Over the next couple of weeks, the weather held and some of the muddy areas began to dry. Both cows were put out to pasture near the barn and all the children spent breaks in lessons sitting on the fence watching the three calves learning to romp around their mothers. How they laughed at the antics. The twins were inseparable, but Ben and Nettie's special calf was much more adventurous. Her mother had to nudge her back toward the barn more than once.

Soon Emma let her school charges go until after the harvest in the fall; they were needed to help with the planting and care of the crops.

One evening while rocking on the porch, Jed and Ben heard a terrible noise, almost like one of the cows was screaming.

"What's that about, Da?"

"Sounds like one of the ladies is bellowing in distress. Let's go check it out."

All the Thorpes were in the pasture. "What's going on?" hollered Jed.

"One of the calves is missing."

"One of the twins?"

"No, the single one," answered Emma.

"No, not mine," whispered Ben as he frantically looked for Nettie. Seeing her running in the back pasture, he jumped over the fence to go to her.

The cow was actually crying tears. "I've heard about cows grieving for their calves," said Jed, "but this is the first time I've seen it."

"It can be pitiful, at times. But they come out of it, some sooner than others. We just don't know where her baby went. She's going crazy looking for it by the back fence."

"Pop, there's footprints back here," one of the boys hollered.

"Someone took the calf," Nettie cried out to Ben as he ran to her.

"Someone took our calf," he whispered to her as they joined hands to walk the fence. They, too, saw a group of footprints.

"Damn vandals. I don't know which side of this mess decided to try to scare us out of here, but it won't work." Dan was red in the face with anger.

"What will they do to her?" cried Nettie.

Dan gave her a reassuring hug. "They won't harm her. Dairy cattle are very dear in this wilderness."

"Da, can we take the canoe and look for signs of them?" asked Ben.

"You sure? The water is higher than you like."

"Just want to go up east and west a bit to see if we can see anything."

Ben had been trying to get more confident on the water and this was a giant breakthrough.

Over the next few days, Dan tried to persuade the cow to nurse one of the twins to console her, but she would have no part of it. They would just have to wait out her grief as she paced the back fence where she had seen her baby last.

"Da, do humans cry out like that when they lose a loved one?" Ben asked one evening while rocking.

"Some do."

"Do you suppose Uncle Jacob was bellowing in grief when he shouted out at Nuga's dance?"

"It could be a form of that."

"Da. Did you cry out in pain when my Mum died?"

"No, but my heart cried out in pain that only I could hear"

"Is it okay to cry?"

"Always. Whatever eases the pain for you. But remember, the pain will go away in time and wonderful memories will take its place."

And with the rhythmic rocking, the father and son slipped into quiet remembrances.

28   Aroostook War

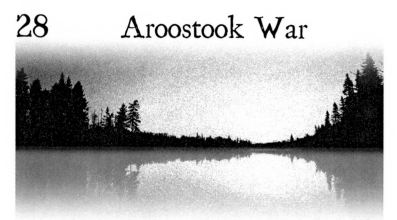

Winter to Spring 1838-1839

The winter of 1838-1839 was far from pleasant and it had
nothing to do with the extreme cold and wild snowstorms.
Although both governments were actively threatening war over
the Aroostook Valley, lumbermen from both Maine and New
Brunswick continued to cut logs and stack them along the banks
of the river, using armed guards to keep the other lumbermen
away.

It was harder for the Canadians to get up river, for more Mainers
were settling in the area and whenever they could, they made
things difficult for the Canadians. Jed went against his very soul
and bought Ben his own rifle in case they had to protect their
cabin. Dan was getting grief from some of the newer settlers for
letting the Smythes live there, for they saw them as squatters. They
complained they were taking trees for their own use, which made
them thieves. Dan told them to mind their own business, for Jed
never took any more than he needed for firewood, to fix his cabin,
or to shave a few stacks of shakes to be traded for supplies. Dan
felt it was a good trade, for he knew that as long as Jed and his
son were there, no one would steal timber from his woodlots; Jed
and Ben would drive them off. It was nobody's business that once
the border was settled and deeds validated, Jed had saved money
to buy an acre around his cabin.

Philippe found himself in quite a mess. He had sent his crew deep
into the valley to cut as usual, but because he hadn't made any
deals with the owners, the Yanks confiscated his supplies and
drove off his men. Then one day he made his way to the Thorpe
property.

"Where the hell is that damn Englishman who's been the bane of the Wingates?" Philippe demanded of Dan. "I heard he is actually a partner in this Buck and Company joke. How come they still log your property, anyway? You're crazy having that half-breed handling your harvest."

"Watch it. The only half-breed I'd be crazy dealing with is you."

With a snarl, Philippe went on. "Let's start again. I really need to see Jedediah. This whole conflict is getting out of hand."

"Never thought I'd agree with you. Hear your men were driven out. How come you never took out any claims for wood lot?"

"Why should I? This is Canadian land and that will never change."

"With a little thought, you could have protected against both sides. Although your father-in-law felt himself better than the rest of us, you had family that could see the writing on the wall. How come you didn't take heed of what they had to say?"

"Who do you mean? My brother and sister and all the Micmac half-breeds they consider family? Jacob's foolish thinking that he will protect his tribe and gain them land once this is over, will take him nowhere. They'll end up in a reservation like all the others."

"And how about you, cousin? Shall we save you a space for a mansion-sized wigwam on government land?" shouted Jacob, who was coming up the path from the lumber camp.

"I have land and a legitimate business."

"Don't you mean your wife has land—or should I say her mother has land and part of that must belong to Mary too? Wait a minute. Doesn't Adelaide's son Ben have some claim to that, too, if he wants? You must think your fair hair and green eyes are all you need. Bullshit."

"Out of my face cousin. It's Jedediah I want to see. He's the only one with business sense and as an Englishman can talk some sense to these Yanks."

"Too bad you didn't acknowledge that business sense years ago. You wouldn't be groveling up here in the wilderness with us ignorant farmers and loggers."

"What's going on?" Jed wanted to know as he came up from the landing. "In the frigid air, your voices are carrying down to the river."

"I want you to get my livestock back. Those damn Maine loggers won't let us in to get my oxen and horses."

"Well, if it isn't my son Ben's uncle."

Red-faced, Philippe yelled, "I'm here to see you! Keep that bastard out of it."

At that Jed blanched, closed his fists, stopped short, turned, and without a word walked back toward the river.

"Good work, cousin. I'd say the camp up river now has some great hauling animals. They'll be no help from this end."

"Just wait, all of you. As soon as New Brunswick secures this river for us, I'll make sure you're all arrested. You can pack up and go back to Ireland, Thorpe. There will be no more potatoes for you here. And Jacob, I will personally put a torch to that village of shacks when you are all dragged off to Bangor or the coast."

"I think it's time for you to float away in your Micmac canoe, Mr. Croteau. You seem to have worn out any welcome here," announced Dan.

"Looks like you messed up an opportunity again, cousin Philippe. My regards to your father and mother."

Philippe's rage could have burned a hole in the canoe and the look he gave Jacob could have set the Thorpe woodlot on fire.

"Guess he hasn't heard that the State of Maine is sending 1,000 militiamen up here to help the volunteer posses keep out the Canadians. He should get his head out of the sand and take a good look at how things are beginning to shape up here," chuckled Dan, who in truth was hoping the Aroostook Valley would be placed within America, as all his deeds were with Massachusetts and Maine.

Mid-February was brutal for the families and workers; temperatures were lower than ever. Wielding frigid axes was not work for the faint-of-heart. The trees seemed to have minds of their own and were harder to fell. Red shirts were more important than ever that winter and Jed made sure Ben did not even go into that part of the woodlot. When he was not in school, he had to work for Dan in the barn or in his own cabin. Once in awhile, though, he was sent to the landing to mark logs, as he was getting good with the "Bc" hammer.

Many of the settlers visited Jed's well; digging a deeper well paid off.

Slowly but surely the piles of logs started to take hold along the frozen river. If they could keep warring crews at bay, the drive would be a good one.

Trying to break up the frosty gloom, Emma decided to try something different and hold a Valentine party for the children. They all made cards for their families and friends, the girls practiced baking skills in Emma's kitchen, making heart-shaped cookies and mixing spices to make warm cider. The boys practiced their carpentry skills and used that day to put up three more bookshelves for the classroom; Dan and his boys had precut the pieces for them. While Emma was busy with the girls, the boys worked on a surprise for her. Ben brought his father's carving set and worked some magic along the edges of the shelves. He engraved a scroll pattern along the rim and a heart on either end, bringing the whole unit together. Then with the time they had left, all of them took rags and rubbed the engravings clean.

Nettie came to the door to warn them that the girls were ready and the boys scrambled to clean up their work and then sat. Everything smelled so good when Mrs. Thorpe carried in the kettle of cider. Just as she placed it on the table, she saw the shelves, threw her hands in the air, and squealed in delight. The girls clapped and jumped and then giggled as Emma hugged and kissed each red-faced boy.

Everyone exchanged red Valentine cards and they all took home cookies wrapped in cloth remnants. It had been a day all would remember, especially Ben and his Nettie. She had made him a card that had a calf inside with heart-shaped markings. He passed her something he had wrapped and when she was alone she opened it to find a small, carved wooden calf with a heart on the side.

That February the Maine militia began to build Fort Fairfield along the Aroostook near where Frank use to board Zeke. Word was that troops would be sent there to camp along what they thought was close to the eastern boundary.

March did not bring much of a break in the weather, but news was that Maine asked the federal government for help defending what they believed was their territory. Congress approved 50,000 men and ten million dollars for the emergency. The state militia at Fort Fairfield was replaced by regular U.S. troops and Fort Kent was under construction at the northern tip of Maine, next to the St. John River.

"What do you think, Dan. Is it getting too dangerous for our families in this strife?" asked a worried Jed. "When I see a strange canoe in the river, I immediately go for my rifle to have it close at hand."

"I know what you mean. But I still think our main concern is the rogue loggers who think they are entitled to anything in the woodlots. I have thought about sending Emma and Nettie to family in Boston, but they won't hear of it."

"I got a letter from Mary and she thinks I should send Ben to her in London. He won't hear of that either, but I'm keeping it in my mind. Tell you the truth, Dan, I think he won't leave Nettie. I don't think he trusts us to keep her safe."

"Guess I'll have to keep an eye on my girl," replied Dan with a half-hearted laugh.

April didn't bring any change in the weather pattern. Buck and Company took advantage of the extended harvest season and increased the yield.

At the end of April, the Aroostook still showed no hint of letting go. For the first time, Ben was going to have his birthday without the hustle of the drive at the same time.

"Come on lazy. Just because you're 14, you don't have to act like an old man."

"Da, just for once, I'd like to let the sun get high in the sky before I have to unroll myself from my quilt. After all, it is Sunday."

"Time isn't for wasting, Ben. You never know how much you have. Make the best of every day."

"But for my birthday, I'd like the best of the day to be staying in bed."

"It's up to you, but don't forget we are having your birthday dinner at the Thorpe's. You might want to take a bit more effort in getting ready."

The kitchen was so warm and cozy. It was not often everyone was there at the same time. The Thorpes, including all four children, were joined by Frank, Peter, Jed, and Ben. Jacob would be there after he fed his crew their Sunday fare.

Thanks to Frank, Emma roasted a turkey. There were lots of boiled potatoes and the end of the carrots, hot baked bread with freshly churned butter. Jed was grateful there was no venison.

"Look Pa, no beans," Peter exclaimed, bringing laughter all around.

"No children's toys in the cake this year, Ben," said Mrs. Thorpe. "Nettie made your cake."

This brought groans from her brothers.

Jacob arrived just in time to see Nettie come from the pantry carrying a tall cake, perhaps just a bit lopsided, but looking grand with a boiled sugar icing. Ben cut the first piece and Nettie put it on his plate. Everyone watched with bated breath as he took the first bite. At first he wrinkled his nose but when he saw the dismay in Nettie's eyes, he laughed, "just kidding. This is great."

That night, Ben stretched in front of the fireplace. "Da, this has been my greatest birthday, ever."

"Do you suppose it is because Miss Thorpe knitted you a pair of mittens? You know; the ones her brothers didn't know she knew how to knit."

"Don't be silly, Da."

Later when Ben snuggled up in his quilt, those mittens were under his pillow.

29 The River is the Master

It was the middle of May before there was any sign the sun was winning the battle over the thick ice on the waterway. On the south-facing edge of the river, where it was shallow, puddles were visible.

There was renewed energy around the camp. It had been a long time since a drive had started this late. Someone said his father once did not get his logs started until June. Heaven forbid.

Frank and Jed worried that the late thaw might make competition on the stream fiercer, but Jacob felt they had great drivers who would get things moving quickly.

Within a week, the landing crew was rolling the first logs into the water. The pitch was coming up nicely and they were moving along at a fairly good pace.

Then trouble. Their drivers came back up to the camp to report that vandals were putting up booms to hold up the logs and they were having a hard time keeping them moving. Sometimes just a small obstruction, like one log chained to the shore, could hold them up. Even though his choppers were finished, Frank stayed around to help them look out for troublemakers. He and Jed were walking the shore east of camp when they saw a couple of men tying up a log on the opposite shore.

"Hey!" Frank shouted out. What the hell are you doing?"

"We're trying to keep the Canadians from getting their logs to the St. John. Those logs belong to Maine lumbermen."

"Not all are Canadian loggers. We harvest for Dan Thorpe and he has a legal claim for his lots, so you are hurting not only the crews from New Brunswick, but ours too."

"So, how we suppose to know that?"

"Ours are hammer-marked with a "Bc," answered Jed.

"You expect us to take time to sort them?"

"No, I expect you not to be so irresponsible. I lost a crewmember very close to here when he was hooked on a shore chain. What if you cause a jam?"

One man threw up his hands. "Let's get out of here." Then to Jed and Frank, "Just tell your drivers to keep their eyes open. If they're worth their keep, there should be no problem."

"There's going to be trouble," said Frank. "I can almost smell it."

"Better have Bill or whoever is free at the landing walk up here every day. Ben and I will use the canoe to go east close to the shore once or twice a day; maybe that will give them the idea to stay away."

That afternoon Dan said his boys would hike the shore, too. Jacob planned to keep an eye out when he moved his outside kitchen to follow the drivers.

The evening air was warm enough to sit on the porch and the May flies were not that bad; maybe they were confused by the late thaw. Ben put two of the rockers out for himself and his father while Jed made mugs of tea.

"This is nice, Da. Did you have nice spring nights like this in England?"

"Not so often. This time of year was quite rainy and when things dried up, I spent most of my time alone with my sheep. Our house didn't have a porch and I sometimes wonder if my Da would have sat out on an evening with me. Our time together was mostly in the winter when we had no outdoor chores."

"I'm glad we are here then, Da."

"So am I."

Then the two went to their rocking and silent togetherness until the late chill sent them in.

The following morning Ben lay in bed thinking about how bright the blue the sky was out his little window when his father called him for breakfast. It was going to be a nice day.

"Ben. Run up to the farm and tell Mrs. Thorpe that you will be with me for a while this morning, and then meet me at Dan's landing. We need to inspect the shore toward Wilson's Corner."

In no time at all Ben was running down the hill to the canoe.

"It has taken a while, but he sure has come a long way, Addie," whispered Jed. "How I wish you could be in the canoe with us this beautiful day."

"Can I sit in the back, Da?"

"Not today son. There are logs in the river now and we need to keep close to the shore to stay out of the way of stronger currents."

"Look, Da. There is a chickadee nest. The mum is bringing in food, so the chicks must be here. We should see some fledglings soon."

Jed raised his eyes to the sky and thought, *he certainly is ours Addie. How he loves the birds.*

"Look out. The logs are piling over there."

"Damn. I need to cross. Any logs coming?"

"It's clear, Da."

"I just don't understand how men can be so malicious. This is a mess. We need some help."

"Is it going to jam?"

"It could. You need to change seats, take the canoe to the other side and paddle close to the shore back to the landing. When you get close, start the distress whistle. That will get Jacob to you quickly."

Ben's heart felt like it was going to break through his chest but he knew he could not be afraid. He needed to get help.

His whistle pierced the warm spring air, chasing some of the birds out of the trees and startling the big turkey in the pine, making him flap awkwardly to the ground. By the time he got to the landing, Jacob, Bill, and Frank were there.

"What's the matter, Ben?" hollered Jacob, who was surprised to see him in the canoe alone.

"Come quick. Someone set a boom and the logs are beginning to get stuck and Da needs help."

"Get in the front Ben, and show me the way," ordered Jacob as he jumped into the canoe with his rifle. "Put some pike poles in your canoes," he yelled to the men, "and follow us."

It seemed like an eternity to Ben, but it didn't take much time at all to get to the growing jam. One of three logs passing them was getting tangled in the   pile. Jed was fighting a losing battle trying to keep the logs in the open channel.

Jacob sprang ashore and pulled the canoe up on the bank with Ben still in it. He checked the chain that was wound tightly around a tree. There was no way he could release it without a big ax. He tried to loosen the secured log but the vandals had done a good job of securing the chain twice around the tree.

"Frank's just behind me with some pike poles. They'll work from the water. Watch your footing. Some of these could slip or turn."

"If I could get to that small one over there, we could break that tangle, but it is too narrow for me." Jed shouted.

In a flash, Ben was out on the logs. "I can do it Da." He managed to break off a small limb to set the log back into the water.

"Good job. That should help me free a couple more of these. Now move back to the safety of the shore."

"But it's like a jigsaw puzzle," Ben noted. "If we can move that third one in, we can set those out too."

On the river, Bill began to move some logs with his pike pole making the channel a bit bigger so other logs could get by without getting stuck.

"Frank!" Jed yelled, "you know what they look like. Take Jacob's rifle and see if you can track them. I don't think they've been gone long. Give them a good scare if you get them in your sights."

Frank pulled his canoe up and took off into the woods.

"It's getting clearer," cheered Bill.

Ben and Jed were on the same log now. Jed put his arm around his son. "Good job, I'm so proud of you."

Suddenly Jacob screamed, "Don't move! It's a trap! They've placed this one to fall if one of the logs under you moves!"

Jed and Ben hugged each other without moving. Bill frantically held his pike pole against the outside log to keep it in place. Jacob did the distress whistle as loudly as he could to bring Frank back, while he tried to secure the treacherous log.

Suddenly there was a loud snap and Jacob shouted, "NO!."

In one swift move Jed picked up Ben, and as he yelled, "I love you son," he threw him as far as he possibly could into the rushing water.

Ben was under the surface when a sickening crushing sound bounced through the valley and it was over.

"No!" Ben was screaming in silence. "I can't see you through the pane. Da, I can't breathe. Where are you?"

As the darkness was beginning to approach, a strong arm was in the water and lifted him up into the canoe. Bill quickly held Ben so he could not see the devastation on the shore. The boy was barely conscious, which seemed a blessing to all. When he did open his eyes, all he could see was that the water was red.

He screamed, "Da! The water is red! Da!" And perhaps because he realized it was his father's lifeblood, he once again lost consciousness.

Tension along the river was nearing the breaking point. It had been twenty-four hours and Ben had not stirred. Dan had placed him in Red's bed, where his Da had stayed while recuperating from his other encounter with a log, but there would be no recovery from this encounter. The settlers were calling it murder.

Nettie was beside herself not only with grief for Mr. Jed but with worry about Ben. Jacob spent as much time as he could with the boy, for there were arrangements to be made and he wanted to be with him when he gained some strength. He sent Red to feed the driving crew.

Frank and Bear had gone off with their boys in search of the two who had set the boom and trap. Frank knew what they looked like and Birdie drew a picture from his memory of them, which he felt gave all a good idea of who to seek. Jacob was torn. He wanted the murderers found and turned in to the law, but he also was afraid that if they did find them, no law would be necessary, as they would handle it their own way.

When Ben began to stir he would not respond to anyone. When he opened his eyes, the loss of his father was deep in his eyes. Just looking at him would break anyone's heart. He would not speak or eat. Dan saw to his personal needs. Somehow, Jacob had to get through to him. Emma thought she knew how, but Dan was not willing to let Nettie see him. However, after two days, Jacob convinced Dan to let Nettie in the room if Emma accompanied her. Emma stayed quiet in the corner.

"Ben," she whispered. "It's me, Nettie."

He opened his eyes, then closed them again without responding.

"Please, Ben. Please talk to me." She took his hand and held it tightly. "I'm right here and I am not going to leave you until I know you're all right." She took his hand and held it against her cheek. Then her tears began to slip down her face even though she had told herself to be strong.

When he felt her tears, Ben opened his eyes and looked into hers. "The water was red," he whispered.

She squeezed his hand.

"The water was red, Nettie."

"I know."

"What am I going to do? The water was red."

"Jacob needs to talk to you about that. Will you talk to him for me?"

He closed his eyes tight, but then tears began to form at the corners. He opened his beautiful blue eyes, which were by then swimming in a pool of despair. "What will I ever do?"

"You need to talk with Jacob. We all love you, Ben. You need to let us help. Please talk with Jacob."

In the corner of the room, Emma was weeping. She had never been prouder of her baby.

Finally Ben nodded 'yes' ever so slightly.

Nettie started to pull away, but Ben would not let go of her hand. "I need to get Jacob but promise I will be back right away."

He released her and closed his eyes again. Nettie went back into the kitchen with her mother's arms around her and nodded at Jacob.

You could have heard a pin drop in the Thorpe's kitchen while they waited for Jacob to have the difficult conversation with the boy he had promised to care for as if he were his own son. This was a promise to Jed that would never be broken.

Over the next two days, Nettie managed to get Ben to take a bit of soup. On the third day the two of them took a walk in the sunshine and stopped by the pasture to see the ever-growing twins, who were lying under the spring leaves of a maple tree with their mother grazing contentedly close by. The other cow ate slowly at the back fence of the pasture; stopped occasionally to look around; then went back to grazing.

"Life really does go on," he whispered to Nettie.

She nodded.

He turned and walked back to the farmhouse where Jacob was waiting with Dan. "It's time, Uncle Jacob."

The service was short. It seemed everyone who had settled in the area was there. Many canoes came up from Jacob's village. Birdie, Martha, Hanna, Ruth, and the children surrounded Ben. Jacob was right next to him, but the only comfort he felt was Nettie holding his hand.

He and Jacob had chosen a place just above where Jed had placed Wilson. It was a pleasant clearing and two other family members of settlers had already been buried there, along with a stillborn child. They buried Jed on the crest of the hill overlooking the river in a plain casket made by Dan. Ben had used his grandfather's carving set to engrave a simple "Da" on the top, along with a chickadee on a pine branch.

When Red and his brothers started to fill the grave, Jacob held Ben tightly by the shoulders. Ben whispered, "It's okay, Uncle Jacob. My father's body is in that box, but the minute that log hit him, he was with my mother. Now I have both of them watching over me." This brought tears to the stern sagamore's eyes.

Ben had told Jacob he didn't want to go back to his cabin right away; he wanted to stay at the village with the people who had once before protected him after a tragedy. After a short lunch at the farm, where Ben spent nearly every moment with Nettie, she walked him to the landing, gave him a kiss on the cheek and watched him settle into Jacob's canoe. As they paddled off, Ben closed his eyes tightly and hung on for dear life with both hands.

He whispered to himself, "Da, my heart is crying out with pain that only I can hear."

30 The Transition

Summer 1839

At Jacob's settlement, Ben searched for a way to deal with his father's death. But he did so as a recluse, refusing comfort from those who knew him and not allowing himself to socialize, not even with his peers. Frank's boys, especially Sean, tried their best to break the hard shell he had wrapped around himself. Jacob only asked them not to give up on him.

Since Birdie was living at the trading post, he had asked if he could stay at her shanty. This was where he felt most safe. Sleeping on the floor in the corner with his quilt was his comfort.

The sweet smell of the maple sap kettle brought back memories that he had buried long before. He asked himself how he could have forgotten how to prepare syrup and pour the thickened sap into molds to dry into sugar. He quietly watched Ruth and her little girl from the shadows of the woods while they filled the carved shapes in the cedar plank his father had made. He did not want to lose this experience again and planned to someday tap the maple trees around his cabin. The sugar season was late because of the late thaw, so he planned to enjoy every day the sap ran.

He took long walks around the village, stopping to sit on and admire the stone wall his father had taught them to build. He was surprised to find that even after all this time, there were gaps along the back around the perimeter. One end came down to the river and was becoming quite a landmark for those traveling east on the Aroostook, as the trading post was not far beyond and the abrupt northern flow was soon to follow. One day out of the blue, he found Jacob laying out his yearly canoe and sat to talk with him.

"Uncle Jacob, would you mind if I work on your wall so we can get rid of the gaps along the back border of the property and perhaps bring the other end to the river so your path is complete?"

Jacob put down his mallet and took a look at the frail shell of his Ben. "I think that would be a wonderful idea."

"I saw many piles of stones where the new garden plots were cleared."

Ben saw this as a task he could complete for his father. Jacob saw it as a major breakthrough.

If Ben were having a particularly bad day, he turned to another sanctuary. He would go inside Nuga's wigwam and curl up in her blankets and feel her presence and look at her treasures, which had not been moved since her death. He would talk to her, for he felt no one else would understand. He knew in time he would get some of the answers he needed.

As summer took over the chilly spring, the days began to be more delightful. Ben wandered out more, mostly to watch the chores being done. Once in awhile he stopped and helped clean out the bean hole, pull a stump, or even do some weeding between the corn rows. But most of the time he worked alone with the fieldstones, taking his time to find the right ones to make a strong wall, just as his Da had taught him.

Each day Ruth would leave a basket of food on the step of the shanty. Women in the village left things for Ben with Ruth, like bread, molasses and corn cake, jerky, dried fruit and so on. Ben had a teakettle on his little stove and brought in his own fresh water daily. All were disturbed at how little he ate, but Jacob wanted them to let him find his own pace at returning to a routine.

Jacob hoped that one night Ben would show up at Hanna's for a warm meal and some company. He had no idea that Ben would first walk in when they were having a meeting.

Nuga's wigwam was still used for all business meetings of the village and Buck and Company. One night while Jacob, Frank and Hanna were meeting, Ben walked in. He looked each straight in the eye and asked if he could join them. Jacob motioned for him to sit.

Hanna spoke first, "How may we help you, Ben?"

"I have spent a lot of time thinking about my future—where I want to be and what I want to do."

Jacob broke in, "That is nothing you need to worry about now. It is more important to take time to heal the wounds in your heart."

"I don't plan to worry, Uncle Jacob. I plan to grow from this and make goals for my future."

All the adults were stunned at his strength.

"How can we help?"

"I know that my father was a full partner in Buck and Company. Does that mean that I am now? Do I now hold my father's share?"

Frank was stunned by the straight-out frankness of the question. "Of course, you are entitled to your father's share of the profit. We know you will need this to keep yourself but there are others who want to keep you right now."

"I'm not talking about money. I trust you when it comes to my share, as my father trusted you completely. What I want is to be part of the business decisions. I have some ideas that I'm not sure you have discussed. I would like to be included in the meetings that take place while I am here and have the chance to meet once in awhile after I go home."

"Ben," said Hanna. "You are still a child. You have plenty of time to learn the business and take your place at the table. You should not take on responsibility at such a young age."

"I may be young in age, Aunt Hanna, but my mind has been forced into adulthood. I feel I am more able to manage and make decisions than most of our crew and they are two to three times my age."

"What makes you qualified to be part of the management of Buck and Company?" wondered Frank.

"There is hardly any part of my father's duties with you that we did not discuss. I know how to schedule and figure the payroll. We spent many hours walking the forest, where he taught me what to look for in a good tree and how to harvest to protect the new growth. He taught me how to figure board feet and what to watch for when dealing with the sawyers. But frankly, with the unrest in the area and the Maine settlers who are bursting for a chance to gobble up unclaimed land for farming, I think the need for a drive in this area is going to get smaller with each year."

"Sounds like you have been doing a lot of thinking," noted Hanna.

"That is all I have been doing. Placing stones does not distract much from thoughts and ideas."

"Why do you think the need for the drive is going away from our area?" asked Frank.

"Da told me about a man who just came over from the coast. He has paid for a deed for ten acres he is improving and has made a claim for 320 more acres he wants to buy when the border is established."

"That's a man who is not afraid to plan for the future. Sort of like our Dan Thorpe. Where are his claims on the river?"

"He's not looking at the Aroostook. He has gone inland a bit and the biggest part of the acres is on the Salmon River. Da bumped into him while walking the woodlots. He plans to build a saw mill on the Salmon. It's going to take a few years, but the lot owners will be able to get their harvest done here and without having to deal with the crooks down by the junction. He also was thinking about taking house shakes in trade that can be shipped from St. John to England."

Hanna piped in, "When was your father going to tell us about this?"

"At the meeting you always have after the drive. He was hoping to get some more information from this settler. He did not have the time." Ben took a deep breath and shuddered.

"Are you concerned about your money, Ben?" Frank wondered.

"No. I heard Birdie telling some people at the funeral that Aunt Amy and Uncle Henri have put in the papers to have the trading post become a branch of the savings bank in Bangor. I would like to start an account that I can add to. I am going to ask Birdie if I can sell some of the carvings and boxes that I do during the winter nights. And I'm sure I can still trade with shakes."

"Sounds like you plan to stay at your cabin."

"That is my home. I will not go to England!"

Jacob finally spoke up. "I am quite impressed with your plans, Ben. You have matured much beyond your age with this tragedy."

Ben started to answer, but Jacob raised his finger and stopped him. "You can participate in any meetings you want, but you are not ready to live alone."

"Uncle Jacob!"

Jacob stopped him again. "You are 14. I promised your father that if anything happened to him, I would look after you like my own son and that is the way it is going to be. You are not alone, Ben."

At this, Ben showed the first sign of his age; his bravado could not hold back his tears.

"Now," Jacob continued, "let's get to the real reason you are here. What are your ideas?"

"I want to write to Governor Fairfield in Augusta."

This took all of them by surprise and left them speechless.

"There's too much fighting going on. People are getting hurt, animals are being killed or stolen, logging equipment confiscated, booms and traps built, my father is dead and I heard another boy up near the fort was shot and they can't figure if it was by accident or on purpose. How can we change the way things are going?"

"What do you want to tell the governor? What can he do?"

"I don't think he knows how bad things are. And I don't think the governor of New Brunswick knows what to do, either. I think if I were a partner in Buck and Company, it would sound a lot more official and he might listen to me more than if I were just a boy."

Jacob slapped his knee, "Now that is a plan! I agree with and you most certainly are a partner of Buck and Company, but since no one in our crew knows any of us are their bosses, you will have to be a secret partner too, for the time being."

Everyone laughed when Ben stood up and held out his hand to shake with Jacob, who grabbed him and gave him a bear hug.

"I think it is about time you get off the floor at Birdie's and stay with me in my shanty."

"On my Da's cot?"

"That can be arranged, and you know that includes supper with

Hanna every night."

Hearing that, the first slight smile appeared on Ben's face.

Buck and Company read Ben's letter before he sent it off to
Governor John Fairfield in Augusta, Maine, and all agreed he
was certainly a man of words like his father and would be a
great addition to their meetings.

It may have had no effect, but the partners believed Ben's letter
helped convince the governor to create Aroostook County, which
effectively claimed the land for Maine. Then President Martin
Van Buren sent a representative to meet with his counterpart from
New Brunswick in the war zone, to come up with an agreement
to end hostilities. Britain agreed to a commission that would
work out a boundary treaty. American statesman Daniel Webster
represented the United States and Baron Ashburton represented
England.

Jacob set up an agreement with Ben that he would stay with Jacob
for two years—the summers of 1839 and 1840 with his Micmac
family, and winters working as Jacob's cookee at the Thorpe
camp. They would share Jacob's wigwam during the harvest
and Ben would do a lot more to run the wangan. He would also
take some lessons with Mrs. Thorpe, who was trying to keep the
children in their studies until they were at least 16 years old. The
last part suited Ben just fine, for that would be his only time with
Nettie. After the drive of 1841, Jacob would decide if Ben was
ready to take over his own cabin.

When Ben was feeling a bit stronger, mentally as well as
physically, Aunt Amy asked if he would come to the trading post
to visit. Jacob wasn't sure he was ready, but Ben had missed Amy
and wanted to go. What neither one of them knew is that Phoebe
was going to be there. The first few minutes were awkward and
Jacob nearly took Ben home, but Ben stood his ground and went
over and kissed his aunt on the cheek.

Aunt Amy grabbed the boy and hugged him tighter than any
bear hug he had ever received. She was crying. "Sweetheart," she
sobbed, "I am so sorry to hear about your father. I loved him so
and I'm sure you know how much Nuga did, too."

"Thank you, Aunt Amy," he whispered. "It means a lot to me to
hear it."

Uncle Henri walked in and shook the boy's hand.

"If there is anything I can do. Do you need a place to stay?"

"No, Sir. I have done a lot of thinking and I have set some plans for my future. But I appreciate your offer."

Henri was stunned by his confidence.

Phoebe spoke up, "Your grandmother and Aunt Mary would like you to move to London. They could take you up to the farm to show you where Jedediah lived. Also, London would be a perfect place to pursue your education."

"Thank you, Ma'am, but I plan to stay on the Aroostook and there could never be a better teacher than Mrs. Thorpe."

"What kind of future could you have in the wilderness?"

"One that my father would be pleased with, Ma'am. And may I pass a message to your husband? If he would allow a bit more time, he could send his crews to chop in the Allagash, where his harvest would still be driven down the St. John. I know this would do away with his short cuts, but he would not need to deal with us hooligans on the Aroostook."

Jacob turned around and faced the door, and Aunt Amy covered her face and giggled, but Uncle Henri slapped his knee and laughed out loud.

"Phoebe, what my son Philippe needs up there on your plantation is a thinker like this young man."

After gathering herself, Phoebe answered. "Benjamin, you may have the business sense of your father, but you are definitely the son of my sister."

"Thank you, ma'am."

31   Last Drive

Winter to Spring 1841

Jacob checked to make sure the wood was stacked along the walls inside the bean hole. He knew Ben was always on top of that job, but it was his habit to do so after training cookees for so many years. The last two harvests had been eye-opening in some ways for Jacob. His bond with Jed had not been expected, as they had come from two different worlds. Now he found a different bond with Ben—one as close as a father and son. Jacob had not allowed himself to have a family, as he felt Nuga, Hanna and her family, and everyone who joined them were his family; he devoted all of his being to caring and planning for them. Now he felt he could open himself to thinking of a personal future; if it happened, he would not fight it. If not, Ben's future would more than fill Jacob's.

As he entered the kitchen off the dining area in the camp house, he nearly had to cover his ears to protect them from the noise.

"What's the problem, Ben?" shouted Jacob, trying to make him self heard above the clatter.

As his cookee tossed some more dishes into the wash water, Jacob was glad they were tin and not china.

"That newest crewman just drives me crazy!"

"You mean Caleb? He may be loud, but he's strong and a great worker. "

"He's a bully at times. I see him making fun of some of the men and he can be mean."

"What did your father tell you about barrels and men?"

"The more empty they are, the louder the noise."

"Well, next time he gets to you, just picture him as a molasses barrel."

That actually brought a chuckle from Ben. "I don't join in the jokes and logger chatter, so he thinks I'm stupid."

"He should wish to be as stupid as you."

"I don't understand it when he talks about the dense red men. He wanted to be a part of this crew because you are the cook and he thinks you are the best. And I don't really see you as being red. Where did that come from?" questioned Ben.

"Some people think it is because the sun keeps the skin ruddy on the native people out west, but our faces don't get that much sun in Maine. Nuga said the term 'red man' comes from the war paint we once used in war parties. I believe our people stopped using red paint after the French and Indian War , when Nuga's father fought against the British."

"Now I understand why she had hard feelings against the British. Da told me that her father ran away to France before the British could deport him."

"That was a terrible time. Some families were torn apart and never saw each other again. Many of the Acadians were sent to Louisiana, but some were sent to colonies along the east coast. Nuga remembered that some of her playmates at the convent school had to leave."

"What's going on in here? History lessons? I thought you were a cook, not a teacher," Frank hollered to Jacob.

"Ben can't understand why most of the settlers look down on Indians."

"They've never taken time to understand them. They've been taught they are animals and know nothing different."

"How did you learn to get along with the Indians, Uncle Frank?"

"That's easy. Hanna. She is the most beautiful, intelligent woman I ever met."

"That's my sister," Jacob smiled. "Then on the other hand, there are many Micmac families that don't want to associate with settlers. They don't like the way they treat the land and that they force tribes out of their traditional migrating areas." Jacob continued, "We no longer see the families that used to set summer wigwams not far from here. They said I was foolish to try to claim land for my family, yet we are still trying and they are most likely on the reservations in New Brunswick."

"You are a leader, Uncle Jacob. They should respect that."

"Have you ever seen me in the general store at the junction? I know my place in the scheme of things and don't plan to make any problems that might hurt our little settlement."

"That's not fair, Uncle Jacob."

"A lot of things aren't fair. You should understand that. The best way to move forward is not to dwell on that, but to plan for a better future."

"I am planning."

"Perhaps we should settle some of those plans right now."

"How?"

"I've seen you grow from a boy to a young man in just two years. You will make mistakes, but that is how we learn. I have full confidence that you will be a strong sixteen-year-old citizen on the Aroostook River when you move into your cabin after the drive."

Frank and Jacob believed they could see Ben grow a foot in stature when he said simply, "Thank you."

"Have you been to the cabin?" Frank asked.

"I never went last year. Uncle Jacob brought me the things I needed from my bedroom. I just wasn't ready. But I have been several times lately, since the snow has settled and the days are getting warmer."

Jacob seemed very surprised.

"Nettie encouraged me and walked me over the first time. I hesitated at the door, so she took my hand and we walked in together."

"Did that help?" Frank wondered.

"When we stood inside by the fireplace, I started weeping. She took her hankie and wiped my eyes dry." He didn't mention that she kissed him sweetly.

Jacob and Frank just gave each other an eye roll.

"Each trip back, I have gone through boxes and papers that
were scattered around my father's room, straightened what dry
goods were left in the storage room, stacked some wood inside,
and things like that. There are some small repair projects I need
to start when I move back." He didn't tell them that one project
already started was his and Nettie's blossoming love and that
more than one sweet kiss had been shared.

Frank wondered, "Do Dan and Emma know about this?"

"One day was beautiful—too early for pesky spring bugs, yet nice
and warm. We took out two of the rockers and sat on the porch
making up stories about the fluffy sunny-day clouds. We could
hear the river straining against its banks as it tried to free itself
from its frigid prison. Well, we weren't the only ones enjoying
the break in the weather. Red and his brothers were doing some
hunting and saw us on the porch. They could hardly wait to run
home and tell their parents."

"What happened?"

"Nettie was given quite a talking-to. She is not allowed to come
to the cabin unless Mrs. Thorpe or one of her brothers goes with
her."

"She is only protecting her daughter," said Frank.

"From me? There are a lot of loggers around here she should be
concerned about. There is no way I would hurt Nettie."

"Perhaps she'll change her mind this summer."

"I doubt it. She's thinking about sending Nettie to Boston in the
fall to board at a finishing school. She'll turn sixteen there, away
from her family. As far as I'm concerned, she's wonderful just the
way she is and there is no way she could be finished any better."

"How does Nettie feel about it?"

"She's mad; she feels no amount of fancy schooling is going to
make her a better settler's wife. She plans to live on the river
like her mother. And she doesn't plan to wait until she is in her
twenties like her father says she should."

Breaking his silence, Jacob asked, "And whom is she planning on
having for her settler husband?"

Red-faced, Ben quickly changed the subject. "You have a hungry crew coming in pretty soon. I'd better start the biscuits. Thought I'd plump up some apples, too."

Frank just gave Jacob a nod and a wink. "Ben, for future discussion, tell Nettie to ask her parents how old they were when they were married."

Over the next month, the ice gave way and the river started flowing, much to the joy of Ben, who thought *it won't be long now.*

The snowfall in the mountains had been exceptional, so the river ran higher and faster than Ben had ever seen it. He stayed as far away from it as he possibly could. The raging river prevented them from taking the canoes down to Jacob's settlement for the end-of-season meeting as early as Jacob had wanted. Finally, after checking with Frank, he decided to have the meeting at the camp and include Dan, as what they decided would affect his future earnings. They met in Jacob's and Ben's wigwam.

"Before we start," Frank said, "I talked with Hanna about this before we came up to the harvest and she told me she trusts us to make the right decisions for Buck and Company and for the community too."

"What do you have in mind?" Dan asked.

Frank answered, "We are thinking about making this the last drive for Buck and Company; I believe Jacob has thought this out well."

Dan and Ben looked at Jacob and waited patiently for him to gather his thoughts.

Jacob took a deep breath. "We have nearly finished our sixteenth drive. It's easy for me to remember the number, as our Jedediah was a not willing substitute for a mid-wife at the birth of Nettie, and then shortly after the drive we celebrated Ben's first birthday. It is hard for me to believe that these two children have grown so quickly into a fine young couple."

At that, Dan shifted his eyes uneasily to Ben, who was blushing plainly, obviously something he had inherited from his father.

Jacob continued, "We've met most of our goals. Frank has established himself well in St. John and this will help our community a great deal as we continue to grow. He has taken all the help he gleaned from Dan and we now have gardens that produce a harvest that is enough for our people as well as to bring in a profit. My sister is more than delighted at the improvements in her home and in the savings account she never thought possible. Jedediah's generous funding has grown several-fold to meet his goal of making a home for his son, and it also has provided a nest egg that I know Ben will use to secure the future of his own family."

Once again Dan looked uncomfortable, but offered his own thoughts about the sixteen drives. "When Frank first introduced me to Jacob, I didn't know how to react to working with a Micmac, particularly when it came to handling my woodlots. However, once I got myself past my foolish preconceived ideas about the work ethics and trustworthiness of indians, I thought this would be a chance to meet some of my own goals. Honestly, my Emma thought I was crazy. It took her longer to warm up to the idea and she has more than once asked my forgiveness for being so foolish. She respects you very much, Jacob."

Jacob nodded slightly, but in his mind greatly appreciated the words.

Dan continued, "I have also met my goals. Truthfully, I never thought we would accomplish this much. I was so excited to be able to pay off my original deed and buy out some of the others. I have enough money saved to pay off the remaining claim if we ever get this border problem solved. So I would have no problem with ending the harvests."

Jacob continued. "One of the major concerns I have now is the treaty that is being hammered out. I have heard that the negotiations are going well. Some Canadians are not happy because they've learned Ashburton may have some land grants in the area and that granting the land to America could be better for him. Of course, this is just hearsay, but it is looking more positive that Maine is going to be granted the Aroostook Valley. That means in a year or so the land agents will evict those they feel are squatters and grant deeds to others."

Ben looked a bit concerned at that.

"I would like to devote all my time to working to improve our settlement. Philippe was right. We do look like a shantytown. We need to fix the homes and lay some proper paths. Hanna would like us to build a small schoolhouse; she would teach until we get deeded and then we could look for a full-time teacher. She thinks this will impress the land agents. I would like to take my share of this year's drive in board feet of lumber so I can get the repairs and improvements started."

"Wow!" exclaimed Frank. "No wonder you don't talk much. You spend all your time thinking."

That brought an audible giggle from Ben.

"Well Ben. What do you think of all of this?" asked Dan.

"I like the idea of stopping the harvests. I'd like to start working on my cabin. It needs a lot of repairs after not being open for two years. The land around it is starting to get overgrown and I want to bring the flowers my Da planted for my mum back to life. Mr. Thorpe, would I be able to buy that piece of land as my father planned? He had the money all saved and I am adding to it."

"That's something we can talk about soon, Ben."

This was not the answer Ben wanted to hear.

"Can I ask for a favor?" asked Ben of the men.

"Ask away," said Frank.

"If we decide that this is the last drive, will we have to continue to keep the secret of Buck and Company? I would like to give Caleb his pay as a partner in the company."

"I would like to be there to see his face when we announce that the dummy cookee and his crazy half breed boss are two of *his* bosses," laughed Dan.

Frank added, "Well, he thinks he has it figured out that I'm an owner, but wait until we tell him that the other partner is a Micmac woman who represents the shantytown he would like to smash down."

Ben got his wish. Payday for the crew came after the higher-than-normal pitch carried the last of the logs away. Dan and his whole family came down to the clearing to watch the jaws drop as the loggers finally found out who owned Buck and Company. Dan even wore his red timber shirt for the occasion.

When Jacob disbursed the last cash, Dan ran down to the landing to shake his hand, laughing all the way. Just as he got close to the river he tripped over a rock and rolled the rest of the way. He picked himself up, but lost his balance again and fell backward into the churning current.

Emma screamed and the boys and Nettie ran to the edge, to see their father being carried away, tumbling in the water just like one of the logs.

Suddenly Ben ran past Dan faster than even Sean Ryan. He ran along the edge of the water toward the turkey's pine tree. He jumped out onto the limb that hung over the water while the surprised tom flapped haphazardly, trying to get out of the way.

Everyone else followed beside the rushing flow. Emma grew hysterical while Nettie tried to hold her back from the torrent.

Ben pulled himself out over the water and wrapped his legs around the branch. He could see Dan floating powerlessly toward him and reached down as far as he could with his strong right arm. The water was foaming and splashing up into his face, making it hard for him to make out the man, but he could see the red shirt. He knew he was going to have only one chance, but the water and the red brought back sights he had long hidden deep in his soul. The red was getting closer. Ben had to lower himself deeper into the spray.

"Da, the water is red!"

Just as Dan was helplessly rolling beneath him, Ben grabbed for the red.

"Da, Da, the water is red!"

He had Dan by the collar, but it felt as though he was slipping away. Ben yanked as hard as he could and managed to grab Dan's arm, trying to keep Nettie's father from going under. Attempting to keep his own head above water, in his mind he could see his Da's face telling him he could do it.

Suddenly he felt someone holding onto him. Jacob had him around his waist but he could not see that Frank had Jacob around his waist and Red had Frank. They pulled together as a team and slowly Dan began to appear above the froth. *Hurry,* thought Ben; he felt he was losing his grip, but by then Jacob had a hold on the red shirt, too.

The whole incident happened in just a couple of minutes, but to Ben it was hours. The next thing he knew he was laying on the ground and Nettie was holding him in her lap, crying and repeating, "Thank you, thank you. I love you Benjamin Wingate Smythe, with all my heart."

Nearby, Emma was holding Dan, who was coughing up a gallon of the Aroostook.

Ben looked up into his sweetheart's eyes and knew everything was going to be all right. *I beat you, you damn water. I won this time.*

Emma looked over at the two of them and accepted that theirs was a bond that could never be broken.

Back at the farmhouse, they all huddled around the stove and the blazing fireplace; river water right after the ice had gone out was far from warm. The kettle was full of hot black tea. Both Dan and Ben were wrapped in quilts and everyone else had pretty much dried by the fires.

Nettie looked at her parents huddled together on a kitchen bench. She asked the burning question of them, "Just how old were you two when you got married?"

Dan took a quick look at Frank, who just as quickly turned to his tin of tea.

Emma answered, "We were married on your father's eighteenth birthday. I was seventeen."

Ben and Nettie looked at each other and both said, "Sounds good to me."

The future was not that far away.

32   Uncle Jacob's Visit

Mid -Summer 1844

The Aroostook was like glass as Jacob paddled very slowly to Ben's cabin so he could enjoy the beauty of the forest. The trees and shrubs looked as if they were creeping to the shore to dip their toes in the river. He barely made a ripple on the water. Jed would have kidded him, saying that even his canoe crept like an Indian, just a bit above the surface.

It had been over a year since he'd been able to find the time to visit. His last journey had been one of joy—he had stood beside Ben when he married his Nettie at Dan's on the clearing that rolled gently to the waterway. It was Ben's eighteenth birthday, as was planned the day of Dan's tumble in the current. The spring wildflowers formed a carpet for them and the sun decided to bless them with warmth and bright skies. Nettie was stunning in the wedding dress her mother had worn in Ireland on a bluff of emerald green. Ben stood proud and handsome in a white linen shirt with black wool pants. Both he and Jacob wore a brilliant red Micmac ceremonial sash and new m'kusins beaded beautifully by Martha.

The Webster-Ashburton Treaty was signed on August 9, 1842, placing the Aroostook valley in Maine. Since that time everyone had anxiously waited to hear if the claims and deeds would stand up. Dan Thorpe was one of the first to receive the official paperwork. His work improving his farmland and paying all debts to the state worked well for him as had Buck and Company. It was their logging that had allowed him the extra money to prepare so well. Once his papers were filed, Dan in turn deeded the two acres around the cabin to Ben and Nettie as a wedding gift.

Bill Jackson also was deeded his land, as he had taken possession of it prior to August 1836, continued possession of it and had improved it. Not all the new settlers fared as well, for they had come later or weren't able to show they had improved the property where they had put up their shelter; they were considered squatters and were evicted. The settler by the Salmon River hadn't arrived until 1839, but he had a deed from Maine showing he had paid for his land and was already building the first sawmill in the area. Word was that quite a few members of his family were also coming from the coast to settle.

As Jacob approached Ben's cabin, he smiled when he saw the canoe he had built for the couple as a wedding gift. They had cleared a bit of the banking and had made their own landing. Climbing the slope by the big boulder and the flower garden, he saw Ben working behind the cabin with his shake knife. My, he was getting good at it. The thin wooden shingles were just flying.

Jacob walked quietly up behind Ben, but his shadow gave him away before he got there.

"Didn't sneak up on me that time. You must be getting slower with age," laughed Ben as he hugged his uncle.

"I'd say your Micmac instincts are getting quicker with age. Look at you, you're as tall as your father, including the crazy mop of hair."

"Nettie, you'll never guess who is here!" Ben gave a holler.

The two men walked to the front of the house as Nettie peeked out the door. Her dress was made of a delicate flowered material and on her white collar was the small cameo pin.

"Uncle Jacob!" came her squeals of surprise and delight. The young lady leapt off the porch into his arms. "Come. You have someone to meet."

The young couple literally dragged their visitor past the rockers and through the door.

Nettie bent over a lovely hand-carved cradle. "JJ, look who's finally here. It is your Uncle Jacob."

"I heard all about this but had to come and see for myself," spoke Jacob very softly. "I thought they must have been kidding me. Jed's little Benjie and Emma's Nettie, have a child? It can't be."

"Sit here so you can see him better. He'll be waking up before we know it."

"Some tea?" asked Ben from the new cook stove in the corner.

Jacob gave him a nod and looked around the pleasant room. There were curtains at the windows and a matching tablecloth on the table with a large canning jar of flowers at the center. A lovely painting of the Aroostook River hung over the fireplace and the whole wall between the fireplace and the storage room door was a floor-to-ceiling bookcase. On one shelf was a small collection of spruce gum boxes, including the ones Jed had made for Addie and Nuga and Ben's smaller pocket box. Next to them were the double paintings of Addie and Mary and a small herd of carved animals with faded colors from Birdie's dye pots

"Let's sit at the table; we'll be able to see when JJ opens his eyes," said the proud mum.

"Most likely we'll hear him first."

"Ah, takes after his father," teased Jacob.

Ben poured the tea and Nettie placed a plate of molasses cookies and apple cake from the early fruit in their side yard.

"Now, tell us. You must have news about your people," urged Ben.

"It wasn't easy. When the land agents came around they seemed impressed by all the work that had been done. They dealt with Frank and asked him who actually would be getting the deed as they had no way to settle a grant with a group of people. This put a crimp into all our plans."

"There had to be a way," gasped Nettie.

"Frank had to bring me into the conversation. You should have seen the faces on these bureaucrats when they realized this was basically a settlement of half-breeds. It had been up to them not long before to assign the Micmac and other Wabanaki tribes to reservations. None of them had ever tried to get possession of land."

"I wish I had been there." Ben went on, "from what I have read, you met all the conditions laid out in the 1842 treaty and now again by the joint report from Maine and Britain."

"Yes, but that was written for individual settlers. I'm sure the officials had never thought about a group of people asking to claim a piece of land."

Ben just shook his head.

"Don't keep us in suspense," Nettie pleaded.

"No one knew how to handle this bunch of what they would call 'misfits,' and then Frank's Sean spoke up and asked, 'why don't you grant deeds to each of the families?'"

"Leave it to him."

"They brought in a couple of more men from Augusta and started the qualifications. Most of the families had been there before 1836, all had stayed in the same homes, and all had worked on improving the property. They decided each head-of-family would be granted a good parcel of land around the family's home."

"What about the gardens and woodlands?" wondered Ben.

"It was the work of your father and you that saved that land for us."

"How in the world?"

"The man who seemed in charge walked the perimeter of the land with Frank and me. He said he could not break off any piece of land that was enclosed by the stone fence. He was amazed at the workmanship, and said that his family in England had one much like it at their farm. He decided that if each deed-holder agreed, they could sign papers to form a village, then he could deed the communal land to the village. They had to name the town and start papers to form a council of leaders."

"So that's why it has taken you so long to get up here and visit us."

"As soon as everything was legal, I thought you would like to see the village papers."

Ben took a look and was speechless. With a tear in his eye, he handed them to Nettie.

She read aloud, "To all concerned, the State of Maine recognizes from this date forward the village of Smytheville, situated in Aroostook County ..."

She leaned down and kissed Jacob tenderly on the cheek. "My, look who also wants to read it."

In the cradle, two big, beautiful blue eyes were looking up at them. As JJ began to whimper, Ben started shaking a rattlebox to catch his attention.

"Is that the rattlebox your father made for you?" asked Jacob.

"Sure is."

"Don't tell me those are the same pebbles in there."

"Well, not really."

"Go ahead, Ben. Show him," said Nettie with a big smile.

Ben carefully slid open the cover and out dropped a slightly bent brass key engraved with the Roman numeral III."

Jacob just roared. "Did your father know about this?"

"It took awhile, but I finally confessed that I had used my Micmac walk and had given the key just the wiggle it needed to come out. The trespasser was so caught up in trying to shake free that he never saw me and when I heard the others coming back, I rolled back into the bushes and came up the tree. I never showed anyone because I thought Da would be mad."

Jacob couldn't stop laughing and JJ did not like the noise. Nettie picked him up and went out on the porch.

"Hey, you two," she called. "Come join us. It is a lovely day."

When they all had settled in rockers, Nettie placed JJ in the sagamore's arms. "Here, Uncle Jacob. It's time you held your new nephew. See? JJ knows you are family."

"Tell me, just what does JJ stand for?"

Ben held Nettie's hand. "Why, Jedediah Jacob, of course."

Jacob could not say a word. He just looked into those blue eyes and rocked.

The river ran softly, just brushing the shore with its soothing sound. Several turkeys sat high in the pines watching a group of young birds playing in the air.

Chick-a-dee-dee. Chick-a-dee-dee-dee

Epilogue

While Isaac Wilder was working on the construction of Fort Fairfield in 1838, he must have sensed that the strife between Britain and the United States was going to be settled in favor of the state of Maine. The story that passed through the family claimed he "hacked his way up the Aroostook Valley and built a saw mill on Salmon Brook." On the Internet, I found an early list of settlers in Township N 13 3d Range at the Maine State Archives. It noted those willing to purchase their land "whenever the state required." In 1839 Isaac made claim to 10 acres he had improved at Salmon Brook and requested 320 more acres. Although there were other settlers on the Aroostook River, he became the first official resident of the new village where he built his mill. Slowly other families began to migrate to the area, and in 1843 Isaac convinced his brother Robert to move his family to Salmon Brook from the town of Perry on the coast of Maine. Two sons migrating with him, were Benjamin and Robert Waterman. The latter was my husband's great-grandfather.

My husband is a proud Maine native with generations of Wilders that first settled in Massachusetts in 1637 and then migrated to northern Maine in the 1700's. Maine did not separate from Massachusetts until 1820 when it was admitted to the Union as part of the Missouri Compromise. After my husband retired we finally had the time to travel to Aroostook County in northern Maine to look into his father's family roots as potato farmers. We had heard that in the town of Washburn, there was a Wilder Farmstead Museum. Visiting the area triggered my interest in the Aroostook Valley and its history.

The museum is found in the homestead built by Benjamin, Robert's brother. The volunteer curator was generous with his tour of the home and contents once owned by the Wilders and other original settlers. He gave us a booklet about the history of the home and village. In it was a single sentence about the settlers that were there prior to the "pioneers." They were all Canadians who lived along the Aroostook River. I asked about those

Canadians but could not find anyone who knew anything about them, thus setting my imagination in motion.

This prompted me to research the history of the border dispute and stories of logging companies from New Brunswick and Nova Scotia that harvested timber then drove the logs to the St John River as there were no sawmills at that time on the Aroostook. I also learned about Canadian farmers who discovered how fertile the land was along the river. From there, I read about assistant cooks (cookees) in the logging camps and how some Indian men would work as cooks to pick up money during the winter months. Prior to my research, I had never heard of the Aroostook War— also called the Lumbermen's War or the Pork and Beans War by some. Over the next several years, online search engines became my daily friends, helping me uncover pieces of the puzzle while continually creating even more questions to investigate.

I particularly enjoyed learning more about the old logging camps, as my father was the foreman of an independent lumber company in the 1950's. At times he would take me into the lots with him when he chose and marked the trees for the next harvest. He would explain to me how he chose the trees in a way that would allow for the growth and health of the rest. As a result, I gained a great respect for the forest or as I called them–the woods.

The story of Ben developed as I read more about the Aroostook Valley, and was colored by my own love of the forest and all the creatures that dwell within.

In 1845, the early settlers and the Canadians organized the area where Isaac built his mill and named it Salmon Brook Plantation. In my mind's eye, I can see one of the signatures as "Benjamin Wingate Smythe."

I first learned of spruce gum boxes while visiting the Patten Lumberman's Museum in Maine. I had chewed spruce gum as a child but it always came nicely processed in small cardboard boxes. The craft of carving the boxes or as some call, "spruce gum books," fascinated me. The boxes ran the gamut from quite plain with names and/or dates carved on them, to beautiful pieces of folk art. The lumbermen carved them to fill their off-hours on Sunday at the lumber camps, and then they stuffed the boxes with spruce gum they had collected. In the spring, they would take them home as gifts. Today, the largest collection of spruce gum boxes is on display at the Maine State Museum in Augusta.

If you are traveling in Maine, I highly recommend a stop at the Maine State Museum. They also have a wonderful exhibit of the history of lumbering in the state. One of the newest exhibits has a remarkable collection of artifacts and textiles of the native Indian tribes from the area. I also recommend visiting the Patten Lumberman's Museum, as well as the Wilder Homestead Museum of the Salmon Brook Historical Society (which is now registered in the National Register of Historical Places).

Enjoy your journey!

Museum Locations:

Maine State Museum
230 State Street
Augusta, Maine 04333
http://www.mainestatemuseum.org

Patten Lumberman's Museum
16 Shin Pond Road
PO Box 300
Patten, Maine 04765
207-528-2650
http://www.lumbermensmuseum.org

Wilder Homestead Museum
17 Main Street
Washburn, Maine 04786

Note: The museum is usually open on Sunday afternoon but it would be worth a letter to the museum to get up-to-date hours before you visit.

CPSIA information can be obtained at www.ICGtesting.com
Printed in the USA
BVOW011913060912

299659BV00001B/132/P